Chronicles of the Tempus

K. A. S. Quinn was born and raised in California and studied History and English at Vassar. For ten years she was the publisher of the *Spectator*. She has written for *The Times*, the *Telegraph*, the *Independent* and the *Wall Street Journal*, as well as appearing on *Any Questions*, *A Good Read*, *Famous Lives* and *Broadcasting House* for the BBC. She and her husband live in London with their two boys. She still reads children's books in bed, after lights out, with a torch.

Also by K. A. S Quinn

Chronicles
of the Tempus

The Queen Must Die

K. A. S. QUINN

The Queen At War

Chronicles of the Tempus

CORVUS

Published in paperback in Great Britain in 2013 by Corvus,
an imprint of Atlantic Books Ltd.

10 9 8 7 6 5 4 3 2 1

A CIP catalogue record for this book is available
from the British Library.

Paperback ISBN: 978 1 84887 055 0
E-book ISBN: 978 0 85789 679 7

Printed in Italy by Grafica Veneta S.p.A.

Corvus
An imprint of Atlantic Books Ltd
Ormond House
26–27 Boswell Street
London
WC1N 3JZ

www.corvus-books.co.uk

To my father and mother

Marvin Solomon
and
Lugene Sanders Solomon

Tempus fugit, libertati viam facere
(Time flies, making a road to freedom)

The Darkened Room, 1854

A single candle flickered on the bedside table, casting the faces of a boy and girl into light and shadow. The boy bent over the bed, and wiping the girl's forehead with a damp cloth, spoke with a roughness meant to mask his anxiety.

'I am surprised at you, Grace; as the eldest in the family you're supposed to be the responsible one. Yet you've gone against Father's orders and returned from Italy. The climate there was helping you. Father says you were gaining strength each day and were on the road to a good recovery. How do you expect to get well in London's damp and fog? You had to take to your bed the moment you stepped off the mail steamer.'

The candle caught the girl's eyes, bright with something beyond the tears that filled them.

'James, I couldn't stay away any longer. I begged to return. I longed for the mists and rains, the soft green of England. I even yearned for the smoke and bustle of London. And I had to see you and Jack, to be with my dear wee brothers. You're growing so fast, the only truly little one left is Riordan. And then war is coming. Jack's regiment will soon be off to the East, to the Crimea. I know Father says I was getting better in Italy, but each day I woke, feeling I'd lost something, and feared I would never get it back. I am afraid . . .'

A hacking cough made the girl sit bolt upright in bed, struggling for breath. James rubbed her back vigorously, propping the pillows behind her. He busied himself, lighting a spirit lamp and warming a liquid over it, then measuring drops into a glass of water.

'Don't talk, Grace,' he said. 'It tires you so. Here, take this, it will help you to rest. Now do as your "wee brother" instructs, he's a good foot taller than you now.' James tried to smile, but it was a thin-lipped effort. Grace smiled back and, taking the glass of water, drank it to please him.

'You take such good care of me, James. You and Jack, such strapping fine young men now, and darling little Riordan; I want so much to see you grown, to . . .'

James interrupted, placing a finger against her lips. 'Rest, I said. Not talk, but rest. When did you become such a chatterbox? Father says there's nothing wrong with you; that your fatigue is to be expected when a young girl becomes a young lady. It's exhaustion, too frantic a social life, too much dancing in crowded ballrooms. He thinks the waltz is the source of much evil.'

'Father says even worse. Don't you know it's all due to books? He feels I read too much and it's brought on this hectic fever. The lectures I've had on "over-stimulation of the female brain".' James and Grace both laughed, but hers was cut short by the persistent hacking cough.

'Rest,' was all James said, but his eyes said much more as he made her as comfortable as possible. 'I've left a bell next to the bed, and I'll move the candle over here onto the dresser. The Palace has arranged that I can sleep next door. Ring if you need me. Goodnight, dear Grace. Sleep well. I am certain you will feel better in the morning.'

'You are sweet to hope, James, but I doubt it will be so,' Grace murmured. The drops were beginning to take effect. She closed her eyes, breathing more evenly.

In the next room another girl waited for James, a girl with silky brown hair and serious grey eyes. She moved quickly across the room, holding back her long skirts with one hand.

'How is she, James?' Princess Alice asked. 'Do I need to call your father?' James looked bitter and weary, older than his years.

'My father continues to pretend that Grace is simply "delicate". I try to go along with this, but you know as well as I do what the truth is. Grace is an intelligent person and can see through the pretence as well. She's losing hope, and we're losing vital time.'

Alice drew a chair up next to the fire and coaxed James into it. 'If your father could put aside his pride and admit he was wrong about Grace's illness, could he cure her?' she asked.

James stared at the fire, seeing Grace's frightened glittering eyes peering back at him through the flames. His father was at the peak of his profession, physician to the Royal House-hold. 'I'm afraid his ability to charm the Queen holds more sway than his medical talents.' James blushed. 'I'm sorry, Alice. I would never be disloyal to the Queen, and I wish with all my heart I had a stronger faith in my father, but he is more likely to harm Grace than cure her.'

Princess Alice stood behind James, staring into the fire as well. 'Is there anyone else who could help – any other physician?'

James shook his head. 'There are doctors who have had some luck treating an illness like this. But that's the problem, it is just luck. Sometimes patients recover, yes; but at other times they waste away, or are gone within hours through a galloping fever. I've been reading everything I can: doctor's notes, university lectures, medical treatises. Each one contradicts the other. The only certainty is that no one in this world knows enough to cure Grace.'

He slumped in the chair, and Alice looked down on her friend's bent head. 'If the answer isn't in this world, it might be in another,' she said. 'There's only one thing I can think of to do, and I'm going to do it now.' Patting James lightly on the shoulder, Alice went out of the room and into the corridor. Up the stairs and down she went, stumbling slightly on her skirts – they'd only just been let down to suit her years. 'It is a nuisance,' she mumbled to herself. '*She* was right about our clothes.' Moving aside a tapestry, she knocked softly on the door behind it.

'Ah yes, do come in,' said a low foreign voice from within, almost as if she were expected. It was a small room, more like a closet, with stone walls curved upwards to an arched ceiling. It had a strangely medieval feel, a forgotten room in the midst of a modern, bustling palace. Inside she found a tall man of striking pallor, sitting at a desk, poring over a manuscript. He stood as Alice entered, bowing deeply.

'You are up late, Princess.'

'I come from a sad vigil,' Alice replied. 'James O'Reilly's sister Grace. She is deathly ill.'

The tall, pale man offered his chair. 'It is indeed sad,' he said, 'when one so young is found in such a hopeless, helpless state. She has my sympathy.'

Alice did not sit, but stared at his desk absent-mindedly, hardly noticing the strange symbols etched on the manuscript before her. She looked up, into the man's creased white face. 'It is hopeless for Grace,' she said, 'because no one in this world can help her. But you have other means, other ways. You know what brings me here?'

He smiled slightly and nodded.

'*She* must be called,' Alice added. 'I know you can call her.'

He smiled again, but this time shook his head in dissent. 'Are you quite certain you wish to make the call? Death comes to all of you. Grace knows this. She has resignation and fortitude. She has faith.' His lips gave an ironic twist at the final word.

Alice pressed her hands against the desk, palms down. She needed to remain calm. 'Grace can live,' she said. 'You, by making the call, by bringing her here, you might give Grace life.'

Taking up a long black walking stick, the man turned it slowly, examining the curious shapes engraved on its silver tip. 'You do remember the last time? The trouble? And though it's really not something we can discuss, I can tell you in confidence – the worst of that trouble is still brewing, building in fact.' Tapping the walking stick lightly against the floor, he shook his head as if to clear it. 'You talk of my giving Grace the gift of life? I doubt the Archbishop of Canterbury would approve of such talk,' he said in an attempt at a lighter tone. 'Me, creating life? A collective shudder would go through your Church.'

He did enjoy the cut and thrust of conversation, but Princess Alice refused to be put off by his banter. Circling the room, she came and stood before him again, holding out her clasped hands. 'Bernardo DuQuelle, you can help, and you must help,' she cried, losing patience. 'How can you tease me in the face of death? If Grace dies, James's heart will break. If you make the call, Grace might be saved.'

The tall pale man looked down on the princess. 'You are not the only one urging me to call her back.' He sniffed the air and shuddered in distaste. 'The others are pressing me; you'd hardly approve of what Lucia asks of her . . . and even if I did agree, who knows what would happen. To call her back, when there are many questions about what she really is . . .'

'I've never believed there is evil in her,' Alice replied. '*She* can only bring good. *She* is our friend, our companion. You think so too, I know. *She* can help. Please.' Alice took the man's long, cold hand. She had never touched him before.

The touch seemed to affect him strangely. He looked at her hand. It fitted into his palm, delicate and warm as a newly baked pastry. Sighing and shaking his head, he went to his desk and closed his book. Bernardo DuQuelle wrapped his cloak around his shoulders, and taking up his black top hat and walking stick, bowed to Princess Alice. 'As I've always said, you are a true daughter of Queen

Victoria. Yours is a forceful nature, well hidden behind a gentle façade. Let us hope you are strong enough for what lies ahead.' The creases in his face deepened, but it wasn't a face to show much emotion. 'I shall do as you wish. Not for the reasons you think, and much against my better judgement. I shall send the message. But there is no need to clap your hands. I will call, but whether or not *she* hears it, that I cannot say.'

Chapter One

The Stranger in the Bed:
Here and Now

A fire engine ripped down 89th Street, the sound of its blaring sirens ricocheting across the canyon of skyscrapers. It bounced upwards, finally reaching the eleventh-floor bedroom of Katie Berger-Jones-Burg. The many windows in Katie's apartment had no double glazing. 'Who needs the expense?' her mother Mimi explained. 'It's perfectly quiet this far up.' But then Mimi took so many pills at night, she was dead to the world. King Kong could come crashing through the windows, and Mimi would sleep on.

Katie didn't take pills. She had, according to her mother, a drearily non-addictive personality. Mimi was the lead singer of Youth 'n Asia, a fading all-girl pop band. Her life had been filled with adventure, drama and a fair share of hallucinogenic drugs. By contrast Katie was, well, bland. Mimi had once complained that she was the only mother amongst their acquaintance who *hadn't* checked her daughter into the Betty Ford Clinic. 'Don't you have any obsessions?' Mimi goaded her. 'Addictions make a person interesting.'

'I read,' Katie countered. 'I read a lot.'

'Reading,' her mother sighed, 'so outmoded.'

An ambulance followed the fire engine, throwing its wail up through the windows. 'New York,' Katie said to herself. 'The city that never sleeps – well, that makes two of us.' Getting out of bed, she went to check on Mimi. Her mother was splayed across a beige cashmere duvet. On the wall above her, a multitude of Mimis were reproduced in block colours on canvas. Was it a real Warhol? Katie had her doubts. On the ceiling was a large mirror. The real Mimi was wearing a pink velvet eyeshade and earplugs with purple tassels. She wasn't wearing anything else. Katie plodded over to the bed – no need to tiptoe – and took hold of her mother's wrist – pulse rate fine. Mimi occasionally took that one pill too many. 'Goodnight, Mimi,' Katie said. 'Sweet dreams.' Katie wasn't certain anyone could dream through that amount of prescription drugs. Maybe that's why Mimi took them. 'Sleep tight, don't let the bed bugs bite,' Katie shouted towards the earplugs, and was greeted by an answering snore.

She padded into the kitchen, scuffing her fuzzy slippers against the tiles. A quick check of the refrigerator revealed its typical state of emptiness. Mimi was not a big eater. She'd spent enough of her working life in a Spandex catsuit to understand the dangers of food. There were some gluten-free, wheat-free, sugar-free, cereal-free biscuits, a bag full of nettles, six bottles of champagne and fourteen bottles of water. Mimi lived off water – special water, expensive water. Their housekeeper Dolores claimed it was water made from mermaid's sweat. Water and vitamins . . . and pills. Katie crammed a biscuit into her mouth and poured a glass of water. 'The water has more taste than these things,' she spluttered through the crumbs. 'Sawdust, it's like sawdust, only with fewer calories.' Katie talked to herself a lot – there was no one else to talk to.

Still grumbling, she headed back to bed. There was a glow coming from her room, which was strange, since she didn't have a nightlight any more. Something made her stop at the door and, looking in, she practically leapt out of her own skin. The ridiculous storybook words rang through her head: *'Somebody's been sleeping in my bed – and they're still here!'* But she didn't believe Goldilocks could have been as scared.

Lying in Katie's bed was a stranger – a girl, an extremely beautiful girl. She sank back on Katie's pillows, her chest rising and falling in the effort to breathe. She was so thin and pale, her eyes started out of her face – glowing eyes, frightened eyes. She leaned forward to cough, pulling back the ruffles of her muslin nightdress and pushing her long damp red hair from her face; anything to stop the coughing and force that precious element, air, into her lungs. It was a desperate, but silent struggle. No sound came from the girl in the bed. As she turned her eyes towards Katie, words slipped like smoke from her mouth, circling around her head and dissolving into the darkness. '*Can you help?*'

And then she was gone. As vivid as the girl had been, nothing remained. Katie rubbed her eyes hard. She too was struggling for breath. Taking a pink blanket from the rocking chair, she crept into the living room and lowered herself, shaking, onto the big cream sofa. For the life of her, she wasn't getting back into that bed.

The visions were appearing – again. It had all happened before. But what exactly *had* happened the last time, the time under the bed? Katie willed herself to remember. But it was like one of those long complicated dreams. You woke up knowing all the information, but by breakfast it was a blur.

A while back, when the strange package addressed to Katie had arrived, she'd remembered everything. All the details of some huge adventure. But then Mimi had come home from the airport – in the midst of a personal crisis as usual – and by the time Katie had settled Mimi into bed, only the foggiest outline of the great events remained. The next morning the whole thing had gone. She'd lost the facts, but she still had the feelings; the emotions of – well, of whatever it had been. Bewilderment, shock and terror; but there was also happiness – a great friendship had been forged. Who was it with? Why was it all just beyond her reach? She'd been somewhere far away on a journey rich with experience. But where?

Katie could have punched herself. Why hadn't she written it all down, right away? She was a prodigious keeper of diaries. Yet even when she rummaged back through the daily entries of her diary, there were few clues and only a brief mention of some visions: a tall man in a black top hat rising from the steam of the subway and a pretty girl with silky brown hair and serious grey eyes.

The most vivid was of a small plump woman in old-fashioned costume. She'd been wounded somehow, and slumped before Katie, bleeding, in the streets of New York. But then the woman had vanished. They'd all vanished. Like just now with the girl in the bed. Katie couldn't be certain whether any of this was real. Even when she'd written about these visions in her diary, she'd questioned them. Maybe she had an overactive imagination. Or she could be going that little bit insane. Katie read and re-read what she'd written, finally hurling the diary across the room in frustration, trying to knock the truth out of it. Still, she didn't know.

There was one more clue, a big one: the walking stick. It had arrived in a package one day, addressed in elaborate script to Katie Berger-Jones-Burg. The doorman had said some kind of punk Goth had dropped it off. It was a fantastical object: black ebony with an elaborate silver head. Both the wooden base and the metal top were carved with strange letters and symbols. 'Kind of like something a magician uses,' their housekeeper Dolores had suggested. 'Maybe flowers will pop out of the end.'

'I don't think so,' Katie replied, turning the walking stick over in her hands. 'I've always hated magicians, especially at birthday parties. What kind of grown-up spends their life trying to fool a six-year-old? It's pathetic and bogus. But there's nothing bogus about this walking stick. It's the real deal.'

Dolores sniffed, 'Real, schmeal. And you don't know where it came from or why it's here. I'd just put it in the back of the closet and forget all about it.'

That was part of the problem. The walking stick had arrived for a purpose, and that purpose was *not* to forget. It had even come with a card. 'Aide-memoire,' the card said – 'to help her remember.' 'Irony,' Katie said to herself. 'This is a really great example of irony.' At the Neuman Hubris Progressive School they were doing Writers and the Martyrdom of Same Gender Preference – Oscar Wilde, Noël Coward, Truman Capote. Her teacher, 'call me Ted', kept pointing out the writers' use of irony as a weapon to ward off persecution. 'Irony and the walking stick,' Katie thought. 'I'd write an essay on it, but "call me Ted" would think I was bonkers.' She picked up the card and read it again.

'Aide-memoire' – to help her remember . . . she could remember nothing.

Chapter Two

The Walking Stick

She must have fallen asleep on the sofa and slept heavily, despite the night's terrors. It was well past ten when she woke up, the light streaming through the city-stained windows of Apartment 11C. The front door banged, and Dolores stumped in, laundry basket on her hip. 'Well, someone has the life of Riley,' Dolores said, dumping the laundry on the sofa, all over Katie's feet. 'Someone can sleep where they want, and as long as they want. While some others, well, they had to get up at five this morning to get from the Bronx to Manhattan.'

Katie extracted her feet from the laundry. 'I bet Mimi's still asleep,' she said, sitting up.

'Course she is,' Dolores answered, beginning to sort

Katie's socks and shirts from Mimi's more exotic garments. 'Looks to me like she'll be in bed for a week. That Mimi, she's having a crisis.'

Katie lay back down. Mimi in crisis was always a nightmare. 'What's happened this time?' she asked.

Dolores picked up a red thong between thumb and forefinger; shaking her head she dropped it into the pile of Mimi's scanty things. 'Mimi's agent, he just tried to book her on tour. In *Mil-wau-kee*, Wisconsin.'

'What's wrong with that?'

'Didn't you hear me, child? Do you think Mimi's going to haul her bony butt off to Milwaukee?'

'Well, yeah,' Katie said. 'I mean I know, she's played Madison Square Garden, and 20,000 pre-teens screamed their heads off. But that's over. Youth 'n Asia hasn't exactly been in the charts lately.'

Dolores balled up Katie's white cotton socks. 'Youth 'n Asia' she sniffed. 'Now that's the problem. They never did have no Asia in them, and now they've got no youth. Mimi's just too old to go dancing around half naked on stage. She can't let go, and she can't go to Milwaukee. So she's gonna go to bed, and stay there.'

Katie knew what this meant: trays of mood-enhancing foods demanded and then pushed aside; heart-to-heart chats with Katie at two in the morning; and Mimi's special zombie drift through the apartment after yet more pills. She'd once shown up at Katie's school, in her bathrobe, to confess that her maternal aura was tinged in grey. But then, Neuman Hubris was the type of school used to that type of mother. They'd escorted Mimi home, and then signed Katie up for extensive counselling. Katie had thought this unfair. Mimi loved psychoanalysis, cognitive therapy and behavioural reviews – anything so that she could talk even more about herself. Katie loathed counselling and dreaded the sessions. She had nothing to say.

Dolores was still talking about Mimi, in a kind of droning sing-song, a litany of complaint. But Katie had left Mimi and her crisis behind. She'd remembered her own crisis last night – the girl in the bed. '*Can you help?*' She'd seen the girl and the message so clearly. What had that been about? Was it a bad dream or a real vision? Last night she'd been so sure that it was real, like all that other stuff hovering just outside the reach of her mind. Now she wasn't so sure.

Katie was usually an appreciative audience for Mimi-talk, but Dolores noticed she wasn't listening at all. 'Katie,' she said, 'you are a hundred miles off. Girls your age, they just dream and dream all day. What you need is a firm hand, and you're not gonna get it from Sleeping Beauty in there. Really, it's time you got up.'

Katie did get up – shot up in fact. She stood bolt upright, staring out the window. But it wasn't the spires of St Thomas More's she was looking at, or the black silhouette of Mt Sinai hospital. It wasn't the view from her apartment window at all. Just beyond her, on the windowsill, stood a man. He was very tall, a black top hat accentuating his height and a long cloak whipped around him. He shaded his eyes with one hand, strange glittering green eyes, and peered through the window. As he pressed his face closer, she noticed its unnerving whiteness – he was practically transparent. All the time he was tapping on the window with a black and silver walking stick. He tapped and tapped, yet there was no sound. Katie lived on the 11th floor. How was he able to do this? He wasn't even holding on.

'Don't jump!' Katie cried, running towards the window. 'Hang on! I'll call the doorman, and the police. Why can you never open a window in this apartment?'

'They're sealed shut,' Dolores answered, looking puzzled, 'except for the terrace. What are you doing, child?' Katie yanked the doors of the terrace open. Running to the edge, she scanned the side of the building. No one was there. She ran back in and checked the windows. Nothing. Girding herself, she ran back outside and looked down. Had he jumped? Her eyes moved over every inch of the terrace. All she could see was Mimi's Buddhist shrine and some 'medicinal herbs' in pots. Katie listened to the taxis honking far below and felt the icy chill of February in New York. She shivered. No one was there.

'Change of plan,' Dolores said, leading Katie back inside. 'I don't think you should get up after all. I think you're heading right back to bed.'

'But Dolores,' Katie said, 'he was here.'

'I know, honey,' Dolores said gently, 'nothing a warm glass of milk and some rest won't fix.'

'But the man, he'll fall,' Katie protested.

'I'll call the doorman downstairs, sweetie,' Dolores said soothingly. 'I'll make sure he doesn't fall.' Putting her arm around Katie's shoulders, she steered her into her pink bedroom.

At the foot of her bed, Katie stopped. 'Dolores,' she said, 'can you just pull down the duvet, and turn over the pillows.'

Dolores was looking more worried by the minute. She turned the pillows and smoothed the bed. 'There you go, baby,' she said. 'All nice and comfy now. You just slip in and get some rest.' Katie got on her hands and knees and peered under the bed. There were piles of books underneath, and a couple of childhood treasures, but there was no girl with long red hair. Just to be certain, she got up and looked in the closet. All she saw was her school uniform, some unfortunate 'teen' clothes Mimi had picked out for her, and in the back, tangled up with her baseball bat and an old battered kite, was the walking stick.

'It's the walking stick,' she said to herself, climbing into bed. 'He had a walking stick. Just like mine.'

'There now, honey,' Dolores said, giving her an uncharacteristic kiss on the forehead. 'You just forget about the man and the walking stick. Just close your eyes. I'm gonna get you that milk. You just yell out if you feel scared or sick.'

The walking stick – that was the key to remembering. If Katie could crack the secret of the stick, if she could read the symbols carved into it, then she'd understand everything.

She'd been trying to figure out the walking stick for ages. First stop had been the internet, for hours, late into the night. She'd even spent a clutch of Saturdays at the New York Public Library poring over book after book. But she learned nothing. Tap, tap, tap – the stick bounced against her brain, but it couldn't get in.

The most frightening and frustrating part was that someone *did* understand, and they weren't going to help. Quite the opposite. Upstairs in Apartment 23C lived Professor Diuman, the world's leading expert on Parallel Being and the Temporal Psyche of History, Distinguished Professor Emeritus of Ancient and Extinct Languages at Columbia University. More important than that, he was one of Mimi's exes. They'd dated for a couple of months, when Mimi was going through a kind of 'find a guy like Arthur Miller' stage. It hadn't worked out, of course. Professor Diuman might be brainy, but he was also ugly, and Mimi didn't do ugly. She'd decided to climb Mount Everest and ran off with a hunky mountaineer.

Professor Diuman had always been nice to Katie. In the first place, he knew she existed, which was more than she could say for some of Mimi's boyfriends. He asked her what she thought about things, what she was doing. Not in a creepy way – more as a comrade in arms. When Mimi dumped him, Katie and the professor had stayed on good terms. He always said hello in the elevator, and bought Girl Scout cookies from her each fall. He liked the Thin Mints. Sometimes he even lent her books, though Katie found them kind of weird.

In New York city apartment buildings, people do not knock on their neighbours' doors, except to complain about noises or smells or a particularly unattractive Christmas wreath. But Katie had knocked on Professor Diuman's door. Anyone who knew as much as he did about language was sure to recognize the symbols on the walking stick. Katie had been so certain it would be OK. He'd give her a glass of milk, and some of the Thin Mints she'd sold him the year before. And then he'd tell her all about her mystery gift.

Except that wasn't how it happened. Professor Diuman was there when she knocked. Smiling and nodding in his slightly timid way, he'd led her into the living room. He sported a long grey ponytail – grown, Katie suspected, to compensate for the lack of hair on the top of his head. His wispy goatee, divided into three neat braids, was not an attractive addition.

'What brings you up here?' he asked Katie. 'Have you locked yourself out? Is something wrong with Mimi?' His small oval spectacles reflected the things about him – the books on the shelves, the curious objects on the coffee table.

'It's this,' Katie said, holding out the walking stick. 'I really need to know more about it, especially the symbols. I thought you might know . . .'

If the walking stick had grown fangs and attacked Professor Diuman, the change in the room could not have been greater. Diuman pulled away, his spectacles growing dark. She could have sworn the braids on his chin bristled and twitched.

'Where did you get that?' he asked, not at all in his usual absent-minded friendly way.

'It was a gift,' Katie said. 'At least I think it was.'

'From whom?'

'From I don't know. It was left downstairs for me, with the doorman.'

'When?'

'I can't remember.' Katie was getting confused.

Diuman took the walking stick from her, turning it in his hands, his eyes flicking from the carved symbols to Katie, his glasses growing darker, his manner more agitated. She could tell he knew what the symbols meant. But she couldn't work out why he was acting so strange.

'The doorman gave this to you?' Professor Diuman ran his fingers over the symbols. 'Are you certain it was meant for you? I really do think there's been a mistake. This was clearly meant for me.'

None of this was clear to Katie. She only knew that Diuman was acting very strangely. His braided beard was undulating, and the room had taken on a funny smell – like when you plug in the Christmas tree and the wires fuse – a kind of burnt, electric smell. A dangerous smell. The best thing would be to leave – right away.

Leaning forward, she snatched the walking stick, and held it behind her back.

'The walking stick is mine,' she said. 'My name was on the card. Thanks for looking at it, but I really have to be going now.'

She felt shaky, but tried to act natural, walking towards the door. For a moment she thought Professor Diuman would let her go, but he sidled in front of her, blocking her exit, his arms stretched across the door frame. He'd put his 'friendly face' back on, but Katie could see he was as tense as a cobra, ready to strike.

'I am sorry, my dear,' he said. 'I just got rather excited about that artefact of yours. I can take it to Columbia University this afternoon. I'll show it to some of my colleagues. It might be worth quite a lot. I can authenticate it, and sell it for you; make a bit of money for a girl your age. You'd like some pocket money, wouldn't you?' He reached out for the walking stick, but she kept it behind her back.

'It's mine,' she repeated. Diuman flushed red, the sparse hair on his head standing up with static electricity. Katie saw herself reflected in his glasses and she looked scared.

'If I were you,' he said in a tight, shaking voice, 'I'd be more reasonable. Now do be a good girl.'

Katie ducked under his arm and twisted the door knob. It wasn't locked. She'd make a run for it; down the corridor. Professor Diuman followed, and would have caught her, but the elevator opened and Mrs Klapznik stepped out. 'Diuman!' she barked. 'I want to talk to you about those noises coming from your apartment.' She looked from the Professor to Katie. 'Is something wrong here?' she asked. 'I don't want trouble in the building.'

'No, no, Mrs Klapznik,' Professor Diuman said. 'I'm saying goodbye to Mimi's daughter. You know, Mimi in 11C.'

'As if I wouldn't know Mimi!' harrumphed Mrs Klapznik. 'Now there's noise for you – parties and paparazzi and who knows what else goes on in that apartment. But my problem is with 23C, with you, Professor Diuman.'

Katie had never been as glad to see anyone as she was to see Mrs Klapznik. Diving into the elevator, she jabbed 11, and then the *Close* button, several times.

Professor Diuman hadn't come after her. The doorman said Diuman had left, quite suddenly, on some kind of trip. But Katie knew one day soon he'd be back, up there, just twelve floors above, plotting to get the walking stick. She'd hidden it in the back of her closet. Stupid stick; but nothing could be that dangerous without a purpose. She just wasn't smart enough to figure it out.

Chapter Three

Deep in the Looking Glass

Katie spent the rest of the day in – or under – her bed. She figured the closer she stayed to it, the less chance there was she'd find someone else in it. Mimi stayed in bed too, occasionally wailing for herbal tea. At about six she sent Dolores out for a large tub of Ben and Jerry's Cherry Garcia ice cream.

'If Mimi's asking for ice cream, she's hit rock bottom,' Katie said to Dolores. 'Ice cream is a pre-suicidal move. Should I go in and see her?'

Dolores shrugged into her brown and orange plaid coat and pulled her woolly hat down over her ears. 'I told her a little fib: that you're at your daddy's all day, an' you're not back 'til late tonight,' she said. 'Best she don't even know you're here. I know she's carrying on, but you're the one who needs the rest. Don't worry about Mimi; I'll buy her a bumper box of chocolate doughnuts to go with her ice cream. Before you know it, that woman'll be in hog heaven.'

'You don't think she'll harm herself?' Katie asked. 'You know how hysterical she gets *after* she eats.'

'I'll keep an eye on her,' Dolores said. 'And tonight I'll make her that special soup she likes – just ginger and nettles and hot water. She can drink it all day tomorrow. That'll cheer her up.'

Reassured, Katie crept back under her bed, pulling the walking stick behind her. It was a tall Victorian-style bed and she kept anything that really mattered underneath it. A blanket knitted by her grandmother, her diary, a Swiss army knife – a present from her long-gone father. Also the essentials – a box of Oreos, tissues, a flashlight. And then there were the books: an eclectic mix of fiction, biography, poetry and letters – though her obsession at the moment was medical pamphlets. She was fascinated by disease, and if she'd thought more highly of herself, she might have wanted to become a doctor.

She ran her index finger over the spines of her books: *His Dark Materials, Swahili Made Easy, My Life as a Dog, 13 Women Astronauts, Dispatches from the Crimea, Tourniquets and Their Uses* . . . In the corner was a pile of books on ancient languages. There were a couple Professor Diuman had loaned her in the past. 'Well, he's never getting these books back,' Katie thought. 'Last time I saw him, he looked like he might eat me alive . . .'

She pulled one of Diuman's books from the pile. It was very old, with crumbling pages and a strange burnt musky smell. It was in Latin, and Katie's Latin was bad. She could only remember *semper ubi sub ubi*: always wear underwear. *Tempus Fugit, Libertati Viam Facere* the title-page read. She knew this had nothing to do with underwear, but something to do with time flying and freedom. She turned the pages, staring idly at the words. Random letters were illuminated with drawings. The word 'Tempus' thrust itself forward, the 'T' engraved with snakes and patterns. Her eyes seemed to re-focus and she could pick out symbols amongst the patterns – symbols a lot like those on the walking stick.

Turning the pages, Katie made a mental note: try not to sleep through Latin class. Though she looked at the book for a very long time, it was all so much gibberish to her. In frustration she slammed the book shut and a stiff white card fell out. It was embossed in a flourishing script. 'Aide memoire' it read. To help her remember! This was the card that had arrived with the walking stick. How had it ended up in this book? Perhaps she'd left the card as a bookmark? She couldn't think of any other explanation. But even Katie knew she wouldn't have been that careless with something so important.

Dolores stood in the doorway. 'Bathtime,' she said. 'And then bedtime.'

'But I've been in bed all day,' Katie protested from behind the pink dust ruffle.

'You are *under* the bed now,' Dolores said. 'I don't know what you do down there. You are a child, not a groundhog.'

Katie knew she'd never be able to sleep, but the sooner she was in bed, the sooner Dolores would leave, and she could get back to code-breaking; so she diligently had her bath, put on her warmest flannel pyjamas and pretended to sleep. Finally the door slammed.

Slipping back under the bed, Katie found the *Tempus* book and the embossed card. How had they ended up together? Did they connect in some way to the walking stick? It was all such a puzzle and Katie had so few pieces: she had to fit them together any way she could. She simply had to figure this out. Maybe she could find the words 'aide memoire' somewhere in the *Tempus* book. She knew that was silly. Old-fashioned people used the phrase 'aide memoire' to remember a business appointment, or a luncheon party, or a ball. It wasn't magical at all, just functional.

She switched on her flashlight and examined the card over and over. 'Aide memoire' she said to herself. Opening the book she read its title page: '*Tempus Fugit, Libertati Viam Facere.*' She turned from the book to the card, from the card to the book. '*Tempus Fugit, Libertati Viam Facere,*' she repeated to herself, and flipping the card she noticed the watermark. She'd seen it hundreds of times; it was the logo of the paper manufacturer, just a jumbled pattern. But tonight it was clearer. Maybe it was the dark and the flashlight, but she could almost read it. As she held the flashlight closer, the pattern formed words and the words formed lines, then the lines became verses:

> In the dark of the night
> The flicker of light
> Lies deep in the looking glass.
>
> If unable to sleep
> Through blackness you'll creep
> Towards shades who shimmer and pass.
>
> The right eyes read reverse
> Through blessing and curse
> And backwards through time and space.

Katie held the card so tight, it made red dents in her fingers. 'That has nothing to do with the name of a papermaker,' she said aloud. She always talked to herself when she was frightened. Mimi was sleeping through a cocktail of Ramelteon and Temazepam and Dolores was on the subway, hurtling towards the Bronx. Katie might as well be alone in the apartment. 'Poetry', she mumbled, 'I'm being frightened to death by poetry. Whoever heard of death by couplets? Though it's not two lines, it's three . . .' Pedantic humour was her other defence against fear.

Katie looked at the card again. The words were fading, reforming as the original watermark and becoming unreadable. She scrambled around for a pencil and a scrap of paper and quickly wrote the words down. If she lost them, she'd never find the meaning of the walking stick. She wasn't going to make the mistake of forgetting again. This was a message for her, and she had to figure it out. 'Now think, you dummy,' she said loudly. 'What did that card say? And what does it mean?'

'*In the dark of the night,*' she said, hunching over her scribbles. '*The flicker of light lies deep in the looking glass.*' She chewed the end of her pencil. 'It's dark now', she said, 'and it's night. Could this be "*the dark of the night?*" Is it show-time? Whatever it is; can I make it happen?

She pored over the words '*The flicker of light*'. This message she was receiving, could it be from the past? Why else the old book and the aide-memoire card? 'Light,' she said, 'a candle.' But Mimi had all the candles – large scented ones all over her bedroom and bathroom. Katie didn't think she should leave her own room; she might break the spell, or whatever it was. She tapped the flashlight against her chin, and it flickered against the piles of books. If she didn't have a candle she would have to make do with the flashlight.

She turned to the next line. '*Lies deep in the looking glass.*' Looking glass; that was a mirror, but which mirror? There were hundreds in the apartment. Mimi's dressing room was mirrored floor to ceiling with real make-up light bulbs and hundreds of drawers for her creams and lotions. There were eight large chrome-rimmed ones in Mimi's bedroom, set in the cream shantung silk walls. There was even a pop-up mirror in one of the kitchen drawers, so that Mimi could have a final peek at herself over her nettles and water.

Katie lifted the dust ruffle from her bed, and peered around her room. 'Which mirror, which looking glass?' she asked. As if in answer, a tiny shaft of light darted from under the door of her bathroom.

If unable to sleep
Through darkness you'll creep
Towards shades who shimmer and pass.

The strange words on the card seemed to reverberate through her brain. She took a deep breath. There was a choice now. She could get up, telephone her father and ask if she could come over; or she could creep, through the darkness, towards whatever lay beyond her bathroom door. For several minutes she couldn't decide what to do. But then she thought of the girl in her bed. That vision might be connected to this message. *'Can you help?'* had been the question hanging over the girl's head. How could Katie help if she ran away?

'Fine,' Katie said. 'If that's what you want, through darkness I'll creep.' For protection she took the book and the walking stick with her. Wedging them under her left arm, she clutched the white card and the flashlight in her right hand. Flat on her belly, she inched towards the bathroom and pushed the door open. The source of light was the bathroom mirror. Not a reflection of light in the mirror, but the mirror itself. Katie shuddered. There really was something moving inside the mirror. Wands of faint light darted out and then withdrew into the depths.

She almost heard a click in her brain, and then she understood. Had it been Michelangelo, or da Vinci? Which one had written their diary in reverse, so that you could only read it reflected in a mirror? Taking a deep breath she held the card up to face the mirror. Shining the flash light on the card she chanted the final lines of the verse.

'The right eyes read reverse
Through blessing and curse
And backwards through time and space.

The activity in the mirror became frantic. She still couldn't see what was happening, but it was growing, circling. And then the card flashed bright and she could read a new couplet in the mirror, as glaring as a neon sign:

The Tempus will find the message
That leads to timely passage.

She was frightened and excited and still very confused. It was the Tempus that could make it all happen. But what, or who was the Tempus? She looked around the room: the toilet, the towels, the bath soap, the acne cream. She knew, instinctively, that none of this had anything to do with the Tempus. Then, through the darting lights of the mirror, she settled on her own reflection. Again, a brittle click seemed to awaken something in her brain. 'Am I the answer?' she cried. 'Am I the Tempus? Could it really be me?'

'Ah, realization at last. I thought I might doze off, waiting for that revelation.' A low, foreign voice was coming from deep within the looking glass, a voice so bored, it was actually yawning. 'You have a mind that moves like treacle . . . perhaps we could progress now . . . might I suggest the walking stick?'

Of all the things Katie had expected, a sarcastic talking mirror was not one of them. But having got this far, there was no turning back. Taking the mirror's advice, Katie lifted the walking stick high and the whole room galvanized. The symbols carved into the stick's base and head flew through the air, darting into the bowels of the mirror. Image after image formed and then dissolved before her. Things she had never seen, or would never hope to see.

There was the sick and frightened girl with the long red hair, the one in Katie's bed. But this time she was in a different room, with a spirit lamp and a candle burning low

– the end of a long night-vigil. The girl sat up in bed, calling. Katie could hear her now. 'Can you help?' she cried in a pretty Irish lilt, struggling for breath. Katie leaned forward; but before she could answer the girl was gone, the scene had vanished.

In its place was the bustle and action of an army on the move. There were cannons, soldiers, horses, lances and swords. Coming directly towards her was a mounted battalion, horses at a trot, lances prepared, swords at the ready. This was war.

The rumbling of the horses' hooves was echoed by a crash from above. In the mirror, the sky grew dark. Clouds piled thick and black; they swirled and distorted, forming inky black figures in the sky. Lightning split the skies, like swords wielded by giants. It seemed the heavens had an army of their own; two wars waging at once.

Below, the army of men tensed and then surged forward. 'Charge!' the battalion cried as one, picking up speed. 'CHARGE!' The horses' eyes rolled, the men stood upright in their stirrups, arms raised, lances glinting; and in a mad forward dash, headed straight for Katie.

She threw her arms up, ducking, and both battles died away. In their place was a pretty girl with long black curls and big eyes; behind her was a flaxen-haired boy in his teens, dressed in velvet and lace. The girl sang a song in French, sad but soothing. When Katie tried to look directly at the boy, she winced. It hurt even to look at him.

Hundreds of scenes passed through the looking glass. When a serious-faced girl appeared, Katie felt she had found a friend, and reached out to take her hand, only to have this vision replaced by a terrifying, strange and snake-like man. Katie recoiled and involuntarily held the walking stick high. At this the man retreated deep within and the mirror thundered and flashed again. Katie was dizzy, sweating and terrified; but she could not tear her gaze away from the looking glass.

Far in its depths a figure began to form in the swirling clouds, at first a pin-point of dark against the lightning, but growing larger with every passing moment. It was a man, tall and thin, with deathly pale skin. His hooded eyes, beneath a tall silk top hat, gleamed green through the gloom. He was wearing a black cloak, a close-fitting black frock coat and a high white cravat. And he was carrying a walking stick – exactly like the one in Katie's left hand. Tap, tap, tap, she remembered. He'd been on the window ledge, outside her apartment. And now he was within.

This vision, this shade, was different from the others. This one could actually see her. The white-skinned man in the high black top hat – he was looking straight at Katie. He spoke, and his voice was the low foreign voice she had first heard when she faced the mirror, but it wasn't bored anymore. 'SEEK,' he said, 'SEEK'. Katie's heart was pounding and an acid bile was rising in her throat.

'I'm going to pass out,' she panicked, 'and all this will have been for nothing.' Along with the man, she could see herself, faintly reflected in the mirror – rather grey, and gulping repeatedly.

The man had reached the front of the glass. Fixing Katie with his glittering green eyes, so close that she could see their large black pupils, he raised his walking stick. She raised her own with a fierce gesture, but this did not vanquish him. Instead he circled the ebony and silver stick above his head. The strange carved symbols Katie had tried so hard to decipher swirled around it, as if summoned. They reformed and then divided into the words of a thousand languages. With a final, sweeping gesture, he broke through the mirror with his walking stick, the surface rippling into expanding rings.

There were no flying shards of broken glass, just thousands upon millions of words spilling through the opening, encircling Katie. They swirled around her and seemed to fill her. Despite the words she was speechless. For a moment, she could understand everything ever said in this world, but could say nothing. The knowledge inside her was acutely painful. There was no room for her heart, or her lungs. Had the blood stopped moving in her veins? She couldn't breathe. 'Too much,' she finally found the words. And then there was nothing.

Chapter Four

The Reunion

Quiet. Everything around her was quiet and still. She had thought she was dying; yet now she had never felt so comfortable.

'You fainted,' said the low, foreign voice. 'It was amateur dramatics night on 89th Street.' Katie continued to lie on her back with her eyes closed. She needed to think, to figure things out. But then something was prodding her in the side. She remembered that prod, right in the soft spot under the ribcage. Trying not to move a muscle, she opened one eye, ever so slightly, and took a sidelong peek to her left. There was the walking stick – not hers – but his, all carved ebony and gleaming engraved silver, poking her in the side.

Two well-shod feet shifted impatiently on the stone floor. A long, thin white hand, smelling slightly of musk, extended to pull her up. She wasn't on her bathroom floor. Katie knew, with absolute conviction, that this was not a dream; and the time for uncertainty was gone. Though it might be frightening, she must face whatever was coming. Taking the offered hand, she stood, and opening her eyes wide, she looked. She understood.

It was Bernardo DuQuelle. 'I've been plagued and pestered by several different worlds to bring you back,' he said. 'Why they all want you is beyond me.' He looked her up and down, taking in Katie's yellow flannel pyjamas, patterned with orange and green frogs. 'You look a fright,' he added. 'You've never quite been up to our standards, but this time you've outdone yourself. James O'Reilly will be appalled. And really, are you something Princess Alice should see? But she begged and begged, and against my better judgement . . .'

With these two names, happiness replaced Katie's fear. 'Alice! James! Are they here? I've got to see them!'

'*Got* to? You have become presumptuous with time. What you have *got* to do is calm down and be patient.' Bernardo DuQuelle continued to view Katie's pyjamas with distaste. 'James O'Reilly is attending a medical appointment with his father. Princess Alice is attending a concert with the Queen and Prince Albert.'

Of course, Alice was a princess, and her mother was

Queen Victoria. Katie had made this journey before. She'd been here; she knew this man. With every passing moment she remembered more; and not just *who* was here, but *why* she'd come. The Crystal Palace flashed before her eyes, with its slender iron frame and thousands of panes of glass. There was the Queen in her carriage, Prince Albert, a mass of cheering people. They'd been inside the glass structure, and the Chinaman was moving forward to assassinate the Queen. *The Black Tide is rising . . .*

'Victoria, she's alive! And Albert, he's OK too?'

'*Queen* Victoria,' Bernardo DuQuelle said. '*Prince* Albert. There seem to be no manners in your own time. Yes, the Queen is alive and well and so is Prince Albert. They are entertaining a delegation from France. Trying to sort out the trouble in the East, the Crimea, or so they say. They're all in a frenzy against the Russians, and really can't wait for the war to begin. They are defending the Turks – the Turks! As if any of them have ever given the Turks a single thought. Battle strategy all day and music through the night. You would think they'd never fought Napoleon, never lived through the fear and waste of it all. But the past fifty years have turned the soldiers' gore to glory. Wellington would put them straight, but he, alas, is gone. This is a difficult moment. I need to keep an eye on things. Now, if you will excuse me.'

'You've conjured me up,' Katie protested. 'You can't just leave me here.' She looked around, past DuQuelle, for the first time. She was standing on a cold stone floor, in a room with a low ceiling and drab walls. In the corner, amongst the old buckets and mops, leaned a full-length mirror, its glass mottled with age spots. DuQuelle walked over to the mirror, and flicked a bit of old gilt from the frame.

'I didn't conjure you up, to use your own inelegant turn of phrase. I am not a third-rate magician. I assume you remember who I am?' His green eyes caught her own.

Katie found it hard to turn away from his gaze. She gulped a bit, and nodded. 'I remember,' she said. 'I have a good memory.'

'Good memory,' he exclaimed, 'you have a memory like a sieve! I thought when I sent you back you would be able to keep the basic events in your head. I even left my card and my cane; but no, the time seepage was complete.'

'Well, it's not complete anymore,' Katie replied. 'I do remember.' New York seemed a thousand miles and a thousand years away. 'Why am I back?' she asked.

DuQuelle scooped up Katie's things: the book, the card, the walking stick, and opened the door of the broom cupboard. Looking down the narrow corridor, he escorted her quickly up the stairs and down a hall, into the school room. The Japanese screen and chaise longue were still there. Katie had no choice but to follow. But the more she remembered about DuQuelle, the less comfortable she was with him. DuQuelle had never been her ally. He wasn't even human. 'Please tell me,' she said again. 'Why am I here?'

Rolling his eyes upwards, DuQuelle addressed the ceiling. 'Do we really have to start all over again?' he muttered. 'The chosen . . . I wonder. How sad that they should pin their hopes on this *girl* . . . Though I still do hope there are some things she will never know . . . The very idea that she is the survivor . . . or the warrior . . .' He caught himself talking aloud, shook his head, and turned again to Katie. 'You might just run your fingers through your hair. It's standing on end – the travel, the Tempus Fugit, it will do that. Try to make half an attempt to tidy yourself. Such a sight!' Clicking his tongue, he disappeared, leaving Katie alone in the room. She was not sorry to see him go.

Whatever Alice and James were doing, it was taking hours. Katie had ample time to think, to wonder and remember. She had been here before, in Buckingham Palace, at the height of Queen Victoria's reign. She'd made a great friend of the Queen's young daughter, Princess Alice. And then there was James O'Reilly, the son of the Royal Household physician. She blushed slightly, thinking about James – stubborn, intelligent and none too keen on girls. Had she spent the entire time fighting with James? No – she could remember their spats, but also their friendship.

It was still a jumble in Katie's mind, but the events kept leaping out at her. New people, new places, and above all, danger. 'The Black Tide,' she muttered to herself. They said: 'The Queen must die, and with her will die the inequality of mankind.' But the Queen was still alive. And the Black Tide – were they still plotting against the Crown? Katie had no idea which year it was. How much time had passed? DuQuelle was of no help. He didn't age. For all she knew, Alice could be a grown-up now and James married with children. She looked at her yellow flannel pyjamas and became horribly embarrassed. She'd been longing to see her friends, but now . . . Taking DuQuelle's advice, she brushed her hands through her thick frizzy hair.

A rustle of skirts caught her attention, the quick clip of heels and a heavier tread behind. They were coming. Oh, why hadn't she put on one of those nice nightgowns, now lying in the bottom drawer of her bureau in New York? The door swung open and Alice was there. The moment Katie saw her friend she didn't care about her pyjamas or her hair anymore. Alice was just the same, a little older, but the same sweet, grave, thoughtful Alice.

'Katie!' she cried, taking her by the shoulders and then giving her a hug. 'My Katie! I knew you would come!'

James was standing behind the Princess, staring at Katie. When she looked at him, he pretended to study the floor, carefully. 'DuQuelle had warned me,' he said. 'But I hadn't realized you'd look like this. It's worse than the last time. What are you wearing?'

'They're my pyjamas. I wear them at night, in bed. I don't know why you're complaining, James. At least you can't see my knees this time.'

James flushed at the thought of Katie's knees and began to protest, but Alice, always the peacemaker, interrupted. 'Pyjamas, I believe they wear them in the Asian colonies, in India, I think. And they are very practical and modest. And Katie, yellow really is a lovely colour with your complexion.'

'And the frogs,' James added. 'So lovely, the frogs.'

Katie kicked James in the shin, just hard enough so he'd know she meant business, and they smiled at each other.

'I feel a lot better now that you're here,' Katie said. 'DuQuelle, he gives me the creeps.'

'He cannot be trusted,' James added.

Alice smoothed Katie's wild hair back from her face. 'It's not a question of "creeps" or "trust"; it's a question of need. We needed you, Katie, and Bernardo DuQuelle obliged. We would not have been able to call you back without him.'

'What was it like,' James asked, 'travelling through time? Were you aware of what was happening?'

Katie laughed at James. 'You didn't believe me at all last time, you kept saying I was a big phoney, some lunatic babbling on about the future – and now you want all the details. I don't think you deserve to know.'

It looked like the beginning of a typical Katie versus James squabble, but Alice stepped in. 'I do hope we will have much time to discuss all this, but there is a reason you are here, Katie, and we must use our time effectively.'

'I thought so,' Katie said, seeing James's face fall as Alice spoke. 'If there's anything I can do to help, you know I will. Now what's up?'

Alice glanced at James, who looked fixedly at the back of the Japanese screen. It was too hard for him to say.

'Do you know that James has a sister?' she asked Katie.

'My memory is still coming back,' Katie said. 'I remember a name – Grace – but I don't remember meeting her.'

'That's because you didn't,' James said brusquely. 'Grace was in Italy during your last flying visit.'

Katie ignored James's sarcasm. She could tell that something was wrong. When James was worried, or unhappy, he resorted to rudeness.

'Grace has returned,' Alice continued, 'and Katie, she is very ill indeed. She has a terrible, persistent cough and she's become so pale and thin. Any exercise seems to exhaust her, and now she's taken to her bed. Dr O'Reilly is treating her, but it would be so helpful if someone else . . .' Alice's voice trailed off.

'You know I'm not a doctor,' Katie said. 'I'm not a nurse; I'm not even studying medicine. I can only just cope with basic science and biology.'

'But you have interest in those topics,' Alice persisted in her gentle way. 'While you might dismiss your knowledge of medicine, you have a hundred years of progress that isn't at our command. James has spoken so warmly, and with such admiration of what you *do* know.'

James reverted to staring at the Japanese screen, but he did nod his head.

'Couldn't DuQuelle help?' Katie asked.

'DuQuelle,' James snorted.

'We did ask,' Alice replied. 'He was sympathetic, but he explained that he will only intervene in our world to keep history on course. In his opinion Grace is not a historical matter.'

Katie looked at James, who with great concentration was peeling a bit of lacquer off the screen. Grace. Katie remembered now. Grace was his only sister. James's mother had died when he was very young and Grace had tried hard to take her place, supplying much-needed love to James, his older brother Jack and their baby brother Riordan. Grace was not history to James. She was something much more important: the core of his reality.

'What year is it?' Katie asked James.

'Eighteen fifty-four,' James replied. 'What kind of a dim question is that?'

'Then I've been exposed to over a hundred and fifty years of stuff you don't know.' Katie answered. 'I can't guarantee anything. I probably won't be much help. But James, I really will try.'

James finally turned from the Japanese screen, his face relaxing just a bit as he looked at Katie. 'Thank you,' was all he said. Before Katie could ruin things, and give him a hug, Alice spoke up.

'There is nothing like the present. If Katie is not too fatigued, I think we should go to Grace now. Everyone else in the Palace is downstairs, occupied with the Emperor Napoleon III, so we can move with ease through the corridors.'

'Napoleon III?' Katie asked. 'I didn't even know there was a Napoleon III. Is he different from the Waterloo and Josephine guy? Or the same one but you call him something else?'

Alice looked rather shocked. 'He is Mama's guest, and no, he is not the warring traitor you speak of. That person is long dead.'

James shook his head. 'If your medical knowledge is anything like your history, Katie, we don't have a hope.'

Alice led Katie down the corridor, past the empty guards' room, and down a flight of stairs. Opening one of the many doors that lined the hall, they entered a pretty sitting room, bright and fresh, with a fire in the grate. 'Please wait here,' Alice said. 'It's best I explain, just a tiny bit, to Grace.' She went through a connecting door, into an adjoining room.

Katie briefly spied a large mahogany bed before Alice closed the door. It was very quiet. James was now staring at the fire with the same concentration he had applied to the Japanese screen.

'Nice room,' she said, then could have kicked herself.

'The Palace has been very kind to us. They have taken

Grace in until she convalesces, and moved my accommodation here', he said, pointing to another door leading from the sitting room.

'Oh,' Katie said, 'so that's your bedroom?' And could have kicked herself twice as hard. James turned a dull beet red and kept staring at the fire.

After what seemed like hours of silence, Alice returned. 'I didn't know what to say,' she said. 'How can one explain Katie? So I've simply told her you are a friend with much medical knowledge, and we wish her to meet you. She's quite excited. Do come along.'

As Katie followed she wasn't excited, just troubled. Could she help Grace?

Chapter Five
Grace

In the high mahogany bed, piled with pillows, lay Grace O'Reilly. She was a girl – really a young woman – of extraordinary beauty. Katie recognized her at once. The long red hair, the ruffled nightdress, now overlaid with a paisley shawl. But most of all it was the eyes – enormous and glistening with a sad and frightening knowledge. When she saw Katie, she pulled her shawl close and withdrew into the pillows.

James shot Katie one of his special killer looks. 'You should have changed before you came,' he said.

'Oh yeah, I should have packed a suitcase for this trip,' Katie retorted.

Alice came quickly to Grace's bedside. 'I am so very glad

you are able to make this acquaintance,' she said. 'I know it is very late, but we wanted you to meet the moment our guest arrived. Perhaps James has spoken to you of our mutual friend, Katie?'

'No,' James muttered. 'I've managed to keep Katie to myself.' Alice ignored him.

'Katie comes to us from – well, let us just say from very far away.'

Katie nodded stiffly. Here was the girl she'd found in her bed, in New York City, in the middle of the night. But that had been a vision, a sort of time communication. This was the real thing. 'Nice to meet you,' Katie said.

Grace had travelled widely and frequented some of the finest drawing rooms of Europe. She tried to rise to the occasion. 'And it is a pleasure to meet you,' she said, a slight Irish lilt giving her voice a special sweetness. She was making a magnificent effort to ignore the yellow pyjamas with the green and orange frogs. 'Hearing your voice, I believe you are, perhaps, from America? I've met many of your compatriots in Italy. They added much . . . much . . . vigour . . . and . . . originality to society.' She attempted to rise from her bed, but swayed and sank back onto the pillows, gasping for breath. James sprang forward and began to mix a potion from the bottles on her bedside table. 'Please forgive me,' Grace whispered. 'I am not as well as I would like to be.'

'Grace, don't talk,' James pleaded in a soft voice Katie

hadn't heard before. 'You don't have to play hostess. Katie hasn't come for a tea party. She has come to help you.' He looked Katie straight in the eye. 'She's come to help us.' He finished preparing the draught, and held it to Grace's lips. 'This will soothe you,' he said. 'Please drink this and, with your permission, Katie will ask you a few questions. We'll explain everything in the morning. Is it acceptable to you, Grace, if Katie tries to help?'

Grace stroked James's face and ruffled his hair. 'I didn't know you had an American friend, James,' she murmured in her sweet voice. 'You are growing up so quickly.'

James turned red again, and Katie interrupted. 'I'm really Princess Alice's friend. James, well, he puts up with me.' She smiled at him, all the while searching her mind for the right questions. How did the doctors in New York act? Mimi had millions of doctors and healers and analysts. She should be an expert on this. 'Can you describe your symptoms?' she finally asked, immediately thinking 'Dummy! Dumb question!'

Grace pulled her shawl tight. 'Really, I am feeling much better,' she protested weakly.

James took her hand and looking at her, tried to act stern. 'As I said, this isn't a tea party, Grace. If you want help, you need to tell the truth.'

Grace looked at her counterpane for a moment, pondering, deciding. She looked at Alice, who was smiling and nodding encouragement, and then she looked at Katie for a very long time, until she seemed to reach a decision. 'I'd like to speak to your friend alone,' she said.

James immediately shook his head. 'I really don't think . . .'

Alice interrupted. 'Well, I do. I think that is a splendid idea. They can begin to become acquainted.' She pressed Katie's shoulder and then managed to escort James from the room, without even touching him.

Silence fell. As Grace watched the retreating figures, Katie had a chance to get a really good look at her. Despite Grace's beauty, and her illness, there was still a lot of gentle fun in her face. She didn't look anything like her puffed-up, vain father, handsome as he was. 'Do you look like your mother?' Katie asked, and then almost tripped over her own tongue. 'I mean, I know that's a stupid thing to ask. Really wrong. I mean, I know your mother's dead and you might not want to talk about her, and then you are so ill, and . . .' Katie stopped talking and looked towards the door. She was afraid Grace would ask her to leave.

Grace stretched out a pale thin hand. 'Really, my dear, it's cruel to make me laugh, it only makes me cough. But you are such an original. Fancy James finding a bold, bright girl like you? No, I'm not going to ask you any questions. James is scrupulous in his relations, and the Princess is above reproach. If you are their friend, then you will be mine. But I need to talk quickly now. James has given me that potion to make me sleep. I'll have to talk while I still make sense, and am brave enough to say what I must.'

Without thinking, Katie sat down on the edge of the bed. She wasn't self-conscious any more. 'Tell me,' she said.

Grace took a sip of water to steady herself. 'Our lovely mother; do you know what our mother died of?' Grace asked.

Katie searched her memory. 'She died, I think, when your little brother Riordan was born. Is that right?'

Grace nodded. 'Yes, that was hard enough, the birth. But she was so weakened. You see, she was already frail. I know now, it wasn't just the childbirth, or the worry about father, or her homesickness for Ireland and family. She was suffering from the disease we never talk about. It was consumption. That is what really killed her.'

Katie looked at Grace's emaciated figure, the pale skin and the hectic flush in her cheeks. She knew now, she'd really known the first time she'd seen her. 'It's tuberculosis,' she said. 'Where I come from, we call it tuberculosis.'

Grace sank further into her pillows. 'Whatever you care to call it, it's a terrible, agonizing, wasting disease. And I know I have it, like our mother. And I believe, that like my mother, I am bound to die.'

Katie felt the tears well up in her eyes. Grace raised a languid arm and brushed the drops from her cheeks. 'Don't cry,' she said. 'I am trying to reconcile myself to death. The hardest part will be leaving James and Jack and little Riordan. Just look at James. How kind and sweet James is, that he would bring you to me.' Grace smiled sadly, shaking her head. 'And it shows how desperate he is to keep me. I hope you will not be offended, but Miss Katie, you are barely out of the nursery. Not much more than a child.'

Crying was not useful, and with effort Katie stopped. 'I'm not a child,' she protested. 'I've had lots of life experience.'

Grace smiled again. 'Perhaps,' she said, 'but you are younger than me. How can you possibly help?'

Katie walked to the window and, pulling back the pale blue curtains, looked out. It was a dark, clear night. She could hear Grace behind her, coughing slightly, her breath shallow and irregular. Grace was right. How could she help? She wasn't a doctor. And even if she was, she knew that in this time they wouldn't have the medicines she needed to treat Grace. What could she possibly do?

Grace spoke to her in a low, drawling voice. The drops James had given her were taking effect. 'Don't fret, my dear. It was sweet of you to come at all. And I'm so happy to meet a friend of my wee James. Our father pushes him so in his profession. James is young, and yet he has to play the learned doctor, and look after little Riordan . . . such a tearaway, Riordan. James has little time for friends, aside from our brother Jack. And there's Princess Alice. So lovely . . . so kind . . . Princess Alice . . .' Grace's head lulled back, her eyes began to flutter.

'What's that stuff that James gave you, Grace?' Katie asked.

'Laudanum,' Grace murmured. 'Tincture of laudanum. It is soothing, the laudanum . . .' Her eyes closed and her breathing became deep and even. She was asleep. Katie came to stand beside the bed. She smoothed Grace's long red hair back from her face and tidied the blankets and linens around her. Katie knew James and Alice were outside the door, hoping, depending on her.

'I'm such rubbish!' she cried, 'I don't know anything.' She looked at Grace's thin hands and thought about the way she'd laughed at James and ruffled his hair. She tried to give her three brothers the love they'd lost when their mother died. They needed her. There must be some way Katie could help. Though Katie still didn't know what to do, it dawned on her that she knew what *not* to do. While she might not be able to cure Grace, she could keep Dr O'Reilly from actively killing her. With a final look at the sleeping Grace, she squared her shoulders and went out to meet her friends.

'James, you should stop giving Grace the laudanum,' she said. 'It's addictive, and, like, really dangerous.'

'But laudanum is the primary medicine in the treatment of a fatigue like Grace's,' James said defensively. 'My father might not be the finest doctor in England, but I can't refute his administration of laudanum.'

'It's just covering up the disease, not curing it. All you're doing is doping Grace,' Katie argued. 'And it's silly to call it fatigue. Look at Grace, lying in there, gasping for breath. James, you need to call a spade a spade.'

For a moment James looked like he might push Katie right out of the door and back into her own time, but Alice stepped in.

'Jamie, you wanted Katie here as much as I. And now you must listen to her. And, Katie dear, James and I know how serious this illness is. Do you believe we would have disrupted your life for something trifling? You understand James's character, so you will appreciate how hard he is trying. He has been reading, researching – suggesting every known method possible to treat Grace.'

Alice could always put them both in their place, gently but firmly. Katie spoke quietly to James. 'I am sorry,' she said. 'It was rude of me to butt in like that. I guess I just wanted to start helping as soon as I could.'

'Apology accepted,' James said stiffly. 'And since we have summoned you here, we might as well make use of you.'

Katie knew from past experience that this was as close to reconciliation as she would get from James. 'I think – though I'm not sure – that Grace needs a good nutritious diet. We need to take her off all these drugs. Keep her off anything like that. Please tell me your father isn't bleeding her?'

'Father has been discussing the idea with his colleagues. Also cupping.'

'Well, you have to stop him. James, I know your father has the most gorgeous side-whiskers, and says wildly flattering things to the Queen, but really, his medicine! He's not exactly the world's greatest doctor.'

'Now, Katie,' Alice reproached her. 'You should show more respect for the senior medical adviser to the Queen.' But they all knew Dr O'Reilly had obtained his position through social, rather than medical, skill.

'I think your advice is good, Katie,' James said, 'not exactly ground-breaking medicine, but sound and practical.' Katie felt a rush of warmth, as praise from James was high praise indeed. 'Bringing my father to your point of view is quite impossible, though,' James added. 'He is stubborn, and will continue to keep Grace in bed, starve her, and dose her with laudanum and alcohol.'

All three were silent. Overruling the Queen's own doctor was a daunting task. 'If I could somehow be near Grace a lot, then I could make sure she gets the things she needs,' Katie suggested. 'I'd open the windows, get her the right food, take her for walks . . .'

James scowled. 'We've made such a stupid mistake,' he said. 'We called you here, but we forgot something. You don't even exist in this time. You have no family here, no background, no position. What would people think of a strange American girl who simply appears from nowhere – it's not as if you could roam around the Palace giving medical advice.'

'It is a problem,' Alice nodded. 'Entrance into the Palace circle comes either through service or social pedigree. I don't mean to sound snobbish, but you have neither, Katie. Where would you fit in?'

They looked Katie up and down, her tall lanky frame, currently clad in yellow flannel pyjamas, her bushy black hair, her funny foreign accent. Everything about her shouted out 'not one of us'. How could they possibly make her belong? Alice's face was full of concern 'Don't look so crestfallen, Katie. To us you are as family . . . it's just my family is quite particular . . . and . . .'

'It's OK, Alice,' Katie cut in. 'This isn't anything new. I'm kind of a freak in my own time too.'

James snorted, and they lapsed into silence.

With a brisk knock on the outer door, Bernardo DuQuelle entered. 'Princess Alice was lucky to escape the party,' he said. 'Really, what I have to endure in the name of diplomacy. The music! I loathe Liszt! Still ringing in my ears. But Napoleon III says the Empress is entranced by his work, and of course, the Queen adores anything Germanic. And then there's the endless debate on Russia, despite the late hour. All they can talk of is "teaching Russia a lesson, and protecting the Ottoman Empire." Do you truly think the English care a fig for the Turks? It is almost a relief to return to the problem of Katie. How shall she be enabled to help Grace – an exciting challenge I'd say.'

Katie had a sinking feeling he'd been outside the door listening all the time.

'We cannot have her lurking behind screens or doubled over in Chinese chests this time.' DuQuelle tapped the knob of his walking stick against his chin. 'We'll have to make her into someone. Someone important enough to have free reign of the Palace – though looking at her just now, I don't think that importance will stem from the worlds of fashion or beauty.'

Alice pursed her lips slightly. DuQuelle's banter was easy, but always left her with an uneasy feeling. Still, she spoke to him with great courtesy. 'Do you have any ideas, M. DuQuelle?'

'Ah, Princess, I do indeed. Have any of you ever heard of Lewis Tappan Esq.?' They all shook their heads. 'That's a good thing,' DuQuelle continued jauntily. 'Few people will have heard of him, and even fewer met him; but Lewis Tappan is a power to be reckoned with. He is a prominent American, in the fields of commercial trade, finance and credit. An important figure in Boston and New York.'

'How can this Lewis Tappan help me?' Katie asked. Bernardo DuQuelle waved his walking stick in the air, as if painting an imaginary picture.

'Let us pretend that Lewis Tappan is on the Grand Tour, with his family. He has a wife, rather prim and sickly, two strapping sons, and an equally strapping daughter. Ah, the New World, it does raise them big and strong.'

'But what does this family have to do with me?' Katie asked again.

'Imagine the Tappan family, visiting Florence, the cradle of the Italian Renaissance. No American on the Grand Tour of Italy would miss Florence.'

Katie sighed. DuQuelle would answer her questions only when he was ready.

'There the illustrious Tappans meet the beautiful Grace O'Reilly,' he continued, smiling at his own narrative. 'They are taken with Miss O'Reilly. Who wouldn't be? Particularly Miss Tappan, the strapping daughter. They become inseparable, the best of friends in that charming way of young girls. So it only seems natural that when Miss Tappan visits England, she would want to be with her dear friend Grace.'

'But I haven't seen this girl in the Palace,' James said. 'And Grace has never mentioned her.'

'She is standing before you,' DuQuelle replied.

'Me?' Katie cried.

'I understand,' Alice exclaimed. 'Katie will pretend to be Miss Tappan, Grace's dear friend, come to England to visit.'

James spoke up. 'I'm not certain I approve of this plan,' he said. 'We all know Katie is courageous, but she can be foolish and she takes risks. To have her so exposed at the absolute centre of English life could put her in danger.'

'But Grace *is* at the centre of English life,' Katie protested. 'She's tucked up in bed in Buckingham Palace. If I'm to help, I have to be here too.'

'Katie is right,' Alice chimed in. 'I don't wish to see her in any danger, but she will need to stay close to Grace. And she isn't foolish, James – she's just a bit impetuous.' Alice smiled at her friend. 'James and I will be near, ready to help at a moment's notice; and of course Bernardo DuQuelle has abilities far beyond anything . . .' Alice trailed off, slightly embarrassed, while James glared at the floor.

Katie looked up at Bernardo DuQuelle. Could they trust him enough to adopt his plan? The lids drooped over his eyes as he examined the head of his walking stick, humming a tune from *La Traviata*. She noticed that his dark curls were carefully arranged across his creased, white forehead. Did he dye his hair? Did his sort even get grey hair? What was his age? Fifty? One hundred? One thousand? He looked old, but did he even age? Everything about him provoked unanswered questions. They were indebted to DuQuelle. He had once even saved Katie's life. But they knew he was dangerous. They didn't understand him and his motives were questionable. Was it really a good thing to have him nearby? The silence became strained.

DuQuelle sensed what they were thinking, and seemed to revel in the uncertainty he created. 'Then we are agreed: Katie will take the role of Miss Katherine Tappan,' he said crisply. 'Now I will use some of those abilities referenced by Princess Alice. We need letters of introduction to the Palace – the Tappan family might be obsolete here, but they have powerful connections in the United States of

America.' DuQuelle smiled to himself. 'I think I will write one from John Quincy Adams II – a man with a fine future, though not quite of the grandfather's stature.'

Alice's eyes widened. 'But wouldn't that be forgery?'

DuQuelle's smile broadened, deepening the creases around his eyes. 'Please do excuse me, Princess, but bringing Katie here was a violation of the laws of nature and of time – bending the laws of man is child's play in comparison.' He looked at James. 'Don't worry,' he added, 'I'll cover my tracks and intercept any correspondence that might emanate from the Foreign Office or the Prime Minister. The Palace will be easier to handle. I don't believe the Queen is in communication with many Americans – not with Mr Adams, and certainly not with Mr Tappan. She tends to stay within her area of comfort – princely cousins, uncle kings, the occasional grand duchess . . .'

DuQuelle looked down at Katie, shaking his head in disapproval. 'So much to do and so little time. There's the letter to the Lord Chamberlain, the sponsor to be found, the dress, the train, the headdress, the curtsy – though I don't believe Katie will ever handle the curtsy . . .'

'What are you talking about?' Katie asked.

'The presentation,' he replied briskly. 'We need to prepare you for the presentation to the Queen. If you are to be staying in the Palace, you must be presented to the Queen.'

For the first time Katie could remember, James O'Reilly was laughing at DuQuelle. 'This must be a tease,' he said. 'The idea of Katie being presented at court!'

'You may laugh,' 'DuQuelle replied, 'but there is no other way. The Queen is holding a presentation, a Court Drawing Room, in ten days; and Katie, I mean Miss Katherine Tappan, will be presented at that drawing room.'

Katie did not like the sound of this, and James continued to bark with laughter. Only Princess Alice seemed to take DuQuelle seriously. 'But of course,' she said. 'This will liberate Katie, give her stature in the household, making it possible for her to go anywhere with Grace.'

'Do you mean to place her on the marriage market?' James joked. 'Then Katie could find a suitable country gentleman and settle down.' Katie kicked him with her fluffy bedroom slipper, but Alice simply ignored him.

'In truth, she's much too young to be presented,' Alice mused. 'But Katie's so well grown, she can pass for seventeen, or even eighteen.'

'Overgrown,' James commented, looking in amazement at Katie's large foot in the fluffy slipper.

'Oh, do shut up,' Katie replied. 'I want to do this like I want a hole in my head, but the plan does make sense. Now what do I need to do?'

'I'll tutor you,' Princess Alice suggested. 'Though with only ten days – the curtsy in itself can take months to master. We have to acquire the proper court dress. As M.

DuQuelle said, there are the plumes, the headdress, the embroidered train – it takes much practice, to learn to handle the train – and if Katie's coming out, she'll need an entire wardrobe.'

'And a trousseau,' James added. 'Within months she'll need a wedding trousseau.'

DuQuelle's mouth turned up at the corners. 'It would indeed be a problem, if some young nobleman were transfixed by Katie.'

He was looking quite merry – for DuQuelle – but suddenly he stopped mid-stream. He sniffed the air in that odd way of his, and his face became still and very pale. Katie started to ask him a question, but he put his hand up, listening to the silence. He sniffed again. 'Can you smell that?' he asked. 'Can you hear that?' They all shook their heads. 'How very strange,' he murmured. 'What a dank and foul smell; the stench of polluted water. And the sound; it is something falling into that water, from quite a height. Something heavy and lifeless, making a great splash.'

'There is no water here,' James protested. DuQuelle continued to listen and sniff.

'The River Thames,' he said. 'London. Something is afoot in London. Something that bodes ill.' Bernardo DuQuelle looked at Katie. 'Lord Belzen, could he possibly know, already, that you are here?'

Chapter Six

Tower Bridge

DuQuelle was right. Something was afoot in London. Not that one could see much. The inky blackness of night had been overlaid by a particular mix of soot and fog, known by the locals as a London particular. And this February night the cocktail of wet coal dust and icy droplets was foul in every way. It caught in the lungs and left traces of grime running down cheek and cloak. It was weather that invited one to stay indoors, bolt the shutters and draw close to the fire. Yet here was Lord Twisted, exposing both his health and a fine new Chesterfield coat to the harshest of elements.

Lord Twisted was not adverse to midnight revels – nor had he spared himself the baser aspects of the city. Indeed, he had often been spotted in St. Giles in search of the night's pleasures. Yet standing on Tower Bridge, at midnight, with a nincompoop like Sir Lindsey Dimblock, was far from fun.

As if trying to add to his irritation, Sir Lindsey asked for the twentieth time, 'Are you certain he said Tower Bridge? And at this time of night?'

Lord Twisted turned his velvet collar up against the cold and nodded curtly.

'As I said . . .' was his only response.

Sir Lindsey was not used to cold or discomfort, and his pride was wounded. 'But really, dash it, such a demand is impertinent,' he complained. 'And to come from him, a nobody, no footing at court, no position in the country – a man of no standing. Lord Belzen, I swear, is no lord, no lord at all. To have him call the tunes, and for us to dance to them! Tower Bridge – at midnight! If I wasn't so hard up, Twisted, I'd be home, safe in my own bed, and not catching my death of cold on a London bridge at midnight.'

Lord Twisted resisted the urge to throttle his companion. 'But you *are* that hard up,' he reminded Sir Lindsey. 'Your debts at gaming are the talk of society. You have no knack for cards, and yet you play.' Lord Twisted omitted the fact that most of Sir Lindsey's losses at cards had been to Lord Twisted, and most of the money Sir Lindsey so missed had been rehoused in Lord Twisted's pockets. Not that much of that money remained. Lord Twisted lived a life of luxury –

in keeping with his title, but far beyond his means. Jewels, horses, fine wines and women – nothing was too good for him. But it was for him alone: his only daughter, the Honourable Emma, was forced to make her own way as a nursemaid in Buckingham Palace.

Lord Twisted looked at Sir Lindsey Dimblock. 'He truly is an idiot,' he thought, trying to mask his dislike. Sir Lindsey had sold his military commission, his family estates, his forestry, his mining rights, even the Dimblock silver. About the only thing left was the illustrious Dimblock pedigree. If ever an aristocrat needed money, it was Sir Lindsey. Belzen would lend this money to him. Lord Belzen, with his fake title and unknown history, was always generous. For him, the association with the gentry was worth the financial layout.

And yet Lord Twisted feared Belzen. There was something about the man. On first meeting, he seemed handsome, almost a gentleman. But the more one looked at Belzen, the more uncomfortable one became, until it was necessary to look away. What was it? Twisted wondered. Was it the dart of Belzen's eyes, the palsy-like shake of his body, or the way his head swayed strangely, as if not truly attached to his neck or torso.

No, Lord Twisted wasn't looking forward to this meeting, but Sir Lindsey needed the money, and Belzen loved to lend. This was no good deed, though. Lord Twisted knew Sir Lindsey; once he had the money, he would not pay off his debts but go back to the gaming tables. And some of that newly lent money would be Lord Twisted's by the end of the night. And Belzen? He would be grateful for the introduction to Sir Lindsey; yet another aristocrat in his debt, another victim. This might even lead Belzen to turn a blind eye to the vast amount Lord Twisted owed him already.

Sir Lindsey was stamping his feet to stave off the cold, and muttering to himself, 'To keep me waiting, really, to keep ME waiting . . .' And then the wait was over. Neither man had heard a sound, yet Lord Belzen was before them, undulating slightly, and wrapped in a long, hooded cloak.

'Perhaps it is his nose,' Twisted thought, as Belzen bowed to them. It was a large, strangely blunted nose, with wide dark nostrils – more of a snout than a nose. Twisted shivered. Lord Belzen seemed to bring a deeper cold with him, making the uncomfortable weather unbearable.

When Belzen spoke it was softly, quietly, with a pointed politeness. 'Lord Twisted, a pleasure to see you again; and Sir Lindsey, what a pleasure to be introduced to such an illustrious member of the royal circle. I trust the night has not been too much for you? I do apologize for the time and place of this meeting, but such matters, between gentlemen, are best dealt with in secret.'

'I don't know why we couldn't meet at my club, or even a public house, somewhere enclosed and warm,' Sir Lindsey Dimblock complained.

'Servants, waiters,' Belzen murmured, 'so quick to hear everything, to spread the story. This is a case where discretion is more important than personal comfort. We need to be entirely alone.'

Sir Lindsey barely returned Belzen's bow. He was willing to take money from this man, but he was not willing to treat him as an equal. Belzen was a money-lender, someone on the darker side of commerce. 'I believe we are here to conclude a business transaction,' he replied curtly. 'I am ready to do business.'

Lord Twisted looked from one man to the next. Sir Lindsey, bullish, stupid and proud, wanted the money but not the obligation. Belzen was angered by his tone. His body twitched in a weird convulsion; his head darted out from its hood. For a moment Lord Twisted could see Belzen's watery blue eyes. They were angry. And yet his voice stayed soft, though with an ominous hiss. 'Of course,' he replied. 'It is too cold for pleasantries. I will name my terms.'

Lord Belzen's terms were surprisingly generous. Even a dunderhead like Sir Lindsey could see that. He could return the money when he wished, with only a small additional payment for all Belzen's trouble. Sir Lindsey did not bother to question the offer. Money was money, and he needed it. 'I accept your terms,' he said to Lord Belzen. 'Shall we draw up the paperwork?'

'A gentleman's agreement,' Belzen replied. 'A handshake will do.' At this Lord Twisted held his breath. Would Sir

Lindsey take Lord Belzen's hand? Lord Belzen reached under his cloak and, removing his glove, held out a long, slim hand. Even on this night of fog and murk, it glowed with a damp opalescent hue, as if never struck by the sun. It was strangely joined, almost webbed, and curved downward. It was a thing of revulsion.

Sir Lindsey hesitated, staring aghast at Belzen's hand. How much did he need the money? In truth, he was desperate. He did not take off his own glove, but did hold out his hand, touching Belzen's briefly. A shudder ran through his body. 'I believe we are done here,' he said. 'I will await the funds at my club address.' Without a bow, he turned to go.

Lord Belzen then spoke. 'Just one more thing,' he hissed softly into the night.

Lord Twisted knew this was not a good sign. Sir Lindsey, in his arrogance, had angered Belzen. This 'one more thing' was likely to be a large one.

Sir Lindsey had the promise of funds, but as yet no money in his purse. He stopped. 'If you could be quick,' he snapped.

Lord Belzen's head moved forward in that unnatural jerking manner, but his voice stayed even. 'It has to do with the war.'

'There is no war,' Sir Lindsey replied.

'But there will be,' Belzen retorted, a new edge to his voice. 'There will be war declared against Russia, and very soon. We are already gathering troops, they are being shipped out as we speak, travelling to Constantinople and then on through the Black Sea. Only for exploratory purposes, at this point, only to observe, but war there will be.'

Lord Twisted spoke up. 'But of course. Sir Lindsey knows this. Why else would Napoleon III be visiting at this time? The French will ally with Great Britain to save the Ottoman Empire. We will be partners in war. We will defeat Russia.'

'But will we?' Lord Belzen asked. 'That is a question for another day. I have a great interest in this war brewing in the Crimea. I would be grateful for any information I can receive on this war . . . financially grateful.'

'I am neither willing, nor equipped for any such exploit,' Sir Lindsey retorted. 'I am no longer a part of the military; I have no knowledge.'

'But you could,' Belzen insisted in his soft insinuating way. 'You have a military background, come from a military pedigree; and so does Lord Twisted.' Underneath his cloak, Belzen rolled his shoulders in excitement. Sir Lindsey stared in shock. Even Lord Twisted felt rising alarm as Belzen continued to unveil his plan. 'With a letter here, a string pulled there, you could attach yourselves to the highest echelon of the military campaign. Raglan, I believe, will be in command. From there you could inform me. I will set up the line of communication. You will go un-detected, but not unrewarded.'

Lord Twisted liked the sound of financial reward, but there were so many questions about Belzen. Which side of this war was he actually on? How dishonest was this activity? And the line of communication, how secure could it be? Underhand deeds did not bother Lord Twisted so much as getting caught.

Sir Lindsey Dimblock had no such questions. He had made up his mind. Belzen was not a lord, not a gentleman, and probably not even British. In short, he was a traitor, and he was asking Sir Lindsey to become a spy. Gambling and gaming debts were one thing, but betraying Queen and country were another.

He'd had enough of the bitter foul night. He'd rather face financial ruin and social disgrace than go any further. Turning to Belzen, he roared into his face. 'I am no informer, no spy, no traitor. For that is what you are asking. I will pay my gaming debts some other way. Twisted, I suggest you leave with me, immediately. Any further communication with this . . . this . . . creature will only incriminate you further. It is below us to speak to him.'

Belzen darted forward, blocking Sir Lindsey's way. His soft voice had turned into a high rasping hiss, painful to the ear. 'You call me a creature,' he fairly shrieked, 'below you, when you are the lowest form of man . . . and man himself is so low. My followers would tear you to pieces – you are stupid, arrogant and swollen with false pride, feeding off the world. You think you can leave . . . it is too late . . .'

It was dark and the atmosphere was thick with fog. Lord Twisted could never be certain of what he saw. One moment Belzen stood writhing and hissing before Sir Lindsey Dimblock, the next moment Belzen's head darted from underneath his hood – but was it his head? The beaked, blunted nose, the striking movement; he seemed more serpent than man. Sir Lindsey could see more. He cried out and backed against the rail of the bridge, flinging his arms up to protect himself. Belzen struck and struck again, his cloak rippling around him, his hissing mixing with Sir Lindsey's shrieks.

Sickened and terrified, Lord Twisted tried to run, but his legs were too weak. Behind him came the inescapable sound of Belzen, the angry hissing turning into a noxious gagging. Sir Lindsey's cries grew weaker and weaker – and then all was silent. Almost against his will, Lord Twisted turned to see the aftermath of the assault. Belzen was gone, but Sir Lindsey Dimblock lay slumped against the side of the bridge. His body was slit from groin to chin and his mouth was filled with a strange black tar.

Lord Twisted swayed and staggered as he looked down on his friend's mutilated body. 'You were a weak man,' he muttered, 'and a foolish one; but you did not deserve this. You must not be found.' Gathering what strength he could, Lord Twisted grasped Sir Lindsey by the heels and manoeuvred him on to the rails of the bridge. With a final push the body was over, plunging into the River Thames below; the splash of the befouled, lifeless object reverberating through the dead of night. 'At least you have escaped,' he said quietly, 'while I am left tied to this devil of a man. I am to be the spy, the traitor, and I must keep this dreadful secret.'

Twisted had the sinewy stubbornness one often finds in the true coward. Lord Belzen might be Lucifer himself, but to stay alive Twisted would follow his every command. For now, it was best to try and forget all that he had seen. 'I need a drink,' he muttered to himself, 'or something stronger.' He searched his mind for public houses nearby, but again his strength failed him. Weak and dazed, Lord Twisted leant over the rails of Tower Bridge, and vomited into the dark River Thames below.

Chapter Seven

The Queen's Drawing Room

Katie, in her role of Miss Katherine Tappan, sat very straight in a carriage on the Mall, leading up to Buckingham Palace. She had never been more uncomfortable. Her bushy black hair had been temporarily tamed – swept up tight at the back of her head, the curls laboriously tucked and pinned. Atop her hair was a headdress, a strange confection of tulle and flowers and large ostrich feathers, two of them, the middle one over a foot high. For a court presentation, Queen Victoria insisted on feathers, white feathers, very *large* white feathers. 'I don't want any fiddly fluffy things in their hair,' she was reported to have said. 'I want to *see* the feathers, from a long way off, as the girls come towards me to curtsy.'

'Well, she won't miss these, that's for sure,' Katie muttered. The feathers were so tall that they touched the roof of the carriage. She felt like she had a 30-pound wedding cake planted just above her forehead. She jerked her chin up in defiance and felt the whole thing lunge to one side.

'Oh, do sit still,' came a weary voice from the other side of the carriage. It was the Honourable Emma Twisted and she was Katie's sponsor for the presentation. Usually girls were presented at court by their mothers, but this was not possible for Katie. First of all, Mimi was stuck in another century. Second, Mimi was, well, Mimi. It was bad enough being presented to the Queen, but being presented to the Queen while standing next to Mimi – probably in a black satin 'body stocking' – didn't bear thinking about. Besides, a divorced person couldn't be presented to the Queen and Mimi was three times divorced. If the Queen had known who Katie's real mother was, there would be no chance of a presentation at all.

Mimi might not be presentable, but Katie suddenly missed her mother. How did time work between centuries? Would Mimi still be sleeping? And then she thought of Diuman – who might have returned to 23C by now – and was glad to be in another time. 'It could be worse,' Katie said.

'I don't see how,' the Honourable Emma replied tartly. 'You must be the least important person ever to kiss the Queen's hand. How you appeared on the Lord Chancellor's list – and how I ended up as your sponsor – is beyond my comprehension.'

Katie could have told the Honourable Emma Twisted how it happened: Bernardo DuQuelle had had a word in the Lord Chamberlain's ear – that's how she'd ended up on the list. And Lord Twisted, Emma's less than honourable father, had accepted a hefty purse in exchange for his daughter's patronage. Katie looked at Emma Twisted, with her drooping feathers and worn-through velvets. Yes, DuQuelle had bribed her father, but why add to her misery? Katie peered out of the carriage window.

The past nine days had been total agony. Katie had been excited at first, to receive the card from the Lord Chamberlain, requesting her presence at the Queen's Drawing Room. But then the training began. Princess Alice helped whenever she could slip away from her lessons, and Grace gave advice from her bed. But it quickly became apparent that Katie wasn't any good at this sort of thing.

'Walking,' she thought, reviewing the week as the horses snorted and stamped before her motionless carriage, 'You'd think I'd know how to walk.' But walking across a room, towards the Queen, had nothing to do with the heel to toe movement she'd been practising since the age of two. Now, at her advanced age, she was learning to walk all over again.

It was a sort of gliding, mincing movement, mostly around the knees and ankles; the shoulders squared but relaxed, the head held upright but with a sense of modesty. There was certainly no swinging of the hips; and the kind of pelvic thrust Mimi practised on stage might put her in prison. So she'd spent several days in Grace's pretty sitting room, trying to sail across the carpet with small gliding steps.

This new walking was just the first stage. 'You are not allowed to turn your back on the Queen,' Alice informed her. 'You have to back out of the room.' So all the mincing and gliding had to take place in reverse. Hard as Katie found the walking, it was nothing to the curtsy. Not just a curtsy, but a curtsy with a bow in the middle of it. Having crossed the room, Katie would stand, one leg in front of the other. Slowly she would bend her legs until her knees were just above, but not touching, the floor. Holding this position, she had to bend the upper part of her body forward, towards the Queen's hand. Hundreds of women performed this motion every year, but for Katie, with her long lanky legs, it was agony. Tightrope-walking or even lion-taming seemed easier options.

Alice drilled Katie relentlessly. 'You need to hold the positions,' Alice explained. 'Three seconds for each movement.'

'I can't hold the positions for three seconds,' Katie wailed. 'I can't hold the positions at all; not quickly, not slowly, not at all.' But Alice was insistent, three seconds for each movement.

'DOWN, two, three; BOW, two, three; BACK, two, three; UP, two, three . . .' Katie brought her knees down with a jerk, and managed to bend her body forward for the bow. But when she tried to right herself the effort was too much. Her ankles began to wobble, her knees to shake, and before she knew it she was sprawled across the floor.

Bernardo DuQuelle and James O'Reilly had been less than helpful. DuQuelle stared in silence, shaking his head from time to time, while James just laughed out loud.

'I've never thought much of the womanly accomplishments,' James said. 'I've been scornful of the dancing and simpering. But Katie makes it all look so difficult. There must be something to it after all.'

Katie tried to kick James, but this proved impossible. She had bed-sheets tied around her waist doubling as the long skirt she'd have to wear, and a tablecloth attached to her shoulders to replicate the train. Alice had told her the train would be at least three feet long and over fifty inches wide. Katie was used to a school uniform – her short skirt and sweater or, even better, a pair of jeans. All these sheets and tablecloths – it felt like she was being ambushed in the bedding department at Bloomingdale's.

Every time she moved, the sheet would wrap around her legs. When she bent down to untangle it, the tablecloth flipped over her head. She twisted and struggled, but ended up on the floor. Every single time, she ended up on the floor.

'Well done,' James said. 'The Queen will be most impressed.'

'Jamie, really!' Alice remonstrated.

'I'd like to see you do better, James O'Reilly,' Grace chimed in.

Katie continued to sit on the floor. 'He's right you know,' she said, 'I am hopeless.' But she was also stubborn. James would not get the better of her. Staggering to her feet, Katie hitched the sheet over one arm and the tablecloth over the other. 'From the top,' she said.

So for nine days Katie had glided forward, minced backwards, and curtsied, curtsied, curtsied. A special French dressmaker known to Bernardo DuQuelle was smuggled into the Palace for Katie's dress fittings. But it wasn't just a dress she was measured for: Katie now owned several sets of Victorian undergarments – drawers, chemises, petticoats and a corset. The drawers were actually quite airy, the chemise comfortable, and she'd get used to the six petticoats she'd have to wear. It was the corset that drove her mad – a tight panelled thing with ladders of cord in the back. She'd begged not to have to wear one, but Mademoiselle Vernet, the dressmaker, had refused to make the dress unless she was laced into a corset. 'Oh, *mon Dieu!*' she exclaimed. 'What kind of girl has the figure of this? Such bulk in one so young. I will not make the dress for court with a waist beyond nineteen inches.'

The corset went over Katie's chemise, and each day Alice pulled the stays a little bit tighter and measured Katie's waist. 'I think I look like a freak', Katie said, surveying herself in the mirror. 'I can't eat in this thing; I can barely breathe in it.'

It turned out she had an ally in James. Though he'd rather die than see Katie in her corset, he had read a great deal about the damage such restrictive garments did to women's health. 'It isn't good for her,' James told the others, 'it isn't good for any of you.'

Grace laughed from her bed. 'Dear James, you are such a firebrand. Is it rights for women now?'

James shook his head vehemently. 'Women's rights, that's a farce. Women are so silly about everything; clothes are just the beginning.' Katie started to argue, but doubled over with a stitch in her side. 'This had better be worth it,' was all she could gasp.

On the eve of Katie's presentation, Mademoiselle Vernet arrived with the finished dress. As she laid it out on Grace's bed, the girls examined it from every angle. It didn't look like any presentation dress they'd ever seen.

'It is very simple,' Grace commented. 'I thought there would be more flounces and tucks; something to try and counter Katie's height.'

'It's very lovely,' Alice said, 'and will suit Katie's figure to perfection. But it's terribly bare, even for a court dress.'

Mademoiselle Vernet looked at her own handiwork with complete approval.

'There was no point in hiding the girl's great height,' she explained. 'We cannot fight it, so we embrace that she is tall and big, and perhaps beautiful in that she is rugged. She is like her country, the Americas, no?'

Katie stared and stared at the dress. She had imagined herself in the flowery, lacy, ruffled dresses of the day, and had known she would look a fool. But this dress, with its clean lines and beautiful materials, just might work. It had a thick white satin bodice, which crossed over the breast and ended in small capped sleeves. The white satin skirt wasn't the huge, flounced, bell-shaped style of the day, and Katie realized, with relief, that she wouldn't have to wear all six petticoats. Four would suffice to create a soft, billowing movement. The extremely simple design contrasted with a wonderful tulle train, embroidered with thousands of tiny swooping birds.

'They are eagles,' Mademoiselle Vernet explained. 'The bird of your country, a bird of fierceness and freedom. It is a lovely dress, and you will look well in it. Though not in the feathered headdress demanded by *la Reine* Victoria, bah!'

Alice began to protest, but Mademoiselle Vernet was already saluting Bernardo DuQuelle. With a kiss on each cheek, she was gone.

The nine days had whisked by, and now Katie sat in a carriage actually wearing the lovely dress. She had a fan and gloves; and in her lap was an enormous bouquet of white lilies and roses. A long white satin quilted cloak was wrapped around her shoulders, to keep out the February chill. Emma Twisted looked like she could use a nice, warm cloak, but Katie didn't dare offer a corner of hers.

'Do try not to crush your gown,' Emma Twisted admonished. As if in answer, Katie's stomach gave an enormous growl. All guests had to arrive in a carriage, so Katie had left the Palace only to circle the park and return. They'd been sitting in the carriage for two hours now, and Katie hadn't eaten that morning. How could she in that dress?

The carriage finally began to move. They slowly pulled through the gates of Buckingham Palace, and under the wide stone archway, to the internal courtyard. The last time, when she had flown through time and space, it had been 1851. She had often looked out of the windows of the Palace into this very courtyard. Then she'd been an observer, in hiding. Now she was going to be a part of it all.

The excitement surged through Katie and she gave a little skip as she descended the carriage steps. The skip turned into a stumble, and a liveried footman bounded forward to catch her. Righting herself, she followed Emma through broad double doors into a large red and gold room, one of the most opulent public rooms in the Palace. To date, Katie had spent her time in attic rooms, nurseries and secret passages. She looked around her at the red walls and gilt detail. 'It's really gorgeous,' she said.

'Try not to expose yourself,' the Honourable Emma Twisted hissed. 'The less you say the better off we will be.'

Taking Katie by the arm, she led her up the grand staircase. It was extremely tall and wide, giving an unending sense of parade and pageantry. Katie was just beginning to feel terribly important when they reached the top, made a sharp left and found themselves in a crowded corridor, literally crammed with girls. The stark hall was awash with white dresses, huge bouquets, fans, gloves and feathers. Everywhere Katie looked she could see hundreds of twitching, trembling white feathers. 'It's a debutante migration,' she joked; though she knew by now that the Honourable Emma Twisted was immune to her sense of humour.

Some of the girls stood very straight, as if already in the presence of the Queen; others leaned against the wall, fanning themselves in resignation. A few continued to practise their curtsies. The noise was ear-splitting, the particular high-pitched clip and drawl of the British upper class.

Katie felt stiff and awkward at the back of the crowd. She was a good head taller than the rest. Emma Twisted looked at her with distaste. 'I was hoping to get through this unnoticed, but that will not be possible. With your extremely peculiar dress and your bizarre height . . . do you know, they have a name for you already? You're referred to as the *giraffe* up and down the Palace halls . . .'

The *giraffe*. Katie looked down at her bouquet. Red splotches were appearing on her arms, just above her long white gloves. She had thought, just this once, that she looked beautiful. But the Honourable Emma Twisted was right, she was a freak.

'I don't believe *giraffe* is the correct term at all,' a quiet but imperious voice spoke behind her. Katie turned to see Princess Alice, smiling brightly, but the smile faded when she turned to the Honourable Emma Twisted. 'I am acquainted with Miss Katherine Tappan,' she continued, 'and I have always considered her to be one of the finest looking girls of my acquaintance. She is statuesque, yes. Don't you think this gives her a classical Grecian appeal?'

The Honourable Emma Twisted blushed. She worked in Buckingham Palace, as Riordan O'Reilly's nursemaid. Despite her grand pedigree, she was nothing more than an impoverished gentlewoman, taking charity from the Royal Family. Mocking this gawky American, Miss Katherine Tappan, might have been a mistake . . .

Word had rippled along the corridor that the Queen's young daughter, Princess Alice, was already there amongst them. One by one the girls sank into deep curtsies, wave after wave of rustling tulle and silk. The deepest curtsy of all came from Emma Twisted. Katie looked at Princess

Alice and slowly bent her knees – DOWN, two, three . . .

Alice helped her up. 'See', she whispered encouragingly, 'you did that beautifully.'

All eyes were on Katie, and whispers went up and down the line of girls. Who was this Miss Katherine Tappan? Perhaps she should be invited to their ball next week, or to a country-house weekend? They turned to consult their mamas. Katie gave Alice a shaky smile. 'One word from you and I'm a hit,' she said. 'Now I just have to get through the curtsy without landing on my – ' Alice laughed and placed her gloved hand against Katie's lips.

'Your language,' she admonished, 'is far worse than your curtsy. It will all go well, I know it. And I will be standing directly behind the Queen, willing you on. I promise.' Giving Katie's hand a squeeze, she made her way through the crowds of girls, all bobbing their salutation to the daughter of the Queen.

The line began to move and the girls broke off their inquisition. Katherine Tappan might be of interest, but they had a date with destiny, an engagement with the Queen. It took hours, and with each passing moment, the tension mounted. The girl in front of Katie was muttering under her breath, 'Your Royal Highness, your Highness, ma'am . . .'

'These interlopers can't even manage the correct address . . .' Emma Twisted sniffed. 'It's not as if they'll ever see the Queen again . . . not like us . . .' Us! Katie's lips twitched, but she was finally at the door.

To curtsy before loyal Alice was one thing, but to curtsy before the Queen and court – Grace's prettily papered sitting room had not prepared her for this. It had to be the longest room she had ever seen, filled with ornate columns and statues, dripping in gilt detail. The courtiers were five deep down either side of the room: ladies-in-waiting, gentlemen of the court, the crème of the diplomatic corps, the heroes of the military, titled politicians and a scattering of archbishops. Tired of standing and bored by now, they were talking amongst themselves. The new stars of court life had come and gone, all that was left were some dreary daughters of the clergy and a few foreign stragglers. A footman spread out Katie's beautiful embroidered train as she handed her card to the Lord Chamberlain. 'MISS KATHERINE TAPPAN OF THE UNITED STATES OF AMERICA,' he announced.

Katie knew the drill. She had to walk down the central aisle of the room, curtsy to the Queen, perform the ceremonial kiss of the Queen's hand, curtsy to all the other royalty in the room, then walk back up the aisle – backwards of course. There was one slight problem. She wasn't moving at all. Mentally, she was telling her legs to go, but physically nothing was happening. She was glued to the spot. She could imagine two of the footmen picking her up by the elbows and carrying her out by a side door, like a statue being removed from the Great Exhibition. At the very end of the room she could see Princess Alice, looking worried even from this great distance. Then suddenly she was on the go, flung forward into the room. Someone had given her a big push from behind. Had she really been kicked in the . . .?

Staggering, she rebalanced and, looking straight towards the end of the room, put one foot in front of the other. Alice was nodding with each step, as if to will her down the aisle. Next to Alice was Bertie, the Prince of Wales, staring at Katie and her great height with some astonishment. On Alice's other side was her older sister Vicky, the Princess Royal. Vicky was paying no attention to the presentation, but was fussing over a boy with blond curls. As the boy turned his gaze to Katie, she recognized the disagreeable child with bright ringlets, now grown to youth. He tossed back his curls and laughed out loud. This was Vicky's young nephew Felix.

Felix's laugh was picked up by the courtiers, a whisper of a snigger rippling down the room. Katie held her head high, careful not to overbalance the awkward headdress. She recognized a handful of people. She had met them before, on her first foray into times past. Alice's younger brother, Prince Leopold, was seated, because of his illness. When he saw Katie, he opened his mouth and nudged his tutor, the Reverend Robinson Duckworth. 'So Duckworth is still employed,' Katie thought, 'even after all the trouble we gave him last time.' James's father, Dr O'Reilly, was there, delighting in such a pompous occasion. Alice's governess, the Baroness Lehzen, was standing near the Queen, sallow and snaggle-toothed as ever.

And finally, there in front of Katie, was the Queen, seated on a gothic-style throne with her husband Prince Albert at her side. She had grown stouter since Katie's last visit, her nose sharper, her eyes more prominent. The handsome Prince Albert had also aged. There were circles under his eyes, and his hairline was fast receding. The Queen pursed her lips. She was above class herself, and disliked the twittering snobbery of the courtiers, sniggering at this extraordinarily tall girl. She gave Katie an encouraging look.

DOWN, two, three . . . Katie made her curtsy to the Queen. With knees hovering above the floor, she reached forward and kissed the royal hand. With surprise she saw that the Queen's fingernails really could have been cleaner, though this was compensated for by bright jewels on every finger. UP, two, three . . . Katie had done it. Princess Alice smiled broadly as Katie curtsied, really bobbed, to the other members of the Royal Family. Bertie was looking at her with admiration now. Up close, he liked what he saw; there was nothing better than a tall strapping girl.

For Katie, the worst was over. All she had to do was walk backwards, down that long aisle. As she tried to step back, she wobbled badly. Once again, she couldn't move. She lurched dangerously. She seemed to be caught in something; trapped, directly in front of the Queen. Katie began to panic.

'Your train,' Alice mouthed, 'you're caught in your train. Hold out your arms.' Having successfully curtsied to the Queen, Katie had forgotten all about the three-foot-long train. She was hopelessly entangled. Following Alice's advice, her arms shot out, much in the manner of a scarecrow in a cornfield. The Lord Chamberlain had to get on to his hands and knees to release her. He then looped the beautiful embroidered train over her extended right arm; doing so with great dignity, as if this were a revered part the ceremony. Katie had to hand it to the Lord Chamberlain – he had a lot of class. But down the room, the sniggering, in some places, had turned to open laughter. Felix was pointing his finger and shrieking.

'I won't cry,' Katie said to herself, more annoyed than anything else. 'I'd like to see them drive a car, or log on to a computer, or use an iPhone. Who'd have the last laugh then?' As she backed away she could hear the Queen speaking to Prince Albert.

'The Americans are not known for their grace, but they have a certain exuberance, a raw health that one must admire.' She too was annoyed with the courtiers, and swept the room with a stern look. That shut them up. Katie's exit seemed even longer than her entrance. She backed out of the room to a leaden, oppressive silence.

Chapter Eight

Jack

It had been a disastrous presentation, but at least it was over. Katie was desperate to get away from the crowds and the courtiers. But where was the Honourable Emma Twisted? 'I think she's deserted you, my dear,' a voice beside Katie commented. 'I find her a fair-weather friend, the Honourable Emma Twisted.' It was Bernardo DuQuelle.

'You pushed me, didn't you?' Katie exclaimed. 'I mean, right at the beginning, you gave me a big kick. That really got me off on the wrong foot.'

'I don't believe you *have* a right foot,' he replied. 'Yes, I gave you a gentle nudge. I thought you'd never start down the aisle. Stage-fright, perhaps. But when you did, it was quite the performance.'

Katie's annoyance boiled over. 'Yeah, I know I totally bombed; but I don't give a flying . . . anything . . . about all that. What a stupid waste of an afternoon.'

'It wasn't the worst presentation of the day,' DuQuelle consoled her. 'A Miss Anne Moorden McPherson of Canada fell flat on her face, hurling her bouquet in the process. It hit the Baroness Lehzen and knocked her wig askew.'

'Not a waste all,' DuQuelle continued as Katie laughed. 'You have had your introduction to the Queen. Every drawing room in Britain is now open to you. You can stay in the Palace as Grace's special friend and help care for her. There are other uses for you as well, but you must be careful.' He peered around the room, and led Katie to a quiet corner. 'I've heard this morning of a most curious case,' he told her. 'Sir Lindsey Dimblock. Always a man of little use – well, now he is of no use. They've fished him out of the Thames, horribly bloated, dead for some time.'

'Yuk,' Katie shuddered.

'A strange word, yuk. But I believe you use it in context. Yuk it is.'

'Foul play?' Katie asked.

'Most foul,' DuQuelle answered. 'The mutilation was a sickening sight. His eyes had been gouged out, his tongue ripped from its root, and a strange tar-like substance oozed from every orifice.'

Katie searched into the recesses of her memory. DuQuelle seemed to be foraging in her mind too. 'So you remember now,' he said. 'You recognize the mode of attack – the frightful death of Fräulein Bauer. What else do you see?'

'The Black Tide,' Katie said. 'They tried to assassinate Queen Victoria in the Crystal Palace. But this isn't their style.'

DuQuelle shook his head. 'I find *style* a soft word for mutilation and murder. But you are correct. Do you remember your last exit from our time? It was midnight in the Palace and you were bungling it as usual. There was an intrusion and a scuffle. The Black Tide were seized by the palace guards and imprisoned for treason. They are silent for now. You must look further than European revolutionaries for this murder.'

A figure, svelte and snake-like, arose in Katie's imagination along with a name she had tried to blot from her memory. 'Lord Belzen,' she said.

DuQuelle sniffed the air in distaste. 'I can almost smell him from here. But why is he interested in Sir Lindsey Dimblock? I suspect the connection is with Dimblock's gambling companion, Lord Twisted.'

Katie looked across the room for Emma Twisted's father. Lord Twisted was standing next to young Felix, in conversation with the Lord Chamberlain. Usually such a close connection to the Royal Family would have thrilled him. But today, he just looked nervous. 'Lord Twisted is a jerk,' she said. 'And Felix there is worse.'

'You are perceptive,' DuQuelle commented. 'Rather coarse, extremely tall but very perceptive.'

Katie groaned, as more and more unwanted information flooded her mind. She'd almost forgotten about Lord Belzen and the Malum; Lucia and the Verus. There was a world beyond this world, and they were in never-ending conflict. The Malum sought power through brute force. The Verus mined the globe for words and exported communication to their own realm. Both wished to control the actions of this world. Both had champions, the Chosen, who did battle for them. 'Is young Felix enslaved by the Malum?' she asked DuQuelle.

'Can you not feel it when you are near him?' DuQuelle asked her.

She looked down at her bouquet, once so lovely – now wilted. A new, disturbing thought occurred to her. 'Are you really so sympathetic to Grace?' Katie asked; 'or is there another reason I am here?' DuQuelle was silent. 'Have I been brought here as part of your Great Experiment?' Katie ploughed on, 'To stop the war in the Crimea? Or must I participate in another battle: the endless struggle between the Malum and the Verus?'

DuQuelle suddenly looked very tired. He hated the convolutions of his own world. It was a topic that always seemed to age him. 'The war between the Verus and the Malum is more real than this tiff in the Crimea, or what the Queen quaintly calls the East,' he replied, not really answering her question.

Their conversation was cut short, however, as the Queen

and Prince Albert entered the room. At the Queen's side was a military officer. He was well past his prime, between sixty and seventy years old, with grey hair and sideburns that swept down from temple to chin. In his person, he was unassuming – of medium build, with light, mild eyes and a gentle smile. But his dress uniform was gorgeous beyond belief: a scarlet tunic ornamented by gold-fringed epaulettes, an opulent silk sash and more decorations than a Christmas tree. He held his plumed hat under one arm. His other sleeve was empty, and pinned to the front of his tunic.

The Lord Chamberlain stepped forward. 'THE QUEEN,' he announced, as everyone bobbed down. Katie wondered if he spoke like that at home. The Queen seemed to take it for granted.

'I have an announcement to make,' she said. 'It is with great pleasure that the Queen makes the appointment today of Field Marshal FitzRoy James Henry Somerset, 1st Baron Raglan, to command our troops in the future expeditions to the East. Lord Raglan has long served the Crown; first under the Duke of Wellington and now as a commander in his own right. He was vital in leading us to victory at Waterloo, and should the need arise, is certain to do so again.'

A murmur of surprise ran through the assembled courtiers. DuQuelle gave a low whistle. 'Is this really the best we can do?' Katie heard him say under his breath.

The Queen went on. 'Further appointments include the Earl of Lucan to command the Cavalry Division, and the Earl of Cardigan to command the Light Brigade.' The mild-looking Lord Raglan seemed both surprised and annoyed by this additional news. 'The Queen is most pleased to announce that our young German relation, Felix of Hanover, has requested leave to observe in the East, and when the troops are established, he will depart for the Baltic, under the excellent guidance of Lord Twisted.' The Queen continued. 'Some will begin their journey as early as the morrow, and the Queen and her family will salute these troops from the balcony of Buckingham Palace.' At this, the Queen and Prince Albert withdrew from the assembly.

So the dangerous Felix was moving closer to the war. Katie turned to demand answers from DuQuelle, but he had slipped away during the Queen's announcements. Most of the other debutantes were gone too, escorted home by their mamas. Alice and Leopold were the only other people Katie knew, and they'd been whisked away by their own mama, the Queen. They were probably back in their rooms, having toast and hot milk.

Katie felt a pang. All these unanswered questions. She would have liked to have talked it over with Mimi. After all, any mother was better than no mother. And the presentation – Mimi would have loved that. The pang was followed a growl of her stomach, so loud that a nearby archbishop jumped. 'I have got to eat,' she said to herself, hunger driving away a hundred questions. 'I did think that, having been presented, they might give us some food, a sandwich or something, some canapés maybe . . .'

She looked around, but could spot nothing. A door at the far side of the room was slightly ajar. Perhaps it would lead towards the kitchens, or at least to a bowl of peanuts. Sidling along the walls, she nipped quickly through the door, shutting it behind her. The room was empty, except for a young man with his back towards her. She thought she recognized him. So this was where James was hiding. He seemed to be in some sort of court uniform and he was stuffing the remains of a large cake into his pockets.

'Shove over,' Katie said. 'I'm absolutely starving.' As the young man turned around, Katie realized he was taller than James, and broader in the shoulders. It wasn't James at all, but his older brother, Jack.

'Uh, yeah, not James, not good, sorry, gotta go,' she muttered. Jack stared for a moment, one cake-filled hand still in his pocket, and then they both burst out laughing.

'You are right,' he said. 'I am Jack O'Reilly. And you are, I believe, MISS KATHERINE TAPPAN OF THE UNITED STATES OF AMERICA.' His imitation of the Lord Chamberlain was very good, and they began to laugh again.

'Otherwise known as the *giraffe*,' Katie said, sticking out her hand to shake his. But Jack's hands were sticky with cake and Katie wasn't sure if Victorian girls would or could actually touch a boy. They both blushed.

'You have been the talk of the presentations,' he admitted. 'And you *are* tall, but not as tall as I am,' he squared his broad shoulders, while his blue eyes danced with merriment. 'I believe you to be the boon companion of my sister Grace. She says you've cheered her up tremendously since your arrival from the Continent. And James holds you in admiration, though he's usually so tight-mouthed and pompous about girls.'

They laughed at his accurate, if unkind description of James. 'Do you think I could have some of that cake before you stuff it all in your pockets? I'm dying of hunger,' Katie said.

Jack tried to wipe the crumbs from his hands. 'Please don't think I'm a glutton,' he apologized. 'The cake is for my little brother Riordan. The Palace is swirling with excitement and he's stuck in the nursery. I thought something sweet might cheer him up, especially since I leave for the East tomorrow.'

Katie cut herself a generous slice of cake. She had seen Jack before, at a cricket match in 1851. But she'd been dressed as a kitchen maid at the time, and now she was supposed to be a grand American traveller. 'So this war is coming and you're going with the army?' she asked.

'Yes, with the Light Brigade. It's a marvellous commission. My father pulled out all the stops to get it.'

The Light Brigade. Katie felt a twinge. She didn't know why, but the Light Brigade sounded bad to her. She looked uneasily at her new friend.

'Do you have to go? I mean, can't you get out of it?'

'Get out of it?' Jack was astounded. 'It's what I've always wanted – a commission with the nation's top cavalry brigade. Every cadet in my class envies me. It is a wonderful posting for someone of my position in society. Only an idiot would abandon it!' He looked at Katie's downcast face. Perhaps he'd spoken too naturally, but he did feel very natural, very normal, with this American girl.

'Tell you what,' he said. 'You're so tall, why don't you don a soldier's uniform and come with us? You'd make a fetching cavalry officer.'

Now this was flirting. If it had happened at Neuman Hubris School, Katie would have kicked him in the shin, or elbowed him in the ribs. But here, in full court dress, she did what any Victorian girl would do. She blushed, again. Changing the subject seemed a good idea, otherwise she'd spend the entire conversation looking like a tomato. 'So what do you think of your new commander?' she asked.

Jack O'Reilly paused, pushing cake crumbs around the table. 'In some ways he's top drawer,' he said. 'Lord Raglan has been in the army since he was fifteen. He was one of us, the cavalry. He's brave, that's for certain. As a young man he cut a dash serving with the Black Watch at Talavera. The Duke of Wellington rated him; he was the duke's military secretary for seventeen years. And they were close. He's married to the duke's niece. Raglan's industrious, unflappable, tactful, decent . . . the cadets like him, admire him . . .'

'What happened to his arm?' Katie asked.

'Waterloo,' Jack said. 'A musket ball shattered his right elbow. The surgeons had to amputate.'

An amputation like that, on the battlefield; Katie winced, knowing there'd be no anaesthetic, nothing to ease the pain, perhaps a shot of whisky if Raglan was lucky.

Jack seemed to read her face. 'Yes,' he said. 'It was awful. But Lord Raglan showed great bravery, even humour. He endured the operation in silence. It was only when the surgeon tossed his severed arm into a pile of sawn-off limbs, he shouted out "Hey, bring back my arm. I need that ring on my index finger. It was a gift from my wife."'

Katie laughed, and then shook her head. 'Yeah, he sounds really brave. I mean, to still be funny at a time like that. But you don't think he's that good, do you?'

Jack gave her a long stare. 'You're a funny girl, to be so interested in such things. Yes, I do doubt him. I am ashamed to question a man of such standing. I'm only a cadet with the Royal Military College; a cadet with his first commission. But Lord Raglan has not been in active service for many years. And most of his experience is as a second-in-command. He's used to acting on orders, not giving them.'

Jack rolled some cake between his fingers. 'It's almost treason to speak like this. I'm certain to be wrong. I don't know why I should tell you such things,' he said, his merry eyes now solemn.

'I think it's a shame, to put you on a battlefield,' Katie said. 'You seem to really understand things. Wouldn't you rather be in the Foreign Office? Or working as a diplomat?'

Jack looked astonished. 'Are you crazy? Every boy my age dreams of war: the cannons, the charge, the glory of battle.'

'We don't feel that way about war. We think war's really bad,' Katie started to explain, and then stopped, flustered. The 'we' she was discussing was 150 years away.

'You are a strange one,' he repeated. 'And we'll disagree on this to the end. But I would like to know more about you, Miss Katherine Tappan. If I have your permission, I will write to you of the pleasures of the campfire, and the exhilaration of battle. And you can write back to me about the peaceful comforts of court life.'

He was flirting again. Katie suspected that corresponding with a boy she barely knew would be highly improper. The rules had changed over 150 years. She thought about Neuman Hubris School, and the note she'd passed to Michael Fester just days ago: *You stink,*' it had said, with a couple of other pithy comments. And now she couldn't even write a polite letter to a boy. She had to put a stop to this flirtation. What would Princess Alice do?

'I'm afraid I cannot allow the correspondence,' she began in a prim imitation of her royal friend. 'I am surprised and disappointed that you would suggest such an action. It shows a lack of delicacy . . .' Jack looked crestfallen, and Katie suddenly realized that she didn't want to follow Alice's imaginary advice. She wanted to hear about the war, and she wanted to hear from Jack. She began again. 'Perhaps if you write to your sister Grace, then she might be kind enough to read your letters to me. Only sections which cover the colour and tone of military camp life, you know, what you do in the campaign. I'd really enjoy that, and like, it would be, like nice . . .' she ended lamely.

Jack eyes lit up. 'Can't I just write to you?'

'It would be improper.' Katie gave him a nudge, and he began to pelt her with cake crumbs. They were on their way to a full-blown food fight when Bernardo DuQuelle entered the room.

'Jack O'Reilly, your brigade is retiring to barracks. Your commanding officer is looking for you,' DuQuelle said sternly.

'Oh bloody, oh sorry . . .' He pulled the much-mauled cake out of his pockets and threw it to Katie. 'Can you pass this on to Riordan for me?' he asked. 'Give him a hug. Tell him he's my little man, and I'll bring him a Russian sabre from the East.' He ducked his head and with a sheepish grin ran from the room.

DuQuelle looked at Katie with great disapproval, but she could only nod and laugh.

'You're supposed to be timeless,' she said to him, 'but you've certainly picked up Victorian morals. I'm glad to see you, though. There are a bunch of things you need to explain.' She peppered him with questions, but he only responded with a lecture on female decorum. DuQuelle practically pushed her through the door, and then, with a curt nod, he stalked away.

In all the excitement of the day, she'd almost forgotten – she was still wearing her presentation dress. When she looked in the mirror, she stepped back in dismay – the figure reflected was so different from the young lady who had set out that morning. She was, truly, a mess. The headdress had settled into the crook of her neck, with the feathers sticking out sideways. Her hair was springing from its pins, waving about her head like disco-dancing caterpillars. Her cloak was soiled, her train was torn and the seams of the lovely dress were already giving way. She had no idea where she'd left the gloves or the bouquet.

Getting the dress off was nearly impossible. Grace was sleeping, Alice gone, and she certainly had no lady's maid. She didn't want to rip the thing, but she couldn't go to sleep in it. After what seemed like hours, she shrugged the dress off her shoulders, bunched it down, and turned it back to front to detach the elaborate train. Then she had to undo every single tiny pearl button.

There were 115 of them. It must have been one in the morning by the time she was done. When she finally got the corset unstrapped she looked at herself in horror. There were red welts coming up all over her where the tight clothes had rubbed. 'I wouldn't call this beautiful,' she thought. 'I'd call it barbaric.'

Luckily, a loose-fitting white muslin nightgown had been left out for her. She put it over her head and clambered into bed, exhausted. The bed was wonderfully comfortable, with a big goose down mattress. But she couldn't sleep. All the excitement and tension and uncertainty were bubbling within her. Between the presentation, the unanswered questions and Jack, her nerves were a mess. She didn't have anything to read, and besides, there was only about a half an hour left of her final candle.

A noise outside her room arrested her attention: the drawn-out creak of a door opening slowly, then footsteps. Slowly, almost rhythmically, the unknown person put one foot in front of the other. There was a remorseless quality to this tread – far away at first, but coming nearer and nearer. Katie held her breath and stared at the latch to her door. The footsteps continued, the latch did not lift. Whoever walked the corridor at the dead of night, they were not looking for Katie.

'This is silly,' she said to herself. 'It's just a busy hallway. Palace traffic. See, there are more footsteps passing by.' This time they stopped at her room. She sat up in bed and grabbed the brass candlestick. It was large and heavy, a good weapon, just in case.

'Katie?' the voice in the corridor called quietly. It was DuQuelle.

'Yes?'

'Lock your door, Katie.' Her candle spluttered, flared and died.

Chapter Nine

The Soldier's Goodbye

She'd stumbled through the dark and turned the key firmly in the latch. Things were happening around her that she did not understand. Sleep would never come. And yet the next moment it was morning, and DuQuelle was standing over her bed.

'What about your Victorian morals?' she mumbled, hiding her head under the pillows. 'Don't they forbid entering a lady's bedroom?' And then she remembered the night before. 'More than that, how did you get in? I locked the door. You were the one who told me to.' She peered out of the window. 'It's the crack of dawn. Let's just say goodbye now, and I'll stay in bed – maybe until lunch.'

DuQuelle sighed – Katie had noticed he did this rather

a lot. 'Bed! There will be no more bed for you,' he replied. 'Didn't you hear the Queen yesterday? Our glorious soldiers are off to the East. Grace has been invited to wave goodbye to her brother Jack, and you are to be at her side, tending to her. Isn't that why you are here?'

'I just want to sleep!'

'Well, you are going to appear on the Royal balcony. But first you have to be bathed and groomed. Really Katie, we all spend far too much time and energy making you look presentable.'

By the time Katie was ready, the Royal Family was assembled on the balcony. Queen Victoria looked as round as a Christmas pudding, her short frame muffled in cloak, shawl and bonnet. Her tiny plump hands were tucked snugly in a fur muff. Beside her was Prince Albert, who hated the cold, but he had no cloak. It was important for the soldiers below to see him in his Field Marshal's uniform. Bertie, much grown and also in uniform, bellowed with enthusiasm.

Beside him Vicky, the Princess Royal, smiled gamely. Her fiancé Frederick William was the heir to the Prussian throne, but Prussia had already declared itself neutral in this coming war. Vicky was in an uncomfortable position, but for now family was family, and she would stand shoulder to shoulder with her mama and Britain. With dismay, Katie noticed Felix at Vicky's side. He was the most beautiful of youths, his pale creamy skin and silken blond curls further highlighted by his military uniform, donned especially for this occasion. Katie shuddered.

Along the balcony, Katie could see Princess Alice standing with her two younger sisters: Louise, highly strung and 'artistic', and Lenchen, large and placid. As was often the case, the girls were dressed in identical frocks. They were horrendous – magenta and sea-green tartan with heavy purple cloaks trimmed in black and mauve ribbons. 'The Royal Family, are they colour blind?' Katie wondered. Alice spotted Katie and tried to reach her, but the balcony was so crowded. Lenchen, in particular, was too bulky a figure to squeeze past.

The O'Reilly family was out in force to see Jack off. Dr O'Reilly was passing Princess Louise a bottle of smelling salts while he smiled and bowed. Katie could just imagine the elaborate compliments he was paying her. James, at his father's elbow, had not inherited such courtly charms. He scowled at Katie and pointedly looked at his pocket watch. 'Yes, I'm late,' Katie thought, 'but it's so much easier for you James, it's not like you're in these ridiculous clothes . . . now where is Grace?'

Katie sidled over to the clustered royals, looking for her new charge. She tripped over Prince Leopold, in his bath chair. His eyes were on stalks with the excitement of the occasion. When he saw Katie, he gave a little jump. 'Miss Katherine Tappan . . . my foot!' he exclaimed. 'It's you, Katie Berger-Jones-Burg. I *know* it's you! Why have you come back when we went to so much trouble to get rid of you . . . you must tell me. You know how helpful I am. You know I saved the day the last time . . .'

Leopold's tutor, the Reverend Robinson Duckworth, did not greet Katie with such enthusiasm. He glanced sideways from Leopold to Katie to Bernardo DuQuelle. For a few long seconds Robinson Duckworth mulled things over and then turned to Katie with a smile. 'The Prince is mistaken in your identity,' he said, 'please accept our apology.' When Leopold began to protest, Katie saw Duckworth lean forward and hiss in his ear, 'We will discuss this *later*.'

DuQuelle looked straight ahead, humming softly to himself. 'Miss Tappan,' he said. 'You are certain to be searching for Miss O'Reilly. You will find her in the corner of the balcony. I don't think she should be out at all, but she's well wrapped against this bitter February cold.'

The Reverend Robinson Duckworth shot DuQuelle a look full of distrust.

But now the march past was about to begin and Katie took her place beside Grace. Despite her furs and blankets, she shivered with the cold. Spread before them was London, and the entire city seemed to have taken to the streets. The Mall was a heaving mass of people. They spilled down the avenues into the Royal Parks, screaming, waving and singing. The soldiers were still their heroes of fifty years past, the unbeatable victors of Waterloo.

According to the great British public, the 'Rooshians' didn't stand a chance.

Katie could hear the steady tramp of columns of men making their way from Wellington Barracks and down Birdcage Walk until they marched past the balcony of Buckingham Palace. The first to be seen were the Scots Fusilier Guards in their brilliant scarlet tunics, bearskin helmets and tartan trousers. The crowds went wild, a sea of handkerchiefs and hats waving in the air. Grace stopped shivering, her cheeks were pink with excitement, and she managed to get up to wave with the rest of the crowd. 'Everyone is so joyful,' she exclaimed.

'Not everyone,' Katie thought. Hidden within the triumphant crowd lay the exceptions: tired-looking, anxious women, clutching the hands of small children and crying out to the men; these were the wives of soldiers, and they were being left behind. Some held their children high for a last look at their fathers, some whispered prayers for their men. Lord only knew when they would see them again.

The crowds had been shouting and singing 'God Save the Queen' and 'Rule Britannia'. But now the regimental band struck up 'The British Grenadiers' march and the streets heaved with song.

With a tow, row, row, row, row, row,
To the British Grenadiers!

They cheered on the soldiers, as the sun rose over the park.

The Queen was not just on her feet, she was on tip-toes, clutching Prince Albert's arm and waving her fur muff in the air. She was herself the daughter of a soldier; and she felt there was a sacred bond between herself and these men. She was filled with a mix of excitement and dread. As a queen, she applauded her soldiers; but as a wife and mother, her heart ached as well. She knew sorrow lay ahead for some.

The tramp of feet was replaced by the clip of horses' hooves. The Heavy Brigade loomed into sight: the Scots Greys, the Royal Irish and the Inniskilling 6th Dragoons. Column after column of mounted cavalry trooped past the Queen. Leaning heavily on Katie, Grace strained her eyes for the one face she wished to see. 'There he is!' she cried. 'There is Jack!'

Dr O'Reilly's sons had been brought up within the Royal Household and many of the occupants of the balcony now pushed forward to get a glimpse of Jack, straight-backed and bursting with pride, as he rode amongst the 17th Lancers, the Hussars, and the Light Dragoons. These were the divisions that made up the Light Brigade under the command of Lord Cardigan – one of the smartest units in the entire army. Jack was resplendent in his dress uniform, a deep blue jacket with a high collar – at least three inches high – encrusted with gold lace. Enormous gold-fringed epaulettes swung out from his broad shoulders and black feather plumes waved from his distinctive lance cap.

'Jack!' Grace cried, 'Jack!' and she reached out her hands, as if to grasp his through this sea of people. Katie glanced towards James. The look on his face was complicated: a mixture of pride in his brother, worry for his future, and more than a touch of jealousy. James was the kind of boy who shunned the limelight, who had no desire to be a hero. But even a bookish boy like James would envy his big brother at this moment. Dr O'Reilly's face was easier to read. His son, his Jack, was marching towards glory. This could only strengthen his position at court. His vanity and ambition were satisfied.

The Light Brigade moved from a walk to a slow trot. On the command of Lord Cardigan, they halted before their Queen, tipped their lances and saluted her. 'God Save the Queen' the Light Brigade shouted as one. The crowd went wild. There were tears on the Queen's cheek. Katie could see Jack, his head turned, like all others, towards his sovereign; but were his eyes searching the balcony, for his family – for his friends?

Their commander, Lord Cardigan, led his horse in a passage directly below the balcony. Both man and horse bowed their heads to their monarch. The Queen clapped and smiled, but Katie saw James roll his eyes. She had to agree with him. There was something about the scrupulously dressed Earl of Cardigan that Katie did not like. Perhaps it was his bristling ginger moustache, or his air of extreme arrogance. She got the feeling she wouldn't like him to be *her* commander. He looked as if he might be a bully.

For Jack, though, this was a day of high adventure. As the Light Brigade moved away, he reined his horse in, ever so slightly, and against all military rules, waved up to the balcony. Both Grace's and Katie's hands shot up in return. 'Goodbye, dear Jack,' Grace said softly. 'God bless you. And come back to me safe and well.' As the cavalry disappeared, on their way to Waterloo Station, the band struck up again.

But someday I'll return again
If rebels they don't find me
And never will I roam again
From the girl I left behind me.

Directly behind the scarlet and blue uniforms, the glinting lances and the rousing music, came the camp followers. These were the soldiers' wives, the lucky ones, chosen by a draw to accompany their men. The women were shabbily dressed and lugged bundles like pack mules. Amongst them Katie could see one man. He marched along cheerfully, his huge leather boots swinging to the music. In his mouth he clenched a smoking pipe that tipped dangerously towards his enormous curly black beard. A rakish cap was pulled down low on his forehead.

As one woman stumbled, he reached forward, took her arm, and then relieved her of her bundle – slinging it over his back despite his own burdens.

DuQuelle laughed aloud. 'Well, that's all right then,' he said. 'If William Howard Russell is with them, they'll come to no harm.'

'William Howard Russell?' Katie asked as the bearded man doffed his cap and bowed exaggeratedly to a stony-faced Queen.

'Russell of *The Times*,' DuQuelle explained, '*The Times of London*. He's their correspondent covering the war. Not that the politicians or the establishment want a newspaper writer in the Crimea; but where there's trouble, Billy Russell will report it. He is the hero of the downtrodden, and those soldiers' wives look as if they could use a helping hand.'

Along the balcony, Prince Albert did not seem to share DuQuelle's sanguine view. As Russell bowed, the Prince turned away in contempt. 'Miserable scribbler,' he murmured, as Russell cheered the women.

Prince Leopold could no longer contain himself. The pomp, the glory, the sheer excitement of the military parade had gone to his head. 'That's what I'm going to do,' he exclaimed to his tutor. 'When I grow up I'm going to be a soldier!'

Felix, overhearing him, laughed his particularly harsh, unpleasant laugh.

'You, a soldier!' he cried. 'When you can hardly walk, much less march. I leave soon, to find glory. You will not even be able to leave your bed. What an absurd idea!'

'Leopold is better every day,' Alice piped up, looking at her brother's miserable, crestfallen face. 'And even if he cannot be a soldier, I am certain he will help with the war effort in some other way.'

'Come Felix,' Vicky said sharply. 'You must learn to hold your tongue. If you continue in that rude way, there will be no war for you.'

Felix, with his disagreeable manner, had punctured the high excitement of the day. The Royal Family began to leave the balcony, Alice holding Leopold's hand as he was pushed indoors by the Reverend Robinson Duckworth.

'I can't say I am sorry to see young Felix go,' the Queen was heard to say. 'That boy is *not* ideal. Aside from our beloved Frederick William, there is an occasional unpleasantness in the Prussian national character – so brusque, an indelicate aggression . . .' Prince Albert nodded as they trailed inside. Katie gave the crowds below one final glance, catching sight of something she'd rather not see. It was Lord Twisted, leaning against a column, deep in conversation with a slim, sinuous man. Lord Twisted looked both sullen and fearful. The other man swayed in a graceful yet somehow repulsive way. It was Lord Belzen.

Bernardo DuQuelle sniffed the air and shivered. He did not care for the cold, and it was bitter this morning. Besides, he'd seen too much of history, too much of war to believe blindly in its glory. He'd had enough. 'If war is to commence, there is much for me to do,' he said, making his apologies and bowing to those still remaining. To Katie he murmured, 'At our very feet stands something far more dangerous than all the Queen's brigades. I suggest we move inside.'

'And what have *you* to do?' Felix sneered at DuQuelle as he went past. 'Must you dust the Royal Art Collection, or update the Royal Archives? I am now a warrior, while you are nothing. You are no Mars. There are no manly duties for you.'

Those remaining were quiet, shocked at Felix's behaviour. But DuQuelle looked at him – not with anger, but with pity. 'Poor child,' he said. 'There are different ways of being a man. And heroic actions do not always require the blare of the trumpet and the roar of the cannon.' Felix, white with fury, stormed from the balcony.

DuQuelle shook his head, watching him go. 'Poor boy,' he repeated, 'not really a boy at all. Not anymore.' Katie opened her mouth, but DuQuelle continued. 'I know, my dear, I know. Felix has no hopes for glory, no plans for heroism. Quite the reverse, I fear.'

Chapter Ten

Lucia

For Bernardo DuQuelle, it was a war on two fronts. Yes, the Crimea was of consequence, but only in this time, in this particular universe. Elsewhere, another war raged, a war of thousands of years – not between countries or peoples, religions or races, but a war, chilling in its simplicity, a war between good and evil. In comparison, the Crimean expedition was tiny; a pebble in the shoe of history. But throw a small pebble into a vast body of water, and it will create ever-expanding rings. So it was with this war between the British and the Russians. It could bring into motion a war to end, not just this world but many worlds.

'If war is to commence,' he said again, 'there is much for me to do. I will need all kinds of knowledge: history, comment and philosophy. One must be well informed if one is to guide Lucia.' The Royal Family would now be busy at breakfast: kippers and sausages, haddock in puff pastry, mutton, Scottish woodcock, and a large wobbly jelly in the centre of the table. The Queen, in particular, believed in a hearty breakfast; and she was certain to have built up an appetite. It would be hours before they were done. He was free to begin his vital work.

He made his way to his cell-like room, deep within the Palace. Lifting his head, he sniffed the air. It was not just the menace of Belzen he smelt, but something equally powerful, and more subtly dangerous. Turning one last corner, he saw his door, lightly outlined against the wall, bright from within. There was no time to learn, or to plan. Lucia was already there. 'Just what I need,' he muttered to himself. 'I've spent most of the morning chilled to the bone, watching boys march off to become cannon fodder. I've had an upstart, a snooty, *possessed* child insult me. And now Lucia . . .' Clearly, it wasn't Bernardo DuQuelle's day.

To be with Lucia was always an uncomfortable reminder of the past: the Verus and the Malum – good and evil – Lucia and Belzen. Had they ever really had their own civilization, with their own communities, laws and languages? DuQuelle remembered his youth, his exquisite life and his great attachment to Lucia, and his friendship . . . with Belzen. But through greed they had overstepped themselves and destroyed their world.

Lucia had confidence in the power of good. DuQuelle had to admit, she was nothing if not good. It gave her strength. Step by step she had begun to rebuild, taking what they needed from other societies. Language had been the hardest. They needed words, but had lost the ability to communicate. Here, in the nineteenth century, in England, they had struck a rich vein. But war threatened to disrupt everything and Belzen was in revolt – scorning the peaceful export of words, believing that brute force was the key to their vital energies. And Belzen wasn't alone. The Black Tide might be thwarted for now, but there were others ready to take their place, to join Belzen and the Malum.

What had Lucia become? A woman, or the shape of a woman, but burning bright through the zeal of her cause. He entered quickly, locking the door behind him. Lucia flitted from corner to corner. She seemed to pulse and throb with fire and air, but gave out no warmth. Yet he could still see her features, which were lovely, and her wild waving blonde curls. But when he tried to approach Lucia the elements within her rebuffed him.

'What can you tell me?' she demanded of DuQuelle.

He smiled to himself. She had always been direct, even before her great transformation. 'There will be war, and soon,' he told her. 'But it has drawn Belzen as well as you. The Malum are present as well as the Verus. Young Felix is the agent of Lord Belzen. That poor child has been channelled from the dead for a purpose. He is the chosen, the Tempus Occidit, the child who falls through time and brings the war to end the world.'

Lucia wavered, her face becoming clearer and her body more formed. The look she gave DuQuelle was decidedly female. He had long feared the strength of Lucia, but he was more alarmed by these few signs of weakness. 'And how will the princeling Felix achieve this?' she asked.

DuQuelle smiled slightly. He thought about removing his cloak, but instead pulled it tighter around him. One could never tell with Lucia. 'I was present when the Queen announced that Felix leaves for the Crimea. What the Queen does not know is that Felix serves, not the Queen, but Lord Belzen. Felix's mission is to make certain that Britain does not win this war. He will spy, he will betray, he will wreak havoc. Felix will plant the seeds of discontent, envy and rebellion. From what I gather his targets are Lord Lucan, Lord Cardigan and a certain Captain Nolan.'

Lucia was not taking this news well – yet she tried to hold the elements within her in check and gather her strength. Lucia did not look back. The past was nothing to her. And she did not trust Bernardo DuQuelle. She needed him, though, in this world, in the centre of power, as part of the Royal Court. He was the only one capable of living with them. Darting forward, she placed a cold, bright hand just in the crook of DuQuelle's elbow. 'That is well done,' she said in her whistling airy voice. 'But there is still much more to do. War is upon us, as you say, a great war. We must strike first.'

DuQuelle pulled away from her touch. 'No, Lucia,' he replied. 'You do not listen, you never did. This war in the Crimea is a small war, though its trivial actions could set in motion events that lead to the Great War – a war throughout Europe that would last for half a century. You cannot simply unleash the Tempus like gladiators. This must be handled carefully, through diplomacy, through communication; or it could be the beginning of the war to end the world.'

Lucia tried to hold in her impatience and anger. She saw the path of duty, straight before her. Like many ideologues, she was not open to new ideas. DuQuelle was now tinged with humanity. This only got in the way. He must be made to understand her will. 'There are two wars, in two spheres,' she persisted, 'the English and the Russians; the Verus and the Malum. Both can be stopped, but only through the chosen, the Tempus. You have found one. I need all three. The three children must meet in battle. They hold the key to creation or destruction.'

Lucia had seemed diminished, but now it was DuQuelle who sank into a chair by the fire. It was not just the February morning. Lucia's words chilled him to the bone. 'You really wish them to meet on a field of battle?' he spoke quietly, his voice filled with disbelief. 'They are barely out of childhood. You would brutalize them in this way?'

'Sympathy,' she hissed as the elements rose within her. 'It is sympathy which weakens you.'

A very rare rage sliced through DuQuelle, ripping aside his usual urbane mask. 'Listen closely, Lucia,' he said. 'Don't pick a fight. Not with me, not in the Crimea, not with Lord Belzen, not with the Malum. Try everything else before you resort to Belzen's tactics – to brute force. Let me put this in the terms of this world, which is the only language we now have. You are moving towards a crusade. And while crusades are mounted in the name of good, they are executed in sheer evil.'

He was infuriated by his loss of temper, aghast at the abuse implicit in her request. DuQuelle could not bear to look at her, to be in the same room. Yet as he unbolted the door and hurried through the Palace corridors, seeking the human element, he could still hear Lucia's voice, rising like the winds within his brain. *You will bring me the three children. The Chosen. The Tempus. They will fight on the field of battle. And the victor must be the harbinger of peace.*

Despite his fury, he knew what he was, and where his loyalties lay. But his sense of what was right and wrong had been changed by living amongst them. Could he ignore the voice of Lucia? He wasn't sure.

Chapter Eleven

A Crimean Correspondent

As the Verus and the Malum prepared for conflict, battle lines were also drawn in the Crimea. But Katie, James and Alice were engaged in their own war, a fierce fight against Grace's illness. At first Katie feared it couldn't be won. Grace was seriously ill, and there was so much they didn't know. James had been studying tuberculosis since Grace's return from Italy and Katie needed to catch up. Together they pored over medical papers and treatises, including Sir James Clark's hefty *A Treatise on Pulmonary Consumption; Comprehending an Inquiry into the Causes, Nature, Prevention and Treatment of Tuberculous and Scrofulous Diseases in General.*

With each word she read, Katie's frustration grew.

Doctors recommended blistering patients with hot plasters to bring out the sickly vapours, bleeding them to release bad blood, starving them to diminish the appetites. Some doctors were adamant that an almost comatose state of druggedness and bedrest were necessary. Others refuted all medication except extensive fresh air and exercise, even strapping weakened patients onto horses for hour-long gallops.

'This is ridiculous', Katie had told James. 'Your doctors, they write such garbage. They just don't know what causes tuberculosis. It's like a germ that spreads through coughing. Once you get it, it ends up in your lungs and causes pneumonia. And then it can spread all over your body: to the joints, to the throat, to the spine. We all get a shot, in my time, so we can't catch it.'

'A shot?' James wrinkled his forehead. 'They shoot you? With a pistol?' Despite being stressed out, Katie laughed.

'No, not that kind of shot. I mean, what do you call it? An injection, from a needle.'

James looked grim. 'It's too late for preventative medicine.'

Katie thought again. 'There are things you can take, once you have tuberculosis. We don't really get it that much anymore, but it's like an antibiotic or something.'

'Can you make it?' James asked. Katie shook her head.

'There's no way I could make it. I don't really even know what it is. You haven't discovered it yet . . .'

James was getting frustrated too. 'There isn't much point telling me how stupid we all are, Katie. If you can't make this anti-mobotic medication, we'll have to think of something else. Instead of complaining, why don't you come up with some ideas?'

'It's not anti-mobotic, it's antibiotic, and you're a long way from it, you don't even have penicillin yet.'

An equally frustrated voice came from the bedroom. 'The two of you, like bickering babies. Can't you see in front of your very own noses? Every day you're helping me. James never ceases in his care. You'd think I was one of the Queen's wee babes. And Katie brings common sense to everything she says and does. So do stop arguing and come keep me company. Despite what Father says, a bit of mental stimulation does cheer me up.'

They both jumped, shamefaced. They hadn't realized Grace was listening. Katie sloped off to see her. 'We'll have to make do with the stuff we *do* know,' she said to James. 'The important thing is to keep trying.'

He shook his head at Katie. 'You're a very stubborn girl,' he said.

Princess Alice assisted greatly. At the request of her father, Prince Albert, she had been tutored by Dr O'Reilly; though on a far lesser scale than James. Dr O'Reilly wasn't a proponent of the education of women, but James knew, from experience, that Alice was a competent nurse: steady, kind and patient. If the truth be told, he admired her tremendously – not for her royal status, but for herself.

Working together they began to wean Grace off the laudanum. It was highly addictive, and Dr O'Reilly had been increasing the dose as Grace's health failed. They'd have to take her off it, little by little; otherwise the withdrawal symptoms would be too severe. Grace was also receiving a daily dose of digitalis. 'It's just an extract of foxgloves,' James explained, 'it's been proven to slow the heart rate.'

But when Katie looked it up, she almost fainted. 'Digitalis is dangerous. It's an appetite suppressant, and the last thing Grace needs is to eat less. If taken incorrectly, it can poison her. I say, drop the digitalis.'

At the same time, Grace's meals became larger. Katie demanded she have red meat (she could almost hear Mimi shuddering in New York) and the occasional glass of red wine. She tried to remember all those articles she'd leafed through in Mimi's endless women's magazines. 'Grace must eat bright green vegetables,' she told James. 'Spinach, broccoli, cabbage – I mean, what are those super foods they're always blathering about – beetroot, I think, blueberries, avocados . . . Do you have kiwis? No?'

'Are you going to cure her by colours?' James teased. But he sensed she was right.

The Royal kitchens were less than pleased by these dietary requests. They were used to sending up a bit of milk toast or weak broth for Grace. And now they were having to find all these strange vegetables, having to peel and chop them and then barely cooking them! It was a fight to the end, to get the food they needed, but Katie made a game of it, moaning and groaning to make Grace laugh. And laugh she did. Sometimes Katie thought it was the laughter that was really curing Grace.

Or could it be the fresh air? Dr O'Reilly had bolted the windows in Grace's room. It was so close and still, Katie could almost smell the germs swimming through the thick air. As spring came, Katie opened all the windows. Along with the soot of London came the scent of newly-turned earth and opening flowers. Grace breathed in deeply: 'It smells of new green things,' she said, 'it smells of rebirth.'

And it was like a rebirth. Day by day Katie watched a vibrant, happy Grace emerge. But despite having reached this point, Grace was still ill – there was no denying it. But she was standing, and laughing with James and Katie and Alice. 'This is going OK,' Katie thought. 'With time we'll cure Grace, and then DuQuelle will send me back to my own time, New York – to Mimi.' She thought, with a pang, about Mimi. She'd left her, sound asleep, in her career trauma, yet again. Katie never really understood how time worked between the centuries. Would Mimi be awake by now? Maybe Katie was needed there, as well as here. But right now, she'd rather stay with her friends, and laugh.

Much of this laughter was at Katie's expense. Grace was older, and the most experienced member of their group. She guessed much of Katie's encounter with Jack, and teased her without mercy. About a month after Jack's departure, Grace ordered James out of her room. Throwing a shawl around her shoulders, she climbed back into bed and turned, with dancing eyes, to Alice and Katie. 'I have a good reason for us to be alone,' she said. 'For in my pocket is a letter from Jack. I will share it with both of you.'

'But wouldn't James want to hear it?' Katie asked.

'He would,' Grace said. 'But more important, Jack would want *you* to hear it, Miss Katherine Tappan.' It was Alice's turn to stare at her friend and wonder about the future; and Katie's turn to look down and fidget.

'You know, I think everyone would want to hear about the war,' she concluded lamely. Grace laughed and unfolding the letter, began to read.

Scutari, April 1854

My dearest Grace:
What an ungrateful boy I am! My life's desire was this commission with the 17th Lancers. Yet at the last moment I struggled to leave my beloved sister in such precarious health. I can only hope that you are reading this letter with happy eyes; that your cheeks are rosy and the fingers turning the pages are round and plump. I do believe you are in good hands. James and

I might quibble about father's abilities, but he is admired at court. And then James himself has such knowledge and expertise in medicines, though don't let on that I think so; the last thing we need is a swell-headed little brother. As for your new boon companion, Miss Katherine Tappan: she will enliven your time with a strong dose of mischief!

When we did sail, the town of Portsmouth gave us a rousing send-off. The port was crammed to the gills with well-wishers. You will raise your brows, Grace, but some of the men used this time for a last carouse, and there was many a sore head when we boarded the HMS Tribune. Flags waved from the quay and the men clambered up the riggings for one last glimpse of home. As we weighed anchor, a huge roar rose above the waters, and we banged our caps in response.

But after the excitement, came the sea, and such a fierce sea it was. The men who had drunk and danced the night away paid heartily on the passage. Even I, a good sailor, had my head over the rails from time to time. (As a doctor's daughter, you will not mind this detail, but you might wish to remove it should you read this letter to your friend Miss Katherine Tappan.)

We had our mounts on board, and the horses were even more seasick than we were. Don't laugh at the idea of a seasick horse. It was a terrible crossing for them. They were hung in slings, on the deck below us; so as not to be crushed by the roll of the waves. I spent much time with my own mount, Embarr. With legs splayed and head down, he suffered greatly. Several fine cavalry horses went almost insane with the colic. The one doctor on board turned vet, and had these horses shot; but they were too cumbersome to be thrown overboard, so were left in a pile amongst the living. I would not treat a horse so myself, and shielded Embarr as far as possible from the corpses of his friends – some of my regiment thought this soft behaviour on my part, but others understood.

And along with the regiments, the horses, the equipment, and rations – we had the women. They had been chosen by the official military lottery, but several men smuggled their wives on board. They are separated from the men, and bunk below the waterline. The stagnant bilge is directly below them, and the horses neigh and stamp above. A woman is by nature a homely body, Grace. Even in the bowels of a ship she slings ropes, drapes sheets, tries to create some privacy and peace for herself – despite the corpses of horses and the reek of men made sick by the sea. The women are aided much by William Howard Russell, also a stowaway on board. He scribbles for The Times and means to report all our brave actions.

Despite his profession, I must admit, Russell is the heart and soul of the ship; always up for a card game, and with a seemingly unending supply of whisky. (Not that I would drink it Grace, you and your dear friend are not to worry.) He has many jokes and salty stories, and always seems to win at the cards (again, please don't worry). He has tackled our commander on the subject of the women; says they cannot be left below deck for weeks on end, to cry and be sick in buckets. He has negotiated an hour, on deck for them, weather permitting. And when they cannot come up, he goes down to *them, takes up a darning needle, and helps them mend their hosiery! Yet there is nothing unmanly about Billy Russell. He is a puzzle, but an amusing one at that.*

We had hoped for a skirmish when we finally landed at Scutari, but the Russians took one look at us and fled! It is strange to have the French as our allies, and they have a different way of doing things. Lord Raglan camps amongst us in a modest hut under the Cypress trees. The French are commanded by a dapper little man, Saint-Arnaud. He bunks on the European side of the Bosporus in an elegant villa. Our men do not think much of him, and it is rumoured he learnt his English as a dancing master in London!

But all this talk of darning socks and dancing masters is not the stuff of war. Soon we leave for a yet unnamed field of battle, where we will take the Russians on and win! The campsite is a merry place, with tall tales, jigs and songs, but I cannot wait for this war to commence.

Again, Grace, here's to your health. My duty to Father. Tell little Riordan less cake and more lessons will do him good. For James I recommend more cake and fewer lessons. Too much studying will stunt his growth. My respectful wishes to the Princess Alice; she is so kind to you, perhaps she would take out her globes and maps, to show you the lands where we camp. And as for your friend, Miss Katherine Tappan – she has told me not to address her directly . . .

With all my brotherly affection,
Your Jack

Grace handed the letter to Katie. 'My eyesight isn't terribly strong,' she said. 'Would you mind glancing through the letter? To make certain I have missed nothing?' Katie took the letter, and stared down at Jack's boyish scrawl. As she began to read, it was as if she'd left Grace's room. The bed, the billowing curtains, the night table with its books, even the letter in her hand – they were all gone.

She was in Scutari. She could see the men, sprawled under the trees in the spring sunshine. She could smell the sweat pouring through their unwashed shirts, and the smoke of hasty campfires. Their talk was rough, and their laughter sharp; but it was a relaxed and happy camp, a camp of men excited at the prospect of a quick and easy victory. If only they could corner the Russians.

Princess Alice gave her friend a troubled look. 'Katie, Katie, where have you gone? You seem a thousand miles away.' Katie did not respond, and Alice got up to shake her gently.

'I can see it,' Katie said, as her eyes slowly focused on Princess Alice.

'Yes,' Alice said. 'Despite being that bit too ribald, Jack does describe it all so nicely.'

'No,' Katie said. 'It's like something else. I don't know anything about this war; we don't study it in my school. I do remember seeing a book about it once, but that's it. I've picked up that you side with the French and the Turks and it's against Russia, and it takes place in the Crimea. But that's all I know. But when I read Jack's letter I can really, truly *see* it, I can smell it.' She ran her tongue across her teeth. Her mouth was dry and sour and hot. 'I can even taste it.'

Alice squeezed her friend's shoulder. 'It might be the power,' she said, 'the Tempus. The words do something to you. I believe it's tangled up with your gift.'

Grace looked at the two girls. 'This must be yet another part of my treatment,' she said, 'this mystery about Katie. It makes me so curious; it really does quicken my brain.' Alice started to reply, but Grace put her hand up. 'Katie is special,' she said. 'And when I know her better, she will tell me all about it herself. But until that time, I will wait. Now tell me something else: what do you think of my Jack?'

'This is the part I find most mysterious,' Princess Alice said. 'I can be rather blinkered about these things, but it's obvious, even to me, that Jack wrote that letter for Katie to hear. I didn't know they'd met. And it certainly wasn't for a length of time to make such intimacy acceptable.'

Perhaps it had been the European tour, but Grace was less shocked. 'You are quite correct in your decorum, Princess Alice,' she said solemnly. 'Jack has been too eager to make a friend of Katie. But then, my dears, there is a war, and he is young. Don't you think we should forgive him? And grant his wish that Katie should hear his letters?'

Katie interrupted. 'I am here, you know,' she said. 'I can explain things myself.' She turned to Alice. 'I met Jack after the presentation. I didn't think it was a big deal. At least, he was leaving, and I wasn't sure he was talking to me the way he should and I told him he couldn't write to me but anyway, he is James's brother, and Grace's brother too, and little Riordan's big brother, and . . . well, I felt like I knew him already. I mean, I liked him the way I like you and James and . . .' Every time she talked of Jack, she seemed to trail off lamely.

Grace was laughing. 'Katie has shown no impropriety,' she told Alice, 'or at least no more than is normal for her. Jack knows I will read her the letters. I imagine now that my gallant brother will become quite the correspondent!'

All this teasing made Katie grumpy. She liked Jack, even more so after his letter. But she didn't want to be a Victorian girl, mocked about her beau. James would hate it too, and her friendship with James counted for a lot. Besides, there were more important things afoot in the Palace than a wartime flirtation. Felix was about to depart for battle, to do the dirty work of Belzen.

There was little time for brooding. The bouncing tread of a small boy reverberated through the sitting room, and with a leap Riordan was on Grace's bed, pulling her curls and rifling through her pockets. 'You have a letter from Jack,' he cried. 'I want to hear! I want to hear! I wager he's killed all the Russians already!'

Grace began to read, editing out the parts unsuitable for such young ears, and Princess Alice settled down to hear

Jack's adventures yet again. But Katie retreated to her own room. She could still hear the gruff shouts of the men, and see them lazing in the sun. It was as if she was sitting next to Jack, watching him write the letter. She could see him frowning in concentration, then laughing at the thought of little Riordan eating too much cake. Jack might be unsettling, in a boy-meets-girl kind of way, but the scene in her mind was of far greater worry. Though the sun was shining on Scutari, there was one ominous dark cloud. It continued to move, lazily, towards the military camp. And then a shadow fell on Jack's half-written letter.

Chapter Twelve

The Challenge

On the surface, life continued uneventfully at the Palace. Each morning Katie had breakfast with Grace, while James absentmindedly drank some tea, took Grace's pulse and checked her vital signs.

'I am well, James,' Grace protested, 'now, do sit down and eat a proper breakfast with us.'

Katie agreed. 'You can poke and prod Grace and thumb your books all day, James,' she said. 'But Grace is getting pretty healthy; you can see it in her eyes.' When Katie had first met Grace, they were enormous, glittering, desperate eyes. Now they twinkled, if not with full health, at least with mirth.

Princess Alice came to see them mid-morning, and they

all went for a walk in the gardens of Buckingham Palace. She'd had a private chat about Grace with her beloved father, Prince Albert. Unlike the rest of her family, the Prince approved of Alice's interest in nursing. He thought it an excellent skill for women of all classes, as long as it was not taken to an immodest level. 'Young Grace is fatigued,' he said, accepting Dr O'Reilly's incorrect valuation of the case. 'She needs rest and nourishment, but I think you are right to suggest moderate exercise.'

Alice had smiled, and taking her father's hand, held it to her cheek. 'You look fatigued as well, Father,' she had said, gazing up at him with her serious grey eyes. 'Perhaps you need to be nursed too.'

Prince Albert laughed and rubbed his temples with his long pale hand, a larger version of Princess Alice's small one. 'It is this war,' he said. 'It's more complex than the British would have it. I am harried, night and day, by Lord Palmerston. Proposal after proposal on the war; he continues to pretend he is still Foreign Secretary. I am awake all hours, counteracting his directives. The Queen complains that I am wearing myself out. If you are the nurse, then I must listen. I will get more rest.'

So each day Alice, Katie, James and Grace set out – to the lake, the rose gardens, the bedded plants, or the stone follies. As Grace leaned on James's arm, walking through the flower gardens of the Palace, her troubles receded. But Katie's problems multiplied. It had to do with Jack's letters.

Every week or so, Grace took one from her pocket and, seating herself on a stone bench amongst the roses, read aloud to her enthralled friends.

Varna, August 1854

My dearest Grace:

The cholera is amongst us! It is rampant in the Light Division and sixteen men have died of it this day in the Rifles. The men are doubled over in muscle cramps, lying in their own effusions. To hear their cries, their high-pitched, faint voices, calling in thirst, begging for wine or water. Hundreds of men lay in camp before me. I see them through the haze of such intense summer heat, their eyes sunken, their hands and feet filthy and wrinkled. The disease comes on so rapidly, it is so fierce, the poor men age fifty years in five hours. I am glad you cannot see what I see.

The medical care for the British troops is almost non-existent. The French have set up bakeries with fresh bread – they have tents with medical supplies – their men are tended by nurses, sisters of charity in their starched white kerchiefs. We have nothing; sparse rations and no medical supplies to speak of. Our bluff army surgeons are ready to saw off a limb at a moment's notice, but useless in comforting a man in his last minutes. Billy Russell says it is a crime, a form of murder, that the British do not have proper nurses. Grace, we have lived in a doctor's household, so I do not hold back in describing these horrors.

There must be some women, so trained in England. Perhaps, if you soften the tone, you could discuss the situation with Princess Alice. She has a keen interest in nursing, and the ear of Prince Albert. Talk to James too. See what he suggests. It is best to avoid Father. He does not believe in female nurses. He says no woman has the stomach for war.

Please let your friend Miss Katherine Tappan know that I am one of the fortunate few in good health, even if my spirits are shaken. If she were here, I wager she'd start ripping linens for bandages and boiling water. She might even face up to Lord Raglan and command 'strike camp, forrrward march!' And we would all follow. The sooner we leave this godforsaken site, the better.

Tell James I will never tease him about his books again. I can only watch the men die, knowing full well that he has the knowledge to save them. And take care of dear Riordan, his little life is precious to me. I hope your friend Miss Katherine Tappan is as merry and audacious as ever. The thought of her makes me laugh, at a time when I can barely raise a smile.

With all my brotherly affection,
Your Jack

What could they say? The only sound was a tinkling fountain, as Grace passed the letter to Katie. Within months, Jack's merry military encampment had become the sickroom of the Baltics. James stared at the ground, and kicked gravel into the tidy flower beds.

Alice listened with quiet concentration, but for once lost her self-control. 'Oh, that I were a man!' she cried, eyes flared, cheeks red. 'Or that I had the training to aid those men in need. The French provide everything for their men: wholesome food and the care of proper nurses – gentlewomen from religious orders. Yet we, the so modern British, feel our women are too delicate, too fragile to nurse. We must do something. James, tell me what to do!'

James looked closely at Alice, who was alight with indignation. It made her very pretty.

'We must find the right person to talk to,' he said. 'Not your father – not Prince Albert – but someone in the government who is naturally sympathetic to our cause. Much as I dislike this course of action, I think we must go to Bernardo DuQuelle.'

Alice nodded, regaining some calm. 'You are right,' she said. 'He knows everyone and everything. If we can get him to take us seriously, he will help. What do you think Katie?'

But Katie was no longer with them. Clutching Jack's letter, she stared – not at it but through it. Perspiration beaded on her forehead, her bushy black hair curled damply around her neck. Her breathing was harsh and quick. 'There must be water,' she murmured. 'Somewhere in this godforsaken place, there must be water.' She looked up wildly, but did not see her friends. 'You can't just leave him dying in the sun!' she cried, and unwinding her light shawl, threw it up into the air. 'Take this,' she commanded, 'improvise some kind of tent; try to make him cool and comfortable. And damn it, there must be some water!'

Grace stood up and started to say something, but James put out a restraining hand. 'It gets worse when she reads,' he said. 'I think this is like sleepwalking; and I've read that one must never wake a sleepwalker. It affects their heart rate.'

Katie paced the gravel path, talking and talking, into thin air; and then stopped to stare down at the letter.

'Perhaps if we take the letter,' Alice suggested. The letter was tight in Katie's grasp. Taking her friend's hands, Alice stroked them in her own, until Katie's finger's loosened. Slowly and gently, she pulled the letter from Katie, and folding it twice, handed it to James. Katie stood very still, her wild voice subsiding to a murmur. Alice guided her to the bench, and again, with the greatest gentleness, helped her to sit down.

Grace watched them all attentively. Someday James would explain this strangeness of Katie's, and she trusted him enough to wait. As for James and Alice, it had not escaped her how well the two of them worked together. Gradually Katie began to regain her normal self. With a shake of her head, she turned to her friends and wiped the sweat and tears from her face. 'The soldier,' she said, 'he's going to die.'

'I know, my dear,' Alice said softly. 'We are trying to help, I promise. We're asking Bernardo DuQuelle to help.'

'And he'd better help with Katie too,' James added. 'Yes, she's the Tempus, the Chosen, but chosen for what – to frighten the rest of us, I think.' The little group was shaken. This war in the Crimea was not going well. And Katie's gifts were stirring in a troublesome way.

The uneasy stillness was broken by footfall on the gravel. Someone else was walking in the Palace gardens. They could hear him before they could see him. Bernardo DuQuelle's voice was low, but easy to recognize. There was an archness, an irony in his tone, that was both entertaining and irritating.

'I do not expect you to confide in me,' he was saying to his companion, 'as I know you are the *soul* of discretion. And I do sympathize with the danger of your position. All I ask is that you reconsider. Think of yourself for once.'

Before DuQuelle's companion could answer, they turned into the narrow path and came face to face with Katie and her friends. DuQuelle immediately ceased his conversation and bowed low to Princess Alice. He looked singularly out of place in the bright sun of high summer. His white skin took on a chalky grey hue, and the creases of his face could have been carved from old ivory.

But the biggest surprise was his companion. It was Lord Twisted, groomed and moustachioed to within an inch of his life – all lavender gloves and pomaded hair; the least discreet and unselfish man at court. He looked relieved that this tête-à-tête with DuQuelle had been interrupted, and doubly so when he spied Grace. She was very lovely, and so very young – really just leaving girlhood. Out of duty, he bowed to Princess Alice, but ignoring James and Katie, spoke only to Grace.

'Ah, Miss O'Reilly,' he exclaimed, 'I have heard reports from my daughter of your return to health. And now I see it – no, feast upon it – with my own eyes! There was a time when we thought this great beauty was to be taken cruelly from our grasp. Your father is to be applauded for his medical skills. He has vouchsafed a goddess for us mere mortals.'

James looked furious, and Grace hardly less so; but before anyone could respond, Felix came skidding around the corner, spraying gravel into the group before him. He was, as always, in ill humour. 'How dare you leave me?' he spat at Lord Twisted. 'If you are to be my guide, you must stay by my side and do as I tell you!'

Lord Twisted winced, but carefully arranged his face into one of concern. Katie felt that dull pain behind her eyes that Felix always brought on.

Only Bernardo DuQuelle smiled down at the blond curls. 'But Master Felix,' he remonstrated. 'You were so occupied sailing your toy boats on the lake. We didn't wish to disturb your child's play.'

This made Felix even angrier. He was growing up; and to be ridiculed as a baby, in front of the other young people, was unbearable. 'I was not playing with toy boats,' he practically shrieked. 'I was planning a naval attack on the Baltic seaports. I was seeing how the little boats could fire upon the people on shore. I am going to war. I will triumph in battle, while you make garlands of roses. I will be killing your enemies, while you make polite conversation. I am a brave soldier! None of you are the least bit brave!'

It was a shocking way to speak. Alice pursed her lips and James looked as if he might throw Felix to the ground. Bernardo DuQuelle, having egged the child on, leaned back and watched impassively. But it was Grace who responded. The colour had drained from her face, except for two round red spots on each cheek. 'I know of brave soldiers,' she said. 'Every week I receive a letter from one of the bravest. He does not boast or berate. He does his duty manfully, God preserve him, dear Jack . . .' Her voice trembled, and she faltered. The warmth of the day, the emotion of Jack's letter, the strangeness of Katie's behaviour and the sheer cruelty of Felix – it was all too much for her. Though Grace was better, she was still not well. She swayed and sank to the ground.

Everyone sprang forward, except Katie. She was sitting very still on the bench, trying to break free of the visions. As the cholera-infested campsite faded, a new danger appeared. Through her blurred vision, Katie could see Lord Twisted. He was kneeling on the ground, with Grace in his arms. There was something highly unpleasant in the way he caressed Grace's cheek as he smoothed her long red hair from her face. Katie wanted to stop him, but she was still too confused. Now she could see James, leaping forward, pulling Lord Twisted roughly from his sister. Felix's high, unpleasant laugh rang through the rose garden. He seemed to feed off the hostility and anger in the scene before him. Katie stood, but felt so sick she had to sit down again.

James was pushing Lord Twisted away from Grace; bellowing, his face contorted. 'I don't care how grand you are, who your father was,' he was shouting, 'or your grandfather, or great grandfather. You are not fit to touch the hem of my sister's skirt.'

'You! You are little more than a servant, a menial in the Palace!' Lord Twisted pulled off his glove. He whipped it through the air, and threw it at James's feet.

James's angry face became quite still. He knew what the glove meant. James stared at the glove for a long moment, then bent to pick it up. 'If it is a duel you wish, so be it,' was all he said.

'You will be hearing from my second,' replied Lord Twisted. He did not bow. Turning heel, he marched down the gravel path. Felix followed him, practically dancing a jig.

It had been such a lovely summer's day. The roses splashed with red and pink, the flower beds heady with colour and scent. And even now, the bees went along their lively way, while the birds sang in the blue sky. But the little group beside the rose garden seemed wintry and dull.

DuQuelle picked a crimson rose. 'Well, I didn't see *that*

coming' he said. 'You will have to fight him, you know.' James nodded, while Grace and Alice shook their heads in dissent.

DuQuelle looked at Grace, 'It is a pity, that beauty of yours,' he mused. 'It will bring you no joy. But now is not the time to foretell the future. You are still far from well. I suggest you return to your room. And do not fret. We will all try to think of some way to help your brother.'

'Help him with what?' Katie asked.

DuQuelle sighed. 'What a waste of a gift,' he said. 'You'd best go lie down too. I hadn't realized that things had gone this far. Try to remember, forgetful Katie, how much Felix *hates* being called a baby. It might just help you at some future date. Now to bed. We will talk later.'

Alice rallied at this. 'Yes, we'd best go inside. Grace is exhausted, Katie is absolutely green, and James, I don't know what to say . . .' Her voice cracked slightly and trailed off at the thought of James fighting a duel with Lord Twisted. They had often teased Alice about her blind faith in bed rest, but today they were grateful.

Taking Grace by one arm, and Katie by the other, Alice supported them down the garden path. James followed, absorbed in what he had done, and what was to come. Only DuQuelle stayed behind. Turning the rose in his hands, he pricked his finger. Katie, looking back, noticed that he did not bleed.

Chapter Thirteen

The Duel

They'd tried all week to dissuade James. Katie and Alice had argued with him and Grace's newly gained health was fading. But even this would not change James's mind. Lord Twisted had insulted his sister and then challenged him to a duel. He had accepted, and that was final. James had his reasons: anger at his father for his fawning behaviour at court and frustration that he lived in a world where a title was more important than true ability. But these reasons were too personal to share with the girls, so he gave them a more mundane explanation.

'If I refused to fight Lord Twisted, he would spread the word throughout the court. It would destroy my father's reputation. Grace would be ostracized by society and my own medical career would be over before it's even begun.'

'And if you accept the challenge, Lord Twisted will probably kill you,' Katie countered, 'so not just your career, but your life will be over.'

James glared at Katie. 'If you knew anything –'

'I know about staying alive.'

Alice sighed; they were going to have a fight, and then James wouldn't be able to back down. 'James, listen to me,' she said quietly. 'The Palace disapproves strongly of duelling. The Queen would be most disappointed if she heard of this. Even if you survived the duel, it would be a black mark against you forever. I know you well, James O'Reilly. You could not maim or kill another man on such a point of honour. It would be against your personal code of ethics. Can't you put your pride aside? Won't you reconsider?' She looked up at him, her steady grey eyes filled with affection and worry.

He had to look away. 'I'll think about it,' was all he would say.

Alice might have persuaded James, but events were against them. The Royal Court was on the move. It was high summer, and they were all leaving for the Isle of Wight, Alice included. The Queen liked a seaside holiday along with the rest of her nation. Her opinion of cold water was identical to her views on fresh air: one couldn't get enough of them. Each day on the Isle of Wight the Queen would descend to her private beach by Osborne House and climb the wooden steps into her personal bathing machine, a kind of beach hut on wheels. The whole contraption was then pushed into the water by her servants. Exiting a back door, the Queen would splash in the shallows, hidden from view. 'Most refreshing,' was her annual summer observation. Princess Alice, descending from another bathing machine, would cling to a rope attached to the back and shiver, her long, heavy serge bathing costume sagging in the icy waters.

After that the Royal Family would continue on to Balmoral, their Highland home. The Queen loved Scotland even more than she loved sea-bathing. There would be deer-stalking, and reels, torchlight processions and picnics amongst the heather. Scotland in October was hardly a tropical climate and Alice knew she'd spend much of the time sitting outside on a tartan blanket, eating cold venison and half-cooked potato. There would, of course, be more shivering – and she was never offered a nip of Scottish whisky. But go she must.

On her final day at Buckingham Palace, Alice visited Grace, who had taken to the sofa in her sitting room, wan with worry. 'It seems so wrong to leave you,' Alice said. 'You are ill, and James is in grave danger. No one really cares if I am at the Isle of Wight. I simply take up room at Osborne House. As for Balmoral – my mother is much more interested in her sweet little lapdogs and her quaint Scottish servants than she is in me.'

Katie had never heard Alice complain like this. 'Cup of tea?' she asked. 'I've just brewed a cup for Grace. Doesn't that fix everything? A nice cup of tea?'

'I can't laugh,' Alice said. 'It is beyond me at the moment.'

'You don't have to laugh,' Katie responded. 'No one really feels like laughing. But do try to leave us with a smile. I'm here and I really will try to blunder through somehow. I won't let James die, no matter how cranky and disagreeable he is about it. I can be a stubborn brat when I want to. And Grace is one tough cookie, despite lying down all the time.'

Alice did laugh and Grace tried to smile. 'What is a tough cookie?' Alice asked. 'It sounds like a term from the theatre.' Katie poured Alice her nice cup of tea. 'Couldn't we somehow postpone the duel?' Alice said, sipping her tea. 'Make some excuse, about location, or weapons, or his second – the person who assists him . . . or perhaps there could be a problem setting the date or time?'

DuQuelle stood in the doorway of Grace's sitting room. 'The location will be Hampstead Heath. The date is next Thursday, and the time is pre-dawn, by the light of the full moon. The gentlemen have chosen pistols as their weapons, with rapiers in reserve; and the seconds . . . well, I am Lord Twisted's second.'

Alice sprang to her feet. 'You! You are Lord Twisted's second! How could you? To betray us in such a way?'

Katie looked at DuQuelle. '*The gentlemen have chosen pistols*,' she mimicked. 'James is not a *gentleman*; he's a boy – a really nice, smart boy who's way out of his depth. He could no more shoot and kill Lord Twisted than he could eat his own head. Why are you doing this, DuQuelle? I know you're a strange guy, but I'd started to believe you really weren't that bad.'

Bernardo DuQuelle surveyed the trio. Grace was so still, her tea sat untouched on the small wooden table. Princess Alice was tight with anger. Katie, he could tell, understood him better than the others.

'You are very quick to doubt my motives,' he said. 'Better the devil you know . . . and Katie, James had some trouble choosing a second for the duel. He didn't wish to implicate others in this possible scandal. So I have nominated you. Good day.' And with a bow he was gone.

'DuQuelle acting for Lord Twisted, and a girl as a second? It simply cannot happen.' Princess Alice was now shocked as well as worried.

Grace leaned back and closed her eyes. Things seemed to be getting worse.

'It's happened before,' Grace told them. 'But the women were not seconds. They were the duellists themselves. About ten years ago, two ladies, at dawn, in Hyde Park fought with both pistols and rapiers. The challenger managed to draw blood. My father tended the wound. It was a great scandal at court. Neither was ever received again. Oh how I wish . . .'

'Well, I'll have to go,' Katie interrupted. 'I'll dress up like a man, and try and dissuade James until the end. As DuQuelle said, better the devil you know. DuQuelle has no morals, no passions, no sentiment – but I really do think he's acting for some secret, kind of good reason.'

They practically had to push Alice out of the door to leave for the Isle of Wight. Grace was put to bed, and Katie continued to tackle James. But every time she opened her mouth, he became more determined to fight. He was impossible: furious with Lord Twisted, and embarrassed at being lumbered with Katie as a second. He barked at her, insulted her, sulked and ignored her. She took it all with surprisingly good grace. She knew that underneath the bravado, he was very, very frightened.

When she failed with James, she turned to Bernardo DuQuelle. 'It is beyond me,' she said, 'but if you're going to hang around with Lord Twisted, please do something. Make him take back the challenge. James is so young. He doesn't know anything about pistols or rapiers. It was a cowardly challenge from Lord Twisted. He knows James can't win.'

'No, James cannot win,' DuQuelle agreed. 'Lord Twisted might be a knave, but when it comes to duels, he is not a coward. He is an excellent mark, and a first-rate swordsman. It is rumoured he has killed several times in duels, and wounded dozens more – though it is also rumoured that he cheats.' None of this was of any comfort to Katie.

The days ticked by and each one moved them closer to the duel. James would not listen to reason. He simply turned aside, ignoring all arguments. She noticed he spent much of his time at target practice and cleaning his pistols. She suspected he was sneaking off to church. Grace fretted and her appetite disappeared. Her weight plummeted when she realized the duel would, after all, take place. DuQuelle was strangely cheery and, on the whole, unsympathetic. Katie was getting nowhere – and if she failed to persuade him, well, James might just die.

Wednesday arrived, a hot, blustery day. As night came on, the wind picked up: the Palace windows rattled in their frames, making the curtains billow. Katie prepared for the assignation in the dead of night. Passing Grace's room, she found her standing beside her wardrobe, trying to get dressed. 'Do you want to die as well?' Katie exclaimed. 'You can't possibly come.'

'I cannot let James kill himself over my precious reputation,' Grace gasped, flinging a dress over her head. 'You have been a tremendous help to me, and I am grateful. But I am several years your senior. I know what I am doing.'

Katie looked at Grace. Her hair was tangled in the collar of her dress and she was struggling to get it on. 'What would Alice do?' Katie wondered. 'She has such tact. She'd know how to talk to Grace.' Katie gently detached Grace's hair from the dress, and sat her down on the edge of the bed.

'It must be hard for you,' Katie said. 'Both Jack and James are in danger. But if you come tonight, will you really make it any better? Little Riordan needs you here. And you know James. He's going to fight this duel. You can't change his mind. If you are there, he will be even more worried, and distracted. Really, do you think it's a good idea to see Lord Twisted again? If I had a choice, I'd skip that one.'

Reluctantly Grace went back to bed. After weeks of decreasing her laudanum, Katie gave her a double dose. She didn't want Grace rising in the middle of the night to follow them.

At least dressing was less of a fuss than normal. Katie had got used to most of her new clothes – the chemise, the long drawers, the endless petticoats; everything except the corset. The corset was unbearable; she couldn't eat properly, couldn't run, or bend; she could barely walk without getting a horrible stitch in her side. And despite the agony of the corset, her waist, by Victorian standards, was still huge.

So it was with relief that she put on a flannel vest and shorts, a white shirt, cravat and long trousers. She did struggle with the wing collar of her stiff white shirt and made a mess of knotting her cravat, but she actually quite liked the trousers with the braid down the side. The men's black kid boots were comfortable, and a perfect fit on her big feet. Katie bundled her bushy black hair on top of her head, and shoved a black silk top hat over it. She could imagine Mimi wearing the long black coat she put over everything; but with a sequined body stocking and fishnets of course. Looking in the mirror, she found herself quite dashing. 'Next time I come back, it's going to be as a boy,' she said. She always talked to herself when she was nervous, and the impending duel had her on edge.

It was easier to get out of the Palace than she had imagined. As the Royal Family was away, the Palace was functioning with a skeleton staff. There were no soldiers in the guard rooms; the nurseries were not under lock and key. At one time she had hidden all over the Palace – there'd been a lacquered Chinese chest and a large picnic basket and she'd tucked herself into corners and thrown herself under beds. But now Katie simply made her way downstairs, through the upper servants' passage, and out of a back door into the bright moonlight. James was waiting outside for her. His face had been quite pale, but flushed with anger and embarrassment when he saw her.

He held tight to his case of pistols, but thrust a bulky leather bag into her hands.

'What's this?' she asked.

'You look ridiculous,' he replied.

'I didn't ask how I look. I asked what's in the bag.'

'It's my medical kit,' James said. 'If anything happens, please try to use it wisely.'

Katie remembered the pamphlet under her bed at home in New York. *Tourniquets and Their Uses*. Was she really going to use a tourniquet now, tonight? Silently they trudged out of the Palace courtyard, through the wide, cobbled entrance and the broad stone gates, their long black overcoats flapping in the wind.

'Aren't you going to get your horse?' Katie asked, clutching her top hat against the weather.

James snorted. 'I'm not going to ride all the way to Hampstead with you gasping and jabbering behind me. We'll take a hansom cab.'

Katie thought it seemed strange, even prosaic, to take a taxi to a duel. But it also seemed very James. He was scared, and he was trying to make it all as normal as possible.

'I love cabs,' she told James. 'We have yellow ones in New York; millions of them in the streets, motorized ones.' Usually James would have jumped at the chance to discuss twenty-first-century engineering but now he was silent. Katie continued. 'The taxi drivers are from all over the world. They never know where anything is, ever, but if you . . .'

'You are babbling.'

'I know.'

'Well, please try to stop. I need to find a cab.'

They found one halfway down the Mall. Not a hansom cab, but a big, lumbering, four-wheeled growler. The driver balked at the destination, so far from the centre of London, but James agreed to pay double, with a 10s deposit. They bumped along, due north, towards Hampstead Heath. The silence inside the cab was thick and deadening; the weather outside angry and insistent. James stared out of the window, trying to memorize the gaslights in the streets, the straggling pedestrians bent double by the wind, the stars in the sky and the moon.

Finally Katie couldn't take it any longer. 'You can't win,' she cried. 'You're going to get shot, maybe even killed. This must be some really stupid boy thing. Do you want to die?'

James didn't shout or sulk. He was silent for a moment and then turned to her.

'I never really know if you are real,' he said. 'You come through time, or so you say, and then you're gone. I can only question the phenomenon that brings you to us. But I do know you are a friend, a true friend.'

Katie looked at James. He'd never spoken so openly or honestly to her. He seemed much older tonight, but still far too young to take part in a duel against a notorious rake. He meant a great deal to her and, she knew, even more to Princess Alice. And then there was Grace, unable to protect the brother she loved so much . . . and little Riordan, already without a mother. Katie had to make sure James did not die.

'You are my friend, James,' she said, 'If I had a brother, I'd want him to be just like you. And I'd want him to live a long, healthy, happy kind of life. You're, like, the least romantic person I know, James, and you don't believe in this overwrought kind of thing. I mean, a duel! Jesus.

Please, can't we just stop this now?' James shook his head.

'I've seen the way Lord Twisted looks at my sister. It's not healthy and it's not right. I have spoken to my father about it, and he will not act. Indeed, for some vain and worldly reason, he seems to desire the connection. Someone must protect Grace. Jack has gone off to war and Riordan is still so little. It has to be me.'

She leaned forward and took James's hand. For once he didn't recoil. 'I've been reading up on duels,' she said. 'A second can take the place of a participant if the participant is incapacitated. Couldn't I take your place? I mean, who knows if I can even be killed, because I'm not in my own time, and . . .' The intimacy between them was shattered.

James flung himself to the opposite side of the cab. 'Do you think for one moment I would let a girl stand in for me? That I would place you at risk, gamble on your immortality? Do you think that I am a coward? That I would hide behind a girl's skirts?'

Katie held her nerve. 'I don't see us as boy and girl,' she told him. 'At least I try not to. I see us as friends, really good friends. And I see us, as, like, equal. I mean, I'm not even wearing a skirt. I'm offering to do what one best friend would do for another. You've risked your life for me. You have done that before. And just because of the way you view girls, you won't let me do the same for you.'

The horses slowed as they ploughed up a steep incline. They were nearing Hampstead. James knew there was no point being angry with Katie. She had been a loyal friend to him. She was sitting in a musty old growler in the middle of the night. She was offering to risk her life for his. He couldn't accept it, of course. But he could at least be polite about it. He tried to shake off the attitudes of his own time, to see her the way she saw him. 'Thank you,' he said gruffly. 'I know you only wish to help. The best thing you can do now is to familiarize yourself with the contents of my medical kit.'

The cab came to a halt at the top of Prospect Hill. The driver had observed the pistol case, the medical kit and the dark concealing clothes. He knew what he had in his cab; a young duellist and his second – two foolish boys out to defend their honour. 'I reckon you're looking for South Wood,' he remarked. 'Just pass through them oaks. From there you can skirt across the grounds of Kenwood House – don't be worrying about the Earl, he's in Scotland. The meadows are on the one side, the South Woods are on the other. Head southeast and you'll be finding the duelling grounds. If you pay another 10s in advance I'll wait. You might be needing me to carry a message, or fetch a doctor.'

Katie shivered, but James was steady. 'I thank you,' he said and gave the driver twice what he'd asked. 'If you would wait; we will be several hours.' The driver weighed up the coins in his hand and squinted down at James. 'Good luck,' he said. 'You are a young 'un for such doings. I wouldna want my own son out on the heath t'night.'

The wild night wreaked havoc on the heath. The ancient oaks creaked and groaned as Katie and James passed underneath. The tall grasses in the meadow whipped and stung their legs. Katie's hat went flying through the air. She caught it, and jammed it down tighter on her head. In the distance lay the stately manor, Kenwood House. The driver had been right; the house was in darkness, but the white stone glowed, stark and ghostly in the moonlight. In front of them was the dense mass of the South Woods.

The trees, thick with foliage, threw their branches across the sky, crossing and re-crossing the moon. 'Maybe Lord Twisted won't show,' Katie shouted through the wind. 'Maybe he'll get lost.' The woods offered a respite from the fierce squalls. Above them the branches rattled and shook in protest, but the woodland floor was dark and almost still. A whisper of a wind scattered the rotting leaves. The undergrowth rustled with small animals, the underside of a bat's wing caught the glint of moonlight.

Just when they thought the woods would never end, they came abruptly to a clearing. The trees hemmed in the spot, giving it complete seclusion. 'Do you think this is it? I mean, it's really such a small space, maybe we should turn back.' Katie said.

'It's not too small, it's fifty paces, there's room to spare,' said a voice from behind a tree. Bernardo DuQuelle stepped forward, and waved his walking stick. 'I've measured it myself.'

'You're just, like, so helpful, I can't thank you enough,' Katie said, her voice thick with sarcasm. DuQuelle, though, was immune to sarcasm, along with almost everything else.

James looked around the clearing. 'Where is Lord Twisted?' he asked. 'I am ready to begin.'

Bernardo DuQuelle lifted his head, and sniffed the air around him. 'Yes,' he replied. 'I suggest we begin immediately. There's something in the air tonight which I do not like at all.'

Lord Twisted emerged from the woods and handed his case of pistols to DuQuelle. He looked at James, a sneer screwing up his dandified face. 'Let us make quick work of this,' he said. 'I have someone waiting for me, in a supper house in Haymarket. I would not wish them to grow cold.'

James stood stiff as a rod at his words. 'You cannot open your mouth, but to be vile,' he said to Lord Twisted. 'I will never be more ready than I am now.'

'Then you shall never be ready,' Lord Twisted laughed; 'for tonight I take aim. Who knows if you will see tomorrow?'

Bernardo DuQuelle stepped between them. 'There is no need for insults,' he said, 'no need for threats. Do you not think the duel is enough? I am certain each contender will rise and greet the sun tomorrow; let us rethink that turn of phrase. Lord Twisted, you have agreed to a duel of the "first blood" – and both gentlemen shall shoot to *disable*, not *to the death*.'

Lord Twisted smiled, and adjusted his white cuff meticulously. 'Of course,' he said, 'as agreed. But with the winds so high, the light of the moon is fitful, unclear. I cannot vouch for my line of vision. What is meant to be a nick to the leg might become a shot through the heart.'

DuQuelle leaned forward and spoke low. A chance gust of wind carried his words to Katie. 'Dr O'Reilly is much favoured by the Queen. What would she think if his son were to die at the hands of a courtier? My dear Lord Twisted, your sojourn to the Crimea might become an exile.'

Lord Twisted stopped smiling, and Bernardo DuQuelle stepped into the centre of the duelling grounds. 'These are the rules,' he announced. 'At my count, both gentlemen shall turn, back-to-back and walk twenty paces to the end of the grounds. At twenty they will turn to face each other, and then fire.'

Katie bit her lip to stop from crying. DuQuelle just had to put an end to this. He couldn't let James go on, like a lamb to slaughter.

'Do you both agree?' DuQuelle asked.

'I agree,' James said.

'But of course,' Lord Twisted replied. He looked almost bored.

DuQuelle sniffed the air again, and scanned the dark woods behind him.

'One last thing,' he said. 'James O'Reilly, as the challenged, will fire first.'

Lord Twisted was suddenly paying attention. 'We fire together,' he said, 'at the drop of your handkerchief.'

Bernardo DuQuelle shook his head. He was smiling ever so slightly. 'You are familiar with the Code Duello – the first shot is awarded to the challenged? James O'Reilly will fire first.'

Lord Twisted's attention drifted again. 'Fine,' he replied, 'I have little to worry about, a boy like this, at forty paces . . .'

James ignored the insult. He was concentrating with all his might on the next few minutes. Bernardo DuQuelle began to count. 'One, two, three, four . . .' Katie could hear a twig breaking in the woods behind her, but she could not take her eyes off James. 'Nine, ten, eleven, twelve.' He looked even younger than his years, with the tall trees swaying above him. 'Fifteen, sixteen, seventeen, eighteen.' Katie was screaming inside her head. What if Lord Twisted *did* kill James? How could she ever face Alice, or Grace? DuQuelle caught her eye for a moment. What could his look mean? 'Nineteen . . . twenty.'

Both James and Lord Twisted turned. Lord Twisted wasn't even nervous. He looked half asleep. Slowly James raised his arm and pointed the pistol at Lord Twisted.

Katie's heart ached for him. His hand shook badly and his face was crumpled. He looked about eight years old. For a moment James hesitated, aiming for the upper leg, and then deciding on the shoulder. Then his face cleared and his hand grew steady. Looking Lord Twisted in the eye, he raised the pistol and shot. High. High over Lord Twisted's head. 'I will not injure him,' he said. 'It is against my principles.'

For one moment Katie's heart sang with joy – of course he couldn't do it. He was James the thinker, James the healer – not James the killer. She started to run towards him, but stopped as Lord Twisted's voice rang out.

'How dare you,' he cried, now wide awake with fury. 'How dare you choose to shoot above my head? As if I were some novice, some green young bounder who must be protected from his own mishaps.'

James stood his ground. He looked taller now, and older. 'I will live by my principles,' he said.

'Your principles? Don't you know, to shoot above my head, to delope – is the gravest insult? Well, if you live by your principles you shall also die by them.'

Katie gasped as she remembered the rules. James had taken his shot, and now it was Lord Twisted's turn to fire. The man was very, very angry. She turned to Bernardo DuQuelle. 'Please,' she cried, 'you have got to do something. Look at Lord Twisted. He's going to kill James. You have got to stop this.'

Bernardo DuQuelle did not reply. He stood stock still, unblinking, staring at something Katie could not see. Perhaps it was the moonlight, but he appeared bloodless as a statue. She ran over and shook him by the shoulder. No, he was flesh and blood, or at least as much as Bernardo DuQuelle could be. Why then, would he not speak?

'Do something!' she repeated.

Lord Twisted now raised his arm. His pomaded hair was on end, the curls whipped by the wind; he was smiling, laughing, but with no joy, no mirth. With casual expertise he cocked his pistol. He was aiming directly at James – at his heart. Bernardo DuQuelle continued to stare, trance-like, into the dark woods.

Katie followed his gaze, squinting. Then she saw it: a hooded figure, coming towards them, low to the ground, its cloak sweeping the leaves from its path. It was a figure she recognized, and dreaded. 'Belzen!' she cried.

This seemed to rouse DuQuelle. Springing forward, he flung himself between the two duellists, directly into the line of fire. Lord Twisted could not stop himself. His shot rang out, and Bernardo DuQuelle staggered backwards, falling to the ground.

'Run, you fools!' DuQuelle cried. 'There's something far worse than a duel in the woods tonight – if you value your life, run!'

Lord Twisted needed no further invitation. He knew he'd bungled and shot DuQuelle. To kill James was one thing, but to kill Prince Albert's Private Secretary was another. He turned tail and fled.

DuQuelle dragged himself onto his knees. 'Didn't you hear me? Run!' The duelling ground had given them some shelter from the wind, but now it rose up with a roar. The trees around them bent double. Dark clouds scudded across the moon. The ground flickered with light and dark. Around them, large branches began to fall.

'We can't leave you here,' Katie yelled into the storm. 'You've been shot. You need help.' James shook himself, and suddenly seemed to realize what was going on. He ran forward and, taking DuQuelle's arm, hooked it over his neck. Katie understood, and did the same. They held DuQuelle between them.

'We need to get him away from here,' James shouted. 'I pray the cab is still waiting.'

'Are you witless?' DuQuelle gasped. 'Katie knows what's coming, and yet she does not flee.'

Something crossed Katie's foot, slapping against her ankle. She leapt back repulsed. It was a snake, and then a rat. A glance over her shoulder showed Belzen was closing in. She could see his strange blunted nose and his small glittering eyes. She shuddered, but worse was to come. As Belzen took in the three figures, desperately limping, he began to writhe and sink to the ground. With dread, Katie knew that Lord Belzen was about to transform himself. He'd been aroused by their weakness, and was preparing for the kill.

Suddenly Katie's fear turned to fury. 'I will not die like this,' she thought. 'I can't let that ghastly thing drink my blood, fill me with tar and gouge out my eyes. I have nice eyes . . .' Belzen was gaining on them. She could hear the slithering of his great mass even through the wild winds. But she would not abandon DuQuelle, and she had no weapons, no pistol, no knife. Lord Belzen was at their heels. The ground rumbled under his surging weight. She couldn't bear the idea of facing him. How horrible, to see what he had become – a snake, a man, a serpent. That was almost as bad as what would happen next, when he caught them.

Then DuQuelle's voice, soft and slight, was in her ear. 'Use your head, or at the least what is on top of it, Katie.' In a panic, almost without thinking, she pulled the top hat from her head and, turning, pushed it blindly over Belzen's snout and glittering eyes.

Lord Belzen coiled back upon himself; this stopped him for but a moment. Katie urged the others forward. She had gained seconds, but every second counted. The very heavens seemed to rage. With a loud groan, a mighty oak gave way close by, uprooted after hundreds of years. Slowly at first, the tree bowed towards the earth, and then in a rush it crashed to the ground. Branches tore past Katie, ripping her clothes and scratching her skin. But the bulk of the tree landed upon the transforming figure of Lord Belzen.

Then there was silence. The storm had passed, so abruptly that the silence had a violence of its own. DuQuelle's white skin had become almost transparent, the deep lines on his face tinged with green.

James looked at him with growing concern. 'I have my medical kit here, but I doubt it will be much help to you,' he said to DuQuelle. 'Let's get you to the cab. Then you can tell us what to do.' DuQuelle licked his lips and closed his eyes. His breathing was shallow. His arm around Katie's neck was ice-cold.

'I think we should carry him,' she said to James. 'And let's get out of here fast. That thing you saw behind us: I can guarantee the falling tree hasn't killed it. It was never alive in the first place.'

James gave Katie a long look as they struggled across the Heath, DuQuelle between them. 'What was that thing — that came out of the woods? I can tell you know, Katie.'

'It was Lord Belzen,' she answered. 'He must have been drawn by the excitement of the duel. He feeds off brute force. But I can't understand why he would pick this particular duel. There's so much brutality in the world. It wouldn't be a feast for him, really just a snack. Then he changed, he began to transform. Why? Was it the duel, the blood that was coming, the death? Maybe DuQuelle had angered him in some way.'

Though weaker by the moment DuQuelle could still speak. 'You have it wrong,' he said weakly. 'I could never excite Lord Belzen in such a way. I am afraid, my dear, that it was you . . .'

True to his word, the cabbie was waiting for them. He looked astonished by what turned up. The young man was not wounded, but he and his second carried a man who seemed half-dead. The second was in bad shape too, clothes torn, skin bleeding. Long black hair tumbled down his back. He . . . was a she!

Katie reached into Bernardo DuQuelle's pocket and found a gold sovereign. 'Here,' she cried, tossing it to the driver. 'To Buckingham Palace!' They loaded Bernardo DuQuelle into the carriage and the cab lurched forward.

Katie could barely look at Bernardo DuQuelle. His strange green eyes glittered too brightly; his mouth was a thin red line drawn crudely on his white face. His breathing came in sharp pants.

James went to work immediately. Laying DuQuelle down on the carriage floor, he loosened his cravat and took the studs out of his shirt. 'I was concentrating on Twisted,' he said. 'I didn't see what happened. Where did he get hit?'

'I think it was his chest, or his shoulder.' Katie replied. DuQuelle was staring at her. His eyes glowed. James took a sponge and some alcohol from his medical bag.

'There are no blood stains,' he said.

Opening DuQuelle's shirt, James ran his hand across his chest. 'Ah, here is the wound,' he said. 'Close to the heart, but not fatal, I hope.' He soaked the sponge in the alcohol and swathed the area. 'How strange,' he murmured, 'there is no bleeding. Could it be that deep a wound? It is more dangerous than I thought.'

Then Katie remembered the day in the rose garden when Lord Twisted had challenged James to the duel. Bernardo DuQuelle had pricked his finger on a rose.

'He is not bleeding,' she said, 'because he has no blood.'

James looked shocked, and Katie felt quite queasy, but Bernardo DuQuelle smiled up at her. 'I begin to believe you are worthy of the Tempus,' he whispered.

James stared down at his patient. 'This is what I feared,' he said. 'I don't know how to help you. Tell me what to do.'

Katie could see the open wound, near the heart. A silver fluid like liquid mercury seeped from the edges. DuQuelle began to wheeze, but now the sound came from the wound. The silver fluid began to shine. It bubbled slightly and then rose like mist from his chest. Above him it reformed, into a new shape – the shape of words:

It is never too late to be what you might have been.

For a moment the words hung above them in the carriage, then dissolved into nothing.

Men do not stumble over mountains, but over molehills.

The words formed and reformed, seeping from the wound in Bernardo DuQuelle's chest. It was fascinating and terrifying. 'What's happening?' Katie cried. 'You're, like, bleeding words. Why are you doing this?'

DuQuelle's voice was barely audible. 'I am losing what is best in me, what is hard gained, most important . . . I am losing what I have learned from you – the finest ideas, the highest ambitions that you communicate.' Leaking from his chest, the words came thick and fast:

No man is free who is not master of himself.

'Epictetus, Confucius . . . They are the best minds, the great philosophers,' James murmured. 'He is bleeding human knowledge. This is far beyond anything we can treat in this time.'

'Or any time,' Katie said. She wasn't frightened anymore. As Bernardo DuQuelle shed his humanity, she began to believe he was, or had been, human. Taking the sponge from James, she placed it on his forehead, and gently stroked his temples. 'There must be someone who can help you,' she said. 'We need you to tell us. We need to help you.'

DuQuelle closed his eyes for a moment, as if he were having a private debate. Katie held her breath. Was he dying? Was he dead? Could he even die? At last he spoke. 'You must leave me at Half Moon Street. I am too far gone to mend myself. There is only one who can treat me. If she has not already left for the Crimea, I believe you will find her at Harley Street. James, you must send a message . . .'

DuQuelle's voice was so low that James had to bend his ear to his lips. DuQuelle muttered the name and the address, and James's eyes grew wide with astonishment. 'Tell no one . . . not Katie . . . no more . . .' Bernardo DuQuelle's eyes rolled back in his head, and the words seeped and glittered above him:

Death may be the greatest of all human blessings.

Chapter Fourteen

DuQuelle's Nurse

'He bled words? I still cannot believe it.' Alice held on to Katie's arm, as they walked through Green Park on an early autumn day. Princess Alice was not usually allowed out without an adult chaperone, but fate had led her back to London with a tiny grain of independence. The Queen was in a 'delicate condition' – there was going to be yet another little prince or princess. When Alice developed a skin inflammation, Dr O'Reilly feared measles. The Queen's unborn child had to be protected, so Alice was rushed back to London, while the rest of the Royal Family continued on to Balmoral, their home in the Highlands of Scotland. It turned out Alice only had a rash – the result of too much vigorous sea-bathing. It subsided in a few weeks, but she got to stay at Buckingham Palace, albeit under the guardianship of the sour old Baroness Lehzen.

'It was really creepy,' Katie said. 'All this glittery silver stuff came out of DuQuelle. And then it became, like, famous words, stuff they teach you at school. I could have learned a lot, if I hadn't been so afraid that he was dying.' Katie didn't share just how relieved she was that he hadn't died, or that she had been writing to him at Half Moon Street since the accident.

James walked on the other side of Alice, stiff as a sentry. They were out in a public park in London. He must make certain no harm came to the Princess. 'I believe you were right in the first place,' he said to Katie. 'I don't think DuQuelle can die – but he can stop being human.' The conversation came to an abrupt end, as they all contemplated gloomily – just what would Bernardo DuQuelle become if he stopped being human . . . It wasn't a pleasant line of thought.

But such a bright, Indian summer day was not the time for gloom. James was safe, and Bernardo DuQuelle was recovering. Lord Twisted had fled London and was now in the Crimea with the British army, his young ward Felix in tow. Grace's health had improved dramatically with the return of her brother, unscathed, and the departure of Lord Twisted. It even looked as if they might win this war.

'It is wonderful news, the victory at Alma. And I believe Grace had a letter from Jack today,' Alice said. 'Have you seen it?'

Katie hadn't. She was avoiding any type of reading at the moment. She couldn't even read a copy of *Tatler* without seeing hundreds of women swirling around a ballroom. Her reaction to words was worsening.

James had read Jack's letter. 'The troops are marching on Sebastopol,' he told them both. 'It is a major Russian naval base. If Sebastopol falls, the Russians will be powerless in the Black Sea. The war will end. The battle at Alma was the first step.'

'And Jack is OK?' Katie asked, with a tightening in her chest.

'He's fine,' James replied. 'Furious but fine. It seems the Light Brigade did not see action. Once Raglan had gained the intended position, he let the Russians retreat. Jack says there were over a thousand British cavalry looking on at a beaten enemy retreating – guns, standards, colours and all – a wretched horde of Cossacks and cowards who they knew would never strike back. He was certain they would turn tail and flee at the first trumpet. Jack said the Light Brigade were but a ten-minute gallop from the enemy. And yet, Raglan let the Russians go.'

'All Jack wants is to see action, to be in danger – why?' Katie asked.

Princess Alice tried to explain. 'It is serious and dangerous,' she told her friend. 'But it is also noble. My mother says the losses were heavy, that many have fallen and many are wounded. But she also says the troops behaved with a courage and desperation which was beautiful to behold.' Katie still didn't get it.

'Jack also says that Lord Twisted and young Felix have arrived,' James added. 'They've set up camp, with the troops, but in the most luxurious tent possible.'

'Well, that will brighten things up for everyone,' Katie commented drily.

James nodded. 'Yes, they are already making trouble. Because of Felix's position within the Royal Family, he has access to the high command. Everyone knows there is bad blood between Lord Cardigan and Lord Lucan, and Felix seems to have attached himself to both of them and stirred things up.'

'Bad blood? What's the problem?' Katie asked. She noticed Alice was blushing and James chose his words carefully.

'Lord Cardigan is married to Lord Lucan's youngest sister,' he told Katie. 'But they are no longer domiciled together.'

'Well, yeah, divorce,' Katie said, 'it just happens.'

Alice looked at her firmly. 'No, it does not,' she replied.

James hated this conversation. 'It was abandonment,' he said, 'and Lord Lucan will never forgive his brother-in-law. This complicates the military campaign, since Lord Cardigan reports directly to Lord Lucan. Young Felix has observed the friction and seems bent on making a bad situation worse. And that's not all. Jack says Felix has made great friends with a certain Captain Nolan – a brilliant horseman, but a man who bitterly hates both Cardigan and Lucan. Felix seems to be using Nolan to spread discontent among the soldiers.'

'And this is how you run your army?' Katie questioned. 'Where's the ghastly Lord Twisted in all this? Isn't he supposed to be chaperoning Felix?'

James's lip curled at the thought of his enemy. 'Twisted is living up to his reputation,' he replied. 'Jack says he is often observed in the drinking dens of the soldiers, plying them with liquor and asking many questions. Lord Twisted also spends much time writing long letters and sending them off, goodness knows where. One hears that he has got to know some of the officers in the Russian camp.'

Alice looked horrified. Katie guessed they all had the same word at the tip of their tongues – *spy*.

Despite this, the day was still beautiful – one last golden fling before the onslaught of winter. And when they turned into Piccadilly, Alice's mood brightened up considerably. It wasn't the imposing homes lining the street that interested her. Further down Piccadilly were some new shops, with glass fronts and pretty things inside. Princesses did not go into shops, but Alice thought, just this once wouldn't hurt.

Katie could read her mind. A lifetime with Mimi, the mega-shopper, had taught her to recognize that glint in the eye. 'No way,' she said, taking Alice's arm more firmly. 'Do you really think James is going to let you go shopping? He's annoyed enough that you're walking down a street.'

Alice blushed. How shameful to be thinking of trinkets when Bernardo DuQuelle was still so ill. 'I wouldn't dream of stopping,' she said primly. 'It was difficult enough to get away from the Baroness Lehzen. And it is a privilege to call upon Bernado DuQuelle at Half Moon Street to thank him for the protection he has given my friends.'

'We didn't think highly of him when he agreed to be Lord Twisted's second, but he showed great courage,' James agreed, his voice rising over the clatter of horses and carriages on the cobblestones. 'Why he did so, I'll never know. You can be certain it wasn't to save me.' Taking Alice briefly by the arm, he guided her around the pavement – someone's horse had been particularly productive that morning.

They passed Devonshire House and turned into Half Moon Street. A terrible smell hit them as they rounded the corner. The old cesspools underneath Mayfair were no match for the new water closets. They were taxed beyond their capacities. Somewhere underground, something had burst. Sewage bubbled up on to the street. Katie reeled back, gagging, while Alice blinked hard, but carried on steadily. James did not bat an eye. He was training to be a doctor; and if you work with cadavers, you have to get used to some seriously bad smells.

Among the stucco-fronted houses lining the street lay Bernardo DuQuelle's home. It was as individual as the man himself: a half-timbered structure with leaded glass windows. The upper floors loomed over the pavement, as if they might keel over and fall into the gutter. 'Not grand,' James muttered, 'but intimidating in its own way.' Katie tugged Alice onwards, to the front door. She had no desire to linger in the street with its awful stench.

They rang the bell, and then rang it again. After some time, a sleepy-eyed footman opened the door. When Princess Alice handed him her card, he managed to wake up. Hopping on one foot, he pulled up a white stocking and slicked back his hair. 'Your Royal Highness,' he gasped. 'One moment, please, inside, Ma'am.'

DuQuelle's front hall was dark and crammed with furniture, portraits, mirrors and hundreds of years of knick-knacks. But it was cool, after the warm day, and dark after the glare of the daylight. Katie noticed that the smell of sewage did not enter the house. Instead it smelled of DuQuelle – slightly acidic, a bit electric, with hints of powder and musk. The footman bumbled about them, offering chairs, trying to take James's hat, his gloves. He was looking for a silver tray on which to place Alice's card, when a voice from below stairs cut through his apologetic murmurings.

'They'll be wanting some arrowroot and beef tea upstairs, and you know she don't like to be kept waiting!' Katie had been a guest, albeit an uninvited one, in this house before. She recognized the strident tones of DuQuelle's fat cook, a demanding woman with a tight hold on the rest of the staff. Taking a final bow, the footman dashed down the stairs to the cellar kitchen, knocking over a side table as he fled.

'Do you think we'd best stand on courtesy and wait?' Alice asked.

'I'm not sure he'll ever return,' Katie replied. 'That cook's pretty tough. Come on, I think I know where we can find DuQuelle.' The house was dark, the curtains drawn and the candles were not lit. Katie started up the aged oak staircase, resting her hand briefly on a finial shaped like a dragon. This was not what you might call a friendly house. It certainly wasn't a clean one. The stairs were thick with dust, the worn steps blackened with age and dirt. As the three climbed, a series of sour-faced portraits peered down at them. 'Can you imagine anyone ever really looking like that?' Katie said, staring at a painting of a young girl with a stiff white ruff encircling her neck. 'But then you two seemed as strange to me when I first came.' The girl in the portrait stared back. She didn't seem to like what she saw.

Up, up, up they went, to the very top of the house. There was a crack of light from under one door, but all else was darkness. As they hesitated outside the door, a quiet but firm voice came from within.

'Don't fidget in the hallway, please. If you have come to visit, I suggest you enter.' It was the voice of a woman, distinct, crisp and decidedly upper class. It was not what they had expected.

James hesitated and shuffled a bit, but Princess Alice squared her shoulders and pushed the door open. Katie followed, tripping slightly over the threshold. She remembered this room with its soot-stained wooden panels, the furniture carved with leering gargoyles, and the endless clutter of books. But the room they entered was quite a different story. It was clean. Every inch of it had been scrubbed. The tapestries on the walls had been beaten until they were free of dust; the sofas and chairs polished and comfortable cushions placed on them. The mountains of books were carefully arranged in the bookshelves. A fire glowed brightly in the hearth.

Bernardo DuQuelle lay on a sofa by the fire, his long legs tucked into a warm wool blanket. His chest had been bound, and a book lay, face down, upon it. He looked much better, at least for DuQuelle. His green eyes still glittered, but with a less fitful, burning gaze. And there were no big smoke rings of words rising from his chest – that was a relief.

Sitting very straight, on a chair by his side, was the woman who had spoken. She rose to meet them. Katie noticed her graceful walk, and her perfect posture. It was difficult to judge her age, but easy to guess her position in society.

She moved forward with confidence and curtsied to Princess Alice. 'It is good of you to come, Your Highness. M. DuQuelle is dedicated to the service of the Royal

Family; how kind of you to recognize this and to call.' Despite her very good manners, and quiet gentlewoman's voice, there was something of the rebuke in her tone.

Alice looked flustered. 'I should have come before,' she murmured, her voice trailing away.

Bernardo DuQuelle sighed from the sofa. Women – they *would* complicate things. 'I hope you will excuse me from rising,' he said. 'But let me take this opportunity to introduce my friend of long standing, Miss Florence Nightingale.'

She was a tall, slender woman, with rich brown hair pulled back from a perfectly shaped oval face. Her colouring was delicately white, unlike DuQuelle's chalk-like pallor. Katie knew a lot about celebrity. After all, she'd lived with Mimi all her life. And this seemingly modest woman was loaded with star power.

Princess Alice's eyes lit up as she recognized the name. 'But of course!' she exclaimed. 'I have heard Lady Canning speak of you. You are the Superintendent of the Institution for the Care of Sick Gentlewomen. Mrs Sidney Herbert also sings your praises. You have made that institution a model of organization and practice. They say your methods should be adopted by all medical establishments throughout Britain.'

James had also lost his reserve. Katie had never seen him look at a woman with such admiration. 'I have read your pamphlet on the training of nurses in Kaiserswerth,' he said. 'I would like to discuss it with you further.'

Miss Nightingale smiled with great sweetness. Katie noticed she had excellent teeth for a Victorian. 'So now we are all old friends,' she said, 'with the exception of this tall and distinguished young lady; I believe you are Bernardo DuQuelle's colonial acquaintance, Miss Katherine Tappan? And I think you must know of me as well?'

Katie looked her up and down, from the white linen ruffled cap on her head to the white lace tipping the hem of her black silk dress. Florence Nightingale: Katie might not know much about the Crimea but she'd read about Florence Nightingale. They had even studied her at the Neuman Hubris School – the proto-feminist, the reformer, the Lady with the Lamp. She would become the most famous woman of her time, but it hadn't happened yet. Did Florence Nightingale know herself? Katie looked into her grey eyes. Despite the sweet smile and fascinating ways, her eyes were pensive and her mind seemed far, far away. Katie might know a great deal about the Florence Nightingale of history, but the actual woman was still a mystery. Why, for instance, was she a friend of Bernardo DuQuelle?

'M. DuQuelle has been of great assistance to me in the past,' Florence Nightingale explained, 'and when I received a message that he was ill, I came immediately to nurse him.' She seemed to have the uncanny gift of reading Katie's mind, a gift Miss Nightingale shared with Bernardo DuQuelle.

'But DuQuelle's illness wasn't a normal illness,' James blurted out. 'I sent that message, but how can you treat him? There's nothing we can do in the medical profession . . .'

Florence Nightingale caught James's eye. Her far-away look had become very direct, and just a little sharp. 'Hygiene,' she rapped out. 'If Bernardo DuQuelle would take proper care of himself and his environment he wouldn't have reacted so adversely.' As if to underline her theory, she picked up the book lying on his chest and, giving it a quick dust with her handkerchief, popped it onto the bookshelf.

DuQuelle groaned. 'Sometimes the cure is worse than the disease.'

Miss Nightingale laughed and turned back to James. 'I requested arrowroot and beef tea over an hour ago. James O'Reilly, would you kindly step out for a moment and check on this for me?'

James reluctantly left the room. Her comments did not explain anything. He knew he'd been fobbed off.

Princess Alice had been staring at Florence Nightingale in a state of high excitement. Suddenly she remembered her manners. They were there, after all, to visit Bernardo DuQuelle. She crossed the room and took the chair next to him. 'We have been so worried about you,' she said, 'and we are overjoyed to see you making such good progress.'

He looked at her with something akin to affection. DuQuelle admired Princess Alice; found her a higher calibre of person than her slightly oafish older brother, or domineering older sister. Her quiet, serious nature meant she was often overlooked in such a large family – especially by the Queen. He thought this was a pity. 'But you are more overjoyed to meet Miss Nightingale,' he teased, 'and quite right too. How could I not recover with such a nurse at my beck and call?'

Florence Nightingale smiled her sweet smile, but she didn't look like the kind of woman at anyone's beck and call. 'I have heard of your interest in nursing,' she said to Princess Alice, 'and I was surprised. It is considered a low profession – only fit for coarse women or drunkards, or worse.'

'But you are a nurse,' Alice replied before she could hold her tongue.

Florence Nightingale looked at the girl seated in front of her and paused, as if weighing up something very important. Then she began to speak, choosing her words carefully. 'I had a calling, as a young girl; I knew that I was different.'

Bernardo DuQuelle tried to rise, as if to stop her, but she restrained him simply by lifting one hand. 'I had special work to do – though it took me years to understand. I was called to be a nurse, to alleviate the suffering of mankind.'

Alice's cheeks had flushed bright pink. Did Miss Nightingale's family simply let her follow this calling? She thought of her own family, of the Royal Household. The Queen was horrified by the idea of nursing, and nearly had hysterics every time Alice mentioned the word. Her father had some sympathy, though. He was, after all, the one who had instructed Dr O'Reilly to teach Alice the more womanly aspects of nursing. But the doctor scorned the idea of women in medicine. He would insist on talking of ballrooms and society when she longed to hear of diseases and cures. It was only James who really helped, lending her books and his notes from lectures and medical cases. If it hadn't been for James O'Reilly, she would know nothing about the thing that interested her most.

'You are considering your own family, and wondering about mine,' Miss Nightingale said. Katie blinked hard – she found all this mind-reading very sinister.

'Yes,' breathed Alice, 'what did your family do?'

Florence Nightingale's soft face suddenly looked very grim. 'They tried everything to stop me,' she said. 'My mother refused to speak to me; my sister had fainting fits. They would not let me study medicine, they would not let me train for nursing, they would not even let me visit hospitals. For ten years I struggled and I sacrificed much.'

James had come back, with the arrowroot and beef tea. Katie, moving as quietly as she could, stopped him from speaking. This was a story she wanted to hear.

'I have not married,' Miss Nightingale continued, 'and I will not do so. I shall never have the children that most women yearn for. My relationship with my own mother is strained. My sister is but a burden.' These were harsh words, but uttered with no emotion. 'Within days I leave for Scutari. It is the hospital for the soldiers in the Crimea,' Miss Nightingale went on. 'It is a desperate situation for our wounded. No decent provision has been made. There are not sufficient surgeons, no dressers, not even linen to make bandages for the wounded. I travel with the few good nurses that exist on these shores. I can see even greater physical and emotional sacrifice ahead. But this is my destiny, the path I must take – though it is a journey I may not survive.'

After a long silence, she turned to Alice, got down on her knees, looked into her face. It was an unusual gesture for a woman of her dignity. 'What do you think of my story?' she asked. 'What do you think of my life?' Katie suddenly noticed that both Florence Nightingale and Princess Alice had almost identical eyes – deep grey eyes, at first glance mild, but resolute in the depths.

'I think,' Alice said, 'that I envy you above all women. You have fought for your vocation, and you have won.'

Florence Nightingale stood up, jubilant, and turned to Bernardo DuQuelle. 'I knew it!' she told him. 'It is exactly as I thought. You must let me make the request.'

'But she is too young, and too important.' DuQuelle protested. 'It will put us all in the path of trouble, even danger. I cannot allow it.'

Katie had no idea what they were talking about. Alice stood up, very straight. It was almost as if she knew what was coming. Florence Nightingale took Alice by the hands. 'Will you come with me?' she asked. 'Will you sacrifice your life of comfort? Will you nurse with me at Scutari?'

Before Alice could answer, James had flung himself between them. 'No,' he stated brusquely, 'she cannot go. How can you expect a Princess of the royal blood to travel to a country at war? The Queen would never grant permission – and Princess Alice is too young; the idea that she would travel, alone, amid sickness and danger? Her reputation would be destroyed, her health would be broken; she might even die. It is a preposterous idea, far beyond even her sense of duty. You must be insane to suggest it.'

Katie nodded her head. 'It kind of is insane,' she said. 'I mean, James was freaking out because Alice walked through the park without a chaperone. And you expect her to travel to a war zone? I don't see how she can go.'

Bernardo DuQuelle agreed vigorously from the sofa. 'I thought we'd had the final discussion on this,' he said to Miss Nightingale. 'Princess Alice is a girl, still in the schoolroom. It is too dangerous a journey. The Queen would never allow it. And even if the Princess could slip away, it would be too difficult to keep her identity a secret. It would become an international cause célèbre, and destroy all your own good work.'

Princess Alice looked at her friends, the inspired glow in her face fading as she stood, quiet and pensive.

Florence Nightingale understood. 'Everyone has something to say,' she said to Alice, 'everyone except you. I am afraid, Princess Alice, if you do not find your own voice, you will never live fully.'

The painful silence continued. Then Princess Alice suddenly found her voice – a knowledgeable, forceful and frankly angry one. 'Do you think I know nothing,' she said in a voice thrilling in its clarity. 'James talks of my sense of duty. I know my duty. My life will be one of service. I am the daughter of a great Queen, and my position embraces petty burdens as well as privileges. I study the hereditary lines of my family, I can tell you the second cousins twice removed of William the Conqueror. I do needlework – goodness, but I am exhausted by needlework. I am expected to make polite conversation with cardinals and cabinet ministers – with people who have no interest in me, who are only interested in the Queen and in power. I attend the openings of factories and institutions; I accept bouquets of flowers. And though my gifts and talents are limited, they are not *that* limited. I am more than a dressed-up doll. I am more than the Queen's unnoticed third child. I am a person who wants to be something more, to help in a very different way. I want to nurse. This opportunity will never come again. I would risk everything rather than lose this one chance. Would you, my dearest friends, really take this from me?'

Again, the room was silent. Katie had always known that Alice's looks deceived; that she was made of sterner stuff. But still, Katie was worried. To want something was not the same as doing it. James stood frozen in doubt. He had known Alice since they were young children. She was the only person outside his family who called him Jamie. He'd always liked her and admired her. In fact, he thought she was about as perfect as a girl could be. But to let her take this risk – how could it be done?

Florence Nightingale looked at them all. She crossed her arms and leaned her chin on one hand. Her foot tapped in frustration at their slowness. 'Of course it can be done,' she answered James's unasked question. 'It will all depend upon her friends. And Princess Alice has very good friends, does she not?' Miss Nightingale gave James a long glance, not without feminine charm, and this seemed to thaw James.

'If Princess Alice is to nurse in Scutari, I must go with her,' he announced. 'I have medical training and that can only be of benefit to this expedition.'

A great gloom descended on Katie. Princess Alice was the best friend she had ever had. She'd stuck by Katie, through thick and thin. But she couldn't possibly go with her to Scutari. Katie had been called to this time to look after Grace and she could not abandon her now. With a pang, Katie realized she was going to be left behind, in a foreign country, in a long ago time, without the people she depended on most.

The unconquerable Florence Nightingale ploughed on. 'By coincidence I was in the Palace this morning,' she said. 'Did you know my Aunt Mai is a lady-in-waiting? I can tell you are thinking about Grace O'Reilly, Katie. I examined her myself, this very day. She will never be in perfect health, but she is out of danger at present. Katie has other duties besides those of Grace's companion. She should accompany us. She has talents, many still untapped, which can be of use – and her, well, let's just say her *inside out* knowledge of history might be extremely helpful.'

Bernardo DuQuelle shifted impatiently and sat up. 'None of this is what we agreed!' he exclaimed. 'The pressure you have put on me . . . the Princess, travelling incognito, in danger; and then Katie, you are sending her right into . . .' A fit of coughing disrupted his tirade.

Florence Nightingale pounded his back, nodding in satisfaction. 'It's settled,' she concluded. 'You will all go.' James began to look excited. He had envied his dashing brother at war, and now he was going to get a first-hand look. Alice glowed with purpose. Only Bernardo DuQuelle groaned from the sofa. Katie's mouth was open. Miss Nightingale was certainly a tour de force. Just as Katie formed a hundred questions, Florence Nightingale curtsied to Alice and took Katie by the arm. 'It has been the most enjoyable of visits,' she said. 'But a taxing one, I believe, and now Bernardo DuQuelle does need his rest. I thank you so much for calling. I will correspond soon.'

They were out of the door and on the landing before Katie could blink. In their imaginations, Alice and James were already in the East, sailing towards the Crimea, amongst the soldiers and wounded at the hospital in Scutari, but Katie had other things on her mind. 'You go on ahead,' she said to them, 'I think I've left my reticule behind.' As they walked down the dark stairs, Katie stayed behind, leaning against the door, listening closely.

She could hear DuQuelle's coughing, spluttering protests, and Florence Nightingale's soft brisk replies. 'To drag a Princess off to war!' he exclaimed. 'Her governess Baroness Lehzen might be old and slack, but she'll certainly notice when Princess Alice is gone for months. And what of the Royal Family when they return from Balmoral?'

'You will think of something, DuQuelle, you always do,' Miss Nightingale answered.

DuQuelle gave an exasperated wheeze. 'This problem is simplicity itself,' he continued, 'child's play in comparison to the other complication.'

DuQuelle's voice grew low and grim. Katie had to strain to make it out. 'It is insane to take Katie with you,' he said. 'For her the Crimea only spells danger. You know Lucia's plans, I've discussed them with you often enough. She thinks this war is *the* Great War, and the three children, the Tempus: Lucia plots for them to meet on the field of battle. The child who brings peace, the child who brings war and peace, and the child who brings the war to end the world – Lucia believes they must battle to the death. Only then will peace be victorious. One of the three, young Felix, is already on the Crimean Peninsula; for all I know, the other might be there as well. Why take the chance?'

Katie sat down on the landing in shock. She was prepared for the strangeness of Bernardo DuQuelle, but Florence Nightingale? This wasn't the woman who appeared in her history books. Was Miss Nightingale really taking her to the Crimea, only to sacrifice her to Lucia and her vision of a perfect world? Was she really to fight Felix? He wasn't just a brat, he was a supernatural brat. She felt quite sick.

From the other side of the door she could hear Florence Nightingale's special voice – calm, firm, mild and inspiring – seeping through the aged wood. 'Do you think Katie is safe in London, DuQuelle? You know what happened on Hampstead Heath. Belzen didn't come looking for duels, or danger or violence. He was looking for Katie. If it hadn't been for that falling tree, he would have her now. It is only a matter of time and you are still too weak to protect her. She will be safer with me, in the Crimea.'

DuQuelle still objected. 'I should never have summoned her. She is not fit for battle.'

Katie could hear Florence Nightingale moving through the room, making it homely and tidy. But her words were far from comforting. 'Things must come to a head,' she said. 'Everywhere we turn, the weight of power is tipping dangerously. We need harmony in this society. It is the only way to safely harvest those words you love. And you cannot survive unless you take their communication. This meeting of the Tempus, that Lucia so desires, I am more sanguine of its outcome. Bernardo DuQuelle, I know you see far, but perhaps I see that tiny bit further. I am uniquely placed, a foot in both camps. Have faith. You must trust me,' she told him, and then raising her voice, repeated, 'you *all* must trust me.'

Katie could barely breathe as she waited for Bernardo DuQuelle's reply. 'Trust! It is a word I mistrust – and faith is beyond me. But Florence, you are of me, from me. It is my hope that you are the best of me. I will try to trust you. I have little choice; I can barely rise from this sofa. I am too weak to protect Katie now. I am near to useless. I must place her in your capable hands.'

'There is much you can do,' Miss Nightingale consoled him. 'I will leave it to you to explain the absence of Princess Alice.'

DuQuelle groaned again. 'Really, Florence, having saved what life I have, you now saddle me with the most monumental of headaches.'

Chapter Fifteen

Scutari

It really was happening. They were going. Katie sat on her bunk in the ship's cabin, and stared down at her dress. 'I hate these clothes,' she said. They were horrible: a grey tweed gown, a grey worsted jacket and a grey wool cloak. Her bushy black hair was tucked into a plain white cap. Over her shoulders she wore a holland scarf embroidered in red with the words '*SCUTARI HOSPITAL*'. Florence Nightingale had ordered these uniforms for all the nurses, and they had not been designed to make the wearer attractive. They'd left England so quickly – there had been no time for fittings. Katie's dress was hitched up in the back, dragged in the front and pinched her waist. It was as uncomfortable as it was unattractive.

Princess Alice sat down next to her. 'It is an unhappy result,' she said to her friend, settling Katie's cloak around her shoulders. 'But then perhaps it is for the best. From all I hear Scutari is disorderly, with many drink-shops. The troops are quite dissolute. It is right that we are made as unattractive as possible.' For further protection, Alice was swathed in a coarse white gown. An agreement had been reached between Florence Nightingale and her dear friend, the Reverend Mother of the Sisters of Mercy in Bermondsey. Alice would travel as one of the nursing Bermondsey nuns, no longer Princess Alice, but Sister Agnes. Katie stared at Alice's sweet face, encased in a white wimple, her habit flowing behind her.

'It's funny,' she said. 'Your outfit isn't much better than mine, but it suits you. Sure you look really young to be a nun, but it seems, well, right on you.' Alice smiled and pressed her friend's hand. 'I am so grateful to you and James. This is my dream, my calling, and yet you sacrifice so much to go with me.'

Katie looked and looked at her friend. Yeah, she was young and vulnerable, but she glowed with purpose. 'It's not a sacrifice,' Katie reassured her. 'I want to go with you. And everything has turned out OK.'

James burst through the door and heaved a large leather bag onto Katie's bunk. 'I need to leave this in your cabin,' he said. 'The Director of the Army Medical Service insisted that supplies are plentiful at the Scutari Hospital, but Miss

Nightingale knows this to be untrue.' While Alice looked even younger in her nun's habit, James appeared almost grown up in his high leather boots and military cap. 'Miss Nightingale is on board,' he added. 'She has been purchasing supplies throughout the night. The *Vectis* weighs anchor within the hour.' They gave each other nervous smiles. Each, in their own way, was out of their depth.

With a mother like Mimi, Katie was used to independence. How could it be otherwise, when your only parent was either on tour with her pop band, or off with a new boyfriend? But this was a new kind of independence. She'd never been to Europe, or Turkey, or any of these places. To be honest, she didn't even know what or where the Crimea was. And now she was travelling across unknown seas, in a big creaky, smelly boat. Not only was it a foreign country . . . it was a foreign time.

James too had much freedom. Katie might be, for all practical purposes, without a father; but he had lived a life without a mother. Each day the image of his mother's merry eyes and freckles faded from his memory. Each day he was more alone, as boy turned to man. All his life he had taken responsibility for himself and provided for little Riordan as best he could. Now, though, there was a much heavier responsibility: the care of two young ladies – and one of them was a Princess of royal blood. The other, through her actions, could change the future of the world. His shoulders sagged just to think of it.

Yet it was Princess Alice who faced the most uncertain new world. She had lived such a cosseted life. The schoolroom was just down the hall from the guards' quarters and the nursery was locked from the outside each night – her father held the key. She had rarely been left alone without a nursemaid, a governess, a music teacher, a dancing instructor, a chaperone, or a lady-in-waiting. In such a large family, there was usually a brother or sister on hand as well. She had shared a room with the Princess Royal until the previous year, and Prince Leopold still slept in the next room. By a wrinkle in time, a quirk, the domino effect of a series of events, she had been able to escape her family. Her dream to become a nurse was at hand. Here she was, on board a ship, heading to the Crimea, dressed as a nun. Would she be able to live up to Miss Nightingale's expectations?

'The ship is full,' James continued. 'The other nurses are on board, along with new recruits to the army. There are even some military tourists, come along to see the battle sites.' James looked disgusted by these last passengers.

'I've heard there's a theatrical troupe on board,' Alice added. 'Can you imagine, sailing out to entertain the regiments? I'd like to see them myself – do you think nuns are allowed to watch actors? There is so much I do not know of the Roman Catholics.'

Katie watched a large black cockroach scuttle across the cabin's floor. She'd lived all her life in New York City, and New York was famous for its cockroaches – but this one was enormous. 'Well, we certainly don't travel alone,' she said, 'though I could do without some of our travelling companions. Cockroaches are just so yuk! How long until we get there?'

'Two days to Malta, and then a third takes us up the River Bosporus to Constantinople. Scutari is on the opposite bank,' James told them. 'So just three days; that is, if the weather holds.'

But the weather did not hold. On the second day the *Vectis* ran into a storm. The ship had to be lightened and balanced. The crew jettisoned her guns; the steward's cabin and the galley were washed overboard. Katie and Alice were moved into the bowels of the ship. Katie rolled from side to side on a straw mat as wave after wave washed over the ship, and wave after wave of sea-sickness overtook her. She was prostrate, weak as a baby, moving only to heave herself onto her side and be sick into a bucket. 'I'm not much of a sailor,' she mumbled to her friends. James didn't ridicule her, but set to work making her as comfortable as possible.

'Many people suffer from sea-sickness,' Alice reassured her friend. 'I hear Miss Nightingale too is confined to her bed.' It turned out Alice was a very good sailor. She and James tended Katie daily, and did the rounds of the ship together, caring for others on board. Even through her nausea, Katie noticed what a good team they made.

After a brief stop at Malta, the *Vectis* steamed up the Bosporus. As sea turned to river, the ship calmed. Katie was able to rise, and her friends led her on deck. They dropped anchor in the centre of the river, as the rain poured down. Constantinople stood on one bank, its minarets piercing the rain. On the opposite shore stood the great barrack hospital of Scutari.

'It's beautiful,' Alice exclaimed. A tiny fleet of gondola-like boats, the painted caiques, bobbed next to the *Vectis*, ready to take the nurses to their new place of work. Other small crafts followed in their wake, the boatmen shouting out the virtues of their boats. 'I cannot wait to be of help – to nurse the poor wounded,' Alice added.

Florence Nightingale slowly walked across to them, her black silk dress sweeping the deck. Katie could tell by her thin pinched face, she'd had a very bad crossing. 'Yes, Constantinople is beautiful. Even Scutari is beautiful,' Miss Nightingale agreed with Alice. 'They are beautiful from here. With closer inspection you will find Scutari a less than lovely site.' She turned to Katie. 'Sea-sickness does sap one's energies, but do not worry, it is a short-lived illness. You will regain your strength. And trust me, we will need it. From the look of that hospital, many strong arms will be needed at the washtubs.'

The *Vectis* now became a hub of activity, as it disgorged its weary, sickly passengers. The nurses were lowered into the waiting caiques with their carpet bags and umbrellas. Katie and Alice shared one, while James travelled with Miss Nightingale. The other passengers scrambled into whatever small vessels they could find. Up on deck, the *Vectis*'s crew both helped and hindered this exodus. From her little painted boat, Katie could hear the sailors laughing and swearing above her. With great sweating effort, they were using ropes to hoist a very large woman into a very small boat. The woman's hair stood on end, and her skirts flew in the whipping rain, showing a length of red flannel petticoat and ragged satin boots.

'Anchor 'er firm now,' a crewman shouted as the woman swayed above the little rowboat. Her pea-green shooting jacket flipped up, exposing an expanse of stomach and she cried out.

'Thar she blows, Miss Modesty,' another crew member shouted, and the rest howled with laughter. The woman grabbed the ropes, and swinging herself upwards, threw a punch at the roaring men. She was lurching perilously. At any moment she could have toppled into the murky Bosporus.

Still on deck, a pretty dark-haired girl held her arms out to the woman below. 'Calm yourself, dear mother,' she called. She turned to the sailors on deck. 'Please help her. Show her the respect she deserves. The woman you jest at is the Countess Fidelia. In her time, she has played the finest theatres of Europe, and has been saluted by royalty. She has come to entertain our soldiers in the Crimea. You should be ashamed of yourselves.'

The sailors might not have felt much shame, but they were struck by the girl's fine beauty. With greater care they lowered the Countess Fidelia into the little boat, and then helped the lovely girl to join her.

'It must be the theatrical troupe,' Alice commented, watching the scene with interest. 'Do you really believe they've performed before the crowned heads of Europe? They don't strike me as mother's type of entertainment.' Katie felt more worry than interest. She recognized the Countess Fidelia with her green shooting jacket held together by one button and her hair like a haystack. She remembered the lovely girl, her enormous eyes ringed round with long lashes. The girl was older now, thinner and even more beautiful. It was the Little Angel. Though Katie had never spoken to her, she knew they were connected. Katie had met her on the streets of London, on her first visit to James and Princess Alice; she was somehow connected to Katie's time travels. But even more worrying, Katie had seen the Little Angel many, many times since – in terrifying visions of battle.

The Little Angel reached the rocking boat, and wrapping her slender arms as far as she could around the Countess Fidelia, comforted her adopted mother, soothing her indignation. Looking up, she caught Katie's eye, and jumped, her arms tightening around the large woman.

'She knows me too,' Katie thought. 'I wonder if I'm in her dreams. Does she have visions? Does she see the battle too?' A shiver ran from the top of Katie's head down her spine, like an electrical current running through her body. There were three of them, the Tempus: there was Katie,

Felix, and now possibly this girl. All three in the Crimea. Katie struggled to understand, but a cold wave slapped over the little boat, soaking her feet. The here and now demanded her attention. They were nearing the shore.

The slopes leading to the hospital at Scutari were steep and slick with mud. As the caiques approached the shore, Alice shrank back and Katie pulled her cloak over her nose and mouth. The grotesque bloated carcass of a large grey horse washed backwards and forwards on the tide. A pack of starving dogs howled from the rickety landing, desperate to get to the horse and a meal. A few drunken soldiers lay in the mud, while some wretched-looking women shivered in thin tawdry finery on the shore.

It was a difficult end to a very testing journey. The sea-sickness, the stench, the shock of seeing the Little Angel; it was too much for Katie. She leaned over the edge of the brightly painted little boat and vomited, yet again.

It was delicate Alice who maintained her composure. 'We have to stay strong,' she whispered to her friend; 'just as Miss Nightingale says. The strong will be needed.'

The nurses disembarked and struggling up the muddy slope, walked under an enormous gateway, into the hospital of Scutari. As Miss Nightingale passed through, she leaned against James. 'Abandon all hope, ye who enter here,' she said to him. James wasn't certain whether she was joking.

The hospital at Scutari was vast, built in a great quadrangle, with echoing corridors forming a square around a courtyard.

'There must be four miles of beds in here,' Miss Nightingale muttered as they straggled along behind her. The walls streamed with damp, the floors were filthy, and the tiles broken. Peering through a narrow window, Katie could see and smell the inner courtyard. It was a sea of mud and garbage. She remembered there had been a garbage strike in New York when she was little. No one had collected the rubbish for weeks. Rats ran everywhere and the city reeked. But it hadn't been half as bad as this.

They were escorted to their rooms – four rooms in all, for forty nurses. Katie counted two beds and three chairs. There were no tables, and no food. It wasn't exactly a heroic welcome. 'The nurses will sleep in the largest room; the nuns in the other two,' Miss Nightingale rapped out, all vestiges of her sea-sickness vanishing in a flash. 'The few men with us – the male medical assistant and the courier-interpreter – will take this small closet.'

Katie watched in despair as Princess Alice was led off with the other nuns, but within minutes the nuns had returned. The Reverend Mother spoke for them. 'Excuse me, Miss Nightingale, but there is a man in our room.'

Miss Nightingale looked impatient. 'Really, Reverend Mother, we are crowded enough in our quarters. Do not loiter on courtesy. I suggest you ask him to leave.'

The barest flicker of a smile hovered around the Reverend Mother's lips. She had seen much in her time. 'I would, Miss Nightingale,' she responded, 'but I fear he is dead.' It was the body of a general, taken ill with dysentery. He'd been given some privacy because of his status, but after his death had been forgotten by the hospital staff.

'The doctors seem to have remarkably short memories.' Miss Nightingale spoke calmly, but with a tinge of exasperation in her voice. 'We will have the body moved in the morning. There is a sheet in my carpet bag. Take it, and cover the poor man. You will have to sleep as best you can,' Miss Nightingale relented slightly at the tearful glances of the nuns. 'The very youngest of your nuns may bed down with me, in the supply cupboard – goodness knows it's bare enough. Sister Agnes, Miss Katherine Tappan, follow me.'

They were packed tight in the storage cupboard. Katie, bone-tired, spread her woollen cloak on the floor and, lying down, rolled over to make room for Alice. 'I think something just bit me,' she whispered.

'That will be fleas,' Miss Nightingale replied, helping to settle the young nuns. 'I suggest you do not complain. It could have been worse – it could have been the rats.'

Alice was far whiter than her wimple. Between the corpse and the fleas and the stench of the hospital, she was finally undone.

'Now sleep,' Miss Nightingale commanded. 'Today has been easy, compared with tomorrow.'

Princess Alice had spent her entire life sleeping on a feather bed, while Katie had the best mattress Bloomingdale's could provide. But still, within seconds they were asleep, lying on the bare floor with the fleas and rats.

It didn't last nearly long enough. Katie woke in the chill of early morning. The fleas hopped high in the air and rats scurried beneath the floors. She could hear the men groaning in the dank, dark corridors outside. Her first thought was of Princess Alice, and how hard this must be for her. But Alice was already up, dressed immaculately in her nun's habit, and deep in conversation with Florence Nightingale, James and the Reverend Mother.

Katie sprang up and, dusting the filth from her nurse's dress, spoke with remorse. 'I'm such a waste of space,' she said. 'You've all been working while I've been sleeping. I'm so sorry. I'm an idiot.' The little group before her was silent for a moment.

Then James burst out. 'No, you're not a wasting space – whatever that means – and you're not an idiot. It's the doctors here that are the stupid ones.'

Miss Nightingale put a warning hand on James's arm. 'The doctors have refused our help,' she told Katie; 'all our nursing skills, all our stores and supplies.'

'And there is nothing here,' Alice added sorrowfully. 'We have examined the hospital, floor to floor, room to room. There are no medical supplies and no proper food or water.'

'As for the nursing,' the Reverend Mother shook her head, 'the wounded are cared for by the soldier orderlies – uncouth, useless and clumsy, the very scum of the army.

They are the worst of soldiers, so they use them here, to nurse the sick. Nurses, my eye! I have faith there'll be better nurses in hell.'

Alice looked shocked, it was awfully salty talk from a nun, but the Reverend Mother had much worldly experience, and perhaps the situation called for it. Alice was learning a lot. Fast.

Katie, still half-asleep, stood up and rubbed her aching limbs. 'You've got to be wrong,' she said to Florence Nightingale. 'I mean, you were sent by the government. Can't they just tell the doctors to use you?'

Miss Nightingale almost laughed. 'It doesn't work that way,' she explained. 'There are systems . . .'

'We will defy the systems,' James cried. 'We will break down the systems.'

'No,' said Miss Nightingale. 'We must work within the system. I have offered my nurses and my supplies. They have been refused. I must win the confidence of the doctors. I must show them that we are completely subservient to them.'

All this confused Katie. It was obvious to her that Florence Nightingale had great power in this world, and probably in other worlds as well. What was all this subservient woman stuff about? 'You've got to be kidding,' she interrupted. 'I mean, I know what happens with you, the lady with the lamp, blah, blah, blah. There's no way you have to . . .'

Florence Nightingale shot her a look that proved Katie was right about something at least – she was indeed one tough broad.

'No one knows what happens,' she barked. 'Do not presume.' And in a softer, though still steely, voice she added, 'By joining my corps of nurses you are under my authority. And by my authority I am telling you: we will do nothing more until we are asked. I have ordered the nurses to sort the old linens. The nuns will organize the packages and provisions we can find.'

Katie just couldn't believe this. 'But there are men dying in the corridors,' she replied, a muttering resentment in her voice.

Miss Nightingale pinched her lips. 'I am more than aware of that. A few must be sacrificed that the army might be saved. We will wait; and they will need us. The crisis will come soon enough.' Miss Nightingale folded her arms against her chest. Her face looked stoic, resigned, but one foot tapped with repressed anger. She had a great knack for controlling herself, and those around her.

Katie glanced at James. He was staring downwards, grinding his heel into the floor. He too resented this line of action, or non-action. Katie tried one last time. 'Are we really just going to sit here, sorting out rags?' she asked, with her best New Yorker sarcasm.

Florence Nightingale looked her up and down. It was a piercing look, not one that Katie liked at all. She shivered slightly, as the silence grew long. 'No, we are not,' Miss Nightingale finally replied. 'At least *we* are not. You and I have other things to do. The Reverend Mother will take temporary charge of Scutari. On top of the sorting and mending, I suggest she organize some alternative kitchen to the rancid stewed meats the men receive now. We'll cook what they need, and if they decline to serve it, so be it.' The Reverend Mother looked more than up to this challenge.

Miss Nightingale then turned her attention to James. 'Since you are male, you might have more luck with those other men, the doctors. Perhaps the superior merit of your sex will help them see sense.'

The Reverend Mother laughed, loud and warm, a laugh that wouldn't sound out of place in a public house. But Princess Alice turned pink. This type of conversation made her uncomfortable. 'What shall Katie and I do?' she asked.

The moment Miss Nightingale turned to Alice, her expression softened. 'Sister Agnes, you will take charge of correspondence. Miss Katherine Tappan is right on some counts – I do have influence with the government, and they will help me, but it will take time. You must write to Mr Sidney Herbert in the War Office. I have outlined the points to be made here.' She passed Alice a dozen closely written sheets of paper. Katie realized she must have worked through the night.

'Shall I help?' Katie asked.

Florence Nightingale smiled, a thin-lipped affair. 'Miss Tappan will travel with me,' she replied.

'Travel!' They were all astonished.

'This very morning,' Florence Nightingale continued. 'We board the fast steamer for the battlefront. If I cannot be of immediate help here, I will try to aid the field hospitals. I have a colleague there, already hard at work. There is someone I wish Miss Katherine Tappan to meet – and someone Miss Tappan will wish to meet herself.' It was a strange course of action, sudden and quixotic.

The Reverend Mother shook her head. 'You do speak in riddles, Miss Nightingale, but you always make sense in the end.'

Despite the chill of the hospital, Katie broke into a sweat. She didn't want to be separated from her friends, and she definitely didn't want to steam ahead to the battlefront. A battlefront meant a battle; the three of them – the Tempus – on the field of battle. Was she being guided to a terrible destiny? 'You must trust me,' Miss Nightingale had said. But to Katie, none of this seemed trustworthy. 'Couldn't I just stay with Alice – I mean, Sister Agnes?' she asked.

Miss Nightingale tried to reassure her. 'You had best stay with me,' she said. 'And your friend had best stay here. James O'Reilly will guard her fiercely, and you can see the Reverend Mother is far from stupid. Sister Agnes will do much good in *this war*. But aid is needed in another war. I loathe the idea of setting out to sea again, but at least this voyage will be a short one.'

'Always the riddles,' the Reverend Mother laughed again, but no one else felt quite so comfortable. Katie feared what she was hearing. If she was not to be a nurse, was she to be a soldier – a warrior in an otherworldly war?

Chapter Sixteen

Mary Seacole

When Florence Nightingale acted, she did so decisively. She left Alice sitting at the table, inkwell and pen in hand. James was bundled off to try and befriend the stubborn, blinkered doctors. The nurses were sorting and mending linens while the nuns were counting and recording their unused supplies. And Katie was once again on board ship, heading for the battlefront. They left the Bosporus, sailing across the Black Sea to Sebastopol, and the actual site of battle.

By morning, the ship anchored in the port of Balaclava, a small enclosed basin, so filled with ships it looked like a forest of masts; a tiny nook of bustle, hidden from the quiet gloomy sea. As Katie and Miss Nightingale were rowed to land they could see dozens of figures lying prone on the wharf: these were the sick and wounded, unloaded from mules and ambulances, waiting to be transported by sea to the hospital at Scutari. 'Our return cargo,' Miss Nightingale said grimly, 'shipped to a hospital where they are certain to die.'

This time there were no doctors to stop Florence Nightingale. The moment she alighted she was among them; turning a body to a more comfortable position, easing a stiff dressing. 'They are too far from help,' she murmured. 'Why cannot the main hospital be placed closer to the battlefield?' She looked up to Katie, standing open-mouthed beside her. 'Look there, that row of pannikins contains tea. Raise the men when you can and help them to drink.'

Katie ran forward, and fumbling in her carpet bag found her own tin cup. Filling it with tea, she knelt beside a young man, who was groaning in pain. God help him! He had been hit in the forehead by shrapnel and the dressings around his head oozed blood. As he groped and fumbled with his fingers, Katie realized his sight was gone. She raised his head. 'Tea,' she said, and he stopped groaning and smiled. 'There is nothing I would like more,' he whispered. Katie swore, there and then, that she would never again ridicule the English love of tea. 'Is it really the voice of a woman?' he said, and then his fragmented brain wandered. 'Is it you, Mother?' he asked.

They stayed with the men until the sun rose high, giving off a wavering autumnal glow. 'There is much to do here,' Florence Nightingale said, 'but we have further yet to go.' She set to work, negotiating with the Turks and Greeks that swarmed the harbour. Katie could see she was a canny businesswoman. Soon Miss Nightingale had procured two mules: old and bony, but with life in them yet. Loading their provisions, she then grabbed one animal by the mane and swung up over its sagging back. 'Come along,' she barked over her shoulder.

Katie did ride – and in the best English tradition. Mimi thought riding lessons were posh, 'very Ralph Lauren', as she put it. But all that posing and posturing was useless when faced with a very old, very stubborn mule. There were no reins, no stirrups and no mincing English 'riding master' to help Katie now. She circled the animal, and then took a running leap at it. The mule gave her a sour look, and stepped aside, leaving her face down in the mud.

'Really,' Miss Nightingale commented drily, and signalled to an orderly, who was moving pallets of the wounded nearby. Without ceremony he flipped Katie, stomach down, over the mule. The animal bolted and Katie just had time to scramble onto its back and follow Florence Nightingale – who was not only sitting bolt upright, but riding side-saddle – without the saddle. Katie didn't bother to ask where they were going. Miss Nightingale was not one for explanations, and besides, Katie wouldn't have understood the answers anyway.

Katie had pitched and rolled through two sea voyages. She'd only had a couple of hours' sleep. Now she was scrambling to stay on top of a very unhappy mule. She knew that if she fell off, Florence Nightingale might leave her there, all alone, in the mud. So she clung on with every muscle in her body. Long after nightfall they came to a halt in front of a long, low-roomed building – still and dark, except for a brightly coloured Union Jack waving over the door.

Miss Nightingale did not dismount, but called into the darkness, 'I am in need of Miss Mary Seacole of Jamaica.' The stillness exploded into racket and confusion. A dozen boys burst from the house and tugged open a corrugated iron gate. They swatted the mules, who, with a final stumble, passed into a yard crowded with horses, sheep, goats, stables, huts and pigsties. The sheep tried to bolt and the boys threw themselves on their woolly bodies. The pigs squealed loudly.

'Mary Seacole be within,' one of the boys shouted. 'We not be help'n you ladies; we's here to be guarding de pigs.'

This reasoning seemed perfectly civilized to Florence Nightingale. 'Fresh pork, such a delicacy in an outpost like this,' she commented with sympathy. 'I'm certain every man within a ten-mile radius would like to get his hands on your pigs. Guard them well.' She leapt easily from her mule. With a groan, Katie let go and landed with a thud.

Candles flared behind the rough-hewn windows, and voices could be heard within. The door flung open, and silhouetted in the light was a most amazing woman. She wore a bright yellow dress with a red calico scarf tied firmly around the neck. On her ample bosom a large golden amulet shaped like a flask swung from a chain. Her flapping Leghorn hat was royal blue and sported several sweeping feathers. Under the brim was a reddish, brownish face, with kindly eyes and a broad freckled nose.

The woman ran forward and, taking Katie by the arms, supported her up the stairs. 'Child, you do look half-dead,' she cried in a sunny, sing-song voice. 'And you,' she said, turning to Florence Nightingale, 'don't you know better than traipsing through a battlefield in the dark of the night?'

Miss Nightingale took the rebuke calmly. 'So, Mary Seacole, this is your establishment?' was her only response.

The woman gave a little skip and, throwing her arms wide, exclaimed, 'Welcome to de British Hotel!' To Katie, sick with exhaustion, it could have been the Ritz.

It was more of a storehouse than a hotel. The long iron room was chock-a-block with counters, closets and shelves; all heaped with burlap bags, rusting tins and knobbly paper packages.

Mary Seacole pulled a wooden chair up to the metal camp stove and Katie sank into it gratefully. 'Now child, you just warm your bones. I'll get you a bite to eat. It's rice pudding day, nice and hot.' The camp stove, though small, gave out a great deal of heat, and Katie began to doze off. She could hear Mary Seacole bustling about, yelling to the boys in the yard and scolding Florence Nightingale.

After a while, Katie was given a strong cup of tea and a tin bowl of thick rice pudding. Florence Nightingale seated herself nearby, with her own tin bowl. 'I don't know how you manage it,' she said to Mary Seacole. 'A lovely nutritious pudding and you say it's made with no milk?'

'Cow's gone dry,' Mary Seacole replied. 'Poor old Bess. No milk to be had there. I'm thinking of making her into a curry; Tuesday next if you're still about.' Giving Katie a long curious look, she turned to Florence Nightingale. 'Is this the one?' she asked.

'It is one of them at least,' Miss Nightingale replied. 'The only one to which we have access. It was Bernardo DuQuelle who found her. Much against his will, he called her back. A stroke of luck for us.'

'Yes,' Mary Seacole agreed. 'We are lucky to get our hands on her, before she falls into less caring hands. Now let's see what we can do with her.'

Katie shook herself awake. 'I am sitting right in front of you,' she protested. 'I have a name, other than *her*. I am Katherine Tappan – really Katie Berger-Jones-Burg, but you probably know that.'

The two women frightened her. They spoke a kind of coded language and seemed to have some master plan – but they were not choosing to share all the details. She should have put up more of a fight to stay in Scutari. Why had she ever left Alice and James? For that matter, why had she left New York City? It seemed a hundred years since she had held the walking stick high and chanted the strange words. She could have walked away then, and simply gone back to bed. Instead she'd taken up the challenge and left her warm bed, left Mimi sound asleep . . . would Mimi still be sleeping?

Mary Seacole was rummaging through Katie's things. She took the walking stick, examined it closely and pushed it aside. 'There must be something here,' she muttered, plunging into the carpet bag. 'Something that links her to . . . ahhh . . . this looks about right.' She pulled out Katie's yellow flannel pyjamas, patterned with the orange and green frogs. The Nightingale nurses had been under strict instructions about packing: four cotton nightcaps, one umbrella, modest and functional underclothing. Katie had instinctively taken the stick, then jammed the pyjamas in at the last minute, along with her fuzzy slippers. They were certainly functional, if a bit too garish to be modest.

Florence Nightingale fingered the garments with distaste. 'They quite set my teeth on edge,' she said, 'but the design is excellent in terms of comfort and warmth.

There is some type of material in the waistband that allows the trousers to expand with such ease . . .'

'It's elastic,' Katie explained sheepishly. 'Sometimes I eat too much pizza at night, so it's handy.' She reached for her pyjamas, but Miss Nightingale held onto them tight. Searching the pockets, she pulled out a crumpled piece of paper.

'This might make things easier,' she said, sniffing the paper, 'it has that acrid smell, from the friction of travel.'

Mary Seacole took it, and sniffed it too, then rubbed it against the amulet hanging around her neck. Pushing back her hat, she held the paper against her forehead. 'Yes,' she breathed, 'this will do.' Turning to Katie, she smiled and, nodding encouragement, handed her the paper. 'Now, child,' she said in her husky sing-song voice. 'You've had your supper, and warmed yourself. So now you just sit yourself down and read your letter to yourself. That's all you have to do.'

Katie had no idea what the letter was. She could have scrunched it up and jammed it in her pocket at any time. As she unfolded the paper, Mimi's swirling, girlish hand leapt out at her.

Katie-Kid – I'm off to the Hamptons!!! Yeah, I know, suntan equals skin cancer, but I'm gasping for sun. And there's a big rave in the works – bongos on the beach – so the bikini and I have split. Talking of bikinis – NO CARBS FOR YOU

WHILE I'M GONE . . . !!! Take care, be cool, but stay out of the refrigerator!!!

XXXXXXXXXXXXXXXXX Mimi

It was classic Mimi: careless, selfish, unthinkingly cruel; but also warm, vibrant, adventurous and funny. Instead of the usual resentment building up, Katie felt a surge of affection. And then she could see Mimi, hear her, smell her distinct scent of patchouli and chamomile. Mimi was in front of her. She was still asleep, exactly as Katie had left her, her pink velvet eyeshade firmly in place, the earplugs with purple tassels stuck in her ears. Time obviously didn't move in the same way when you journeyed back several centuries. Katie had travelled far, but Mimi continued to sleep through one night.

She still had chocolate crusted around her mouth, a hangover from her doughnut binge. It must have got colder though, because she had wrapped the beige cashmere duvet round and round her. She looked like a large slumbering caterpillar. One arm was flung outside the duvet. Katie could see age spots on the back of her hand. Poor Mimi! When she saw this, there would be a worldwide search for the perfect anti-ageing cream. The panic over the onslaught of age would ratchet up a notch. But for now, Mimi was asleep. Her world was at peace.

The only sound in Mimi's room was her own soft snoring. But something else was going on in Apartment 11C. There was a kind of scratching and clicking. Katie's mind wandered down the hall, she could see the front door. It was moving slightly, rattling gently on its hinges. With a final sharp click, the door swung open. A figure stood on the threshold, dressed entirely in black. Katie knew with dread this wasn't Dolores. She made a point of barging in after her Sundays off, bringing the virtuous bustle of a Baptist church meeting into Mimi's scandalous life. No, it couldn't be Dolores. A stray beam of street light reflected on a pair of oval metal spectacles. A wispy grey goatee was divided into three braids. 'No!' Katie cried out. It was Professor Diuman. He was back and he was breaking in.

He crept down the hallway and through the living room. But this wasn't his destination. Softly opening one door after another, he rejected the kitchen, the guest bathroom, the den. Opening a fourth door, he nodded slightly, and entered silently. Over his shoulder Katie could see her own bedroom. A wad of pillows under her duvet looked like a sleeping body. The light from the bathroom that had transported her to another time was gone. It wasn't exactly dark, as the city lights meant New York was never really dark. Professor Diuman could see quite easily – the large pink bed, the painted white chest of drawers, the wide closet with the fold-back doors. With a drawn-out creak, he pushed back the closet door and began to methodically search through Katie's things. She had a good idea of what he was looking for – the walking stick.

'Stop!' Katie cried, 'stop!' Suddenly she saw he was carrying a thick metal rod.

Dolores was in the Bronx, Katie was in the Crimea, and Mimi was alone in their apartment, with a madman. What would Diuman do when he couldn't find the walking stick? What if Mimi woke up? Katie struggled to try and reach Diuman. She leapt to her feet, the note falling to the floor. Lurching forward, she grabbed for a man who wasn't really there, shouting for police who would not be born for over a hundred years.

Florence Nightingale raised her eyebrows. 'This isn't what I expected.'

Mary Seacole shook her head and whistled low. 'No, it ain't. She's gone to the wrong place. That's one bad trip she's taking. I'll get something to calm her down and cool her off.' Mary disappeared into the kitchen, returning with a tin cup. Taking Katie by the shoulders, and holding the cup to her lips, she coaxed her to drink.

Florence Nightingale leaned forward, sniffing the cup. 'Spirits? For a girl her age?' she questioned.

'Spirits for them who see spirits,' Mary Seacole replied. 'She'll settle now and sleep, and hopefully forget most of it.'

'We'll have to try again,' Florence Nightingale said, 'though with more care, more caution.'

'She's one loose cannon,' Mary Seacole commented. She held the vessel-shaped amulet between her thumb and forefinger as if taking its pulse. 'Her power is great, but where it leads her, who can tell?'

Katie was coming to, shaking her head and rubbing her eyes. Had it been a horrible dream, or was Professor Diuman really alone with Mimi in Apartment 11C? 'I have to go!' she cried.

'Where to, child?' Mary Seacole asked.

Katie's voice grew strong. 'To New York, to 89th Street, to Apartment 11C, to the twenty-first century.'

Florence Nightingale and Mary Seacole exchanged worried looks. 'That is impossible,' Florence Nightingale rapped out. 'Would you desert your friends? And we need your help, there is much you can offer – not just to the sick and infirm soldiers, but to the British army, the British Empire. You could be pivotal to victory in the Crimea – you could be pivotal in the problems that beset this world. Yet you wail, "I want to go home". For shame!'

'But, Mimi!' Katie protested.

'Yes, Me, Me – it is selfish of you to be thinking of abandoning your post.' Miss Nightingale turned to Mary Seacole. 'Whatever is in that tin cup, give her more.' Katie drank again. The room began to darken, her thoughts were growing fuzzy. The note from Mimi was on the floor where she'd dropped it. Stealthily she picked it up, and, careful not to read it again, stuffed it in her bodice. She could hear Mary Seacole and Florence Nightingale, their voices growing further away.

'Could you pick up anything from her vision?' Florence Nightingale asked. 'Anything we need?'

'Yes,' Mary Seacole replied. 'It was hard, with all the interference from her own time, but there was more. Her energies run so high. They are mightily heightened.'

'Heightened?'

'Yes,' Mary Seacole said softly. 'She has linked into something, or someone else. She's made some kind of new connection and this has magnified her abilities.'

Florence Nightingale's voice rose. 'Then that must mean . . .'

Mary Seacole gently pulled a blanket over Katie. 'I think it does,' she murmured, sounding worried. 'It just might be . . . the time has come . . . the three, the Chosen, the Tempus – they are all here.'

Chapter Seventeen

Women Must Weep

Katie knew that if she opened her eyes there would be daylight, and she just wasn't ready for that. It felt as if her head was full of thick, wet cotton balls. She could hear the boys outside – shouting and laughing and chasing each other. Beyond them was another noise, a continual popping and banging far in the distance. Katie listened for a long time, until she figured out where she was. Gradually she recalled another sea voyage, the wounded soldiers and the long mule trek to Mary Seacole's British Hotel. There was something else, something about Mimi, drifting ghost-like through her befuddled brain. It all made her feel very lonely and anxious. She would have given much for the company of

Alice and James. Florence Nightingale, though a nurse, was hardly a comforting companion.

Eventually, the anxiety got the best of her. She opened her eyes and found herself lying on a bed in a room with bare plank walls and a corrugated iron roof. In the corner, a camp stove burned brightly. As she watched the sunshine flicker across the walls there was a brisk knock.

Mary Seacole bustled in carrying a basin and jug. 'How are you feeling, my dear?' she asked. 'Last night was quite a night, but I suppose you don't remember much, being so tired and all.'

'Not much,' Katie said. Mary Seacole's smile broadened. Katie stretched and, rolling on her side, looked at her. She was an even more extraordinary sight by daylight, and had added a violet and pink apron to her outfit. 'I remember meeting you, but not much more. Why can't I remember last night?' Katie asked.

Mary Seacole busied herself, pouring water into the basin. 'There must be a reason. Maybe it was the journey; yes, the journey must have been too long. Florence does push people far too hard. I tell her, not everyone is a martyr, afire with a cause. But does she listen – no, no, no. Then she drives herself harder than anyone else. Just think, she's already on the move. Rushed back to Scutari. You hear those funny, booming noises. That's our men, firing the big guns. The siege of Sebastopol has begun. We're hitting the Russians with everything we've got, we're going to bring that city to its knees – but those Russians won't go down without a fight. Where there's war, there's wounded. Already they're reporting boatloads of our men being shipped to hospital in Scutari. It seems the doctors will need Florence after all. She left in the middle of the night, with plans to sail with the British wounded this morning.'

'She's left me here, all alone?' Katie panicked. Florence Nightingale might be a difficult woman, but she was certainly a competent one. Of course the wounded men needed Florence Nightingale more – but how was Katie to manage without her?

Mary Seacole flashed a genuine smile. 'Don't you worry, Miss. I'll look after you. And you're not so alone as you think. You've got callers. Now quit fussing and have a nice fresh wash.'

Katie swung her legs off the bed as Mary Seacole bustled out of the room. Company? This was hardly the place, or the time – or even century – for her to expect company. She hoped it would be James or Alice. But the voices she heard shortly were not those of her friends. One of them was completely new – a deep, bluff rolling voice with the lilt of the Irish about it. The other she had heard before. There was no mirror in the room, but she tried to tidy her wild hair and smooth out the wrinkled tweed dress. 'I must smell terrible,' she thought, but consoled herself by thinking 'and so must everyone else.' With a final pinch to her cheeks, she threw the grey wool cloak over her shoulders and went to meet her guests.

There were two men. Jack was standing in the middle of the room, blushing and shaking his head as Mary Seacole offered him cakes and brandy. The other man had no such qualms. Patting Mary Seacole on the shoulder, he popped two cakes into his mouth at once, and stuffed a third in his pocket for good measure. Katie recognized him: she'd seen him when the troops had paraded before the Queen at Buckingham Palace. It was William Howard Russell. He was stout, though quite tall, with a round face, black hair and whiskers. As a reporter for *The Times*, he was not in uniform, but had created his own semi-military outfit: a Commissariat officer's cap with a broad gold band, a Rifleman's patrol jacket, cord breeches and a pair of leather butcher's boots with huge brass spurs. Despite the cumbersome boots and spurs, he practically danced across the room and, clicking his heels together, bowed to Katie. 'And this is the young lady,' he said 'ten times more beautiful and larger than life.'

For a brief moment Katie wanted to knock him down – she knew her nurse's clothes were awful. And why did they all find her height so funny?

But Jack stepped in, saying with great courtesy and just a hint of laughter, 'James wrote to me, to tell of your pending arrival. And when the reports came through of a tall American landing with the Nightingale nurses, I hoped it would be you.' Jack had grown decidedly thinner. His thick straight hair was long and unkempt and his fair Irish skin coarsened by rough outdoor life. Experience was fast changing him from a boy to a man.

Katie didn't know what to say, or what to do. In one way, she knew Jack well. He was, after all, James's brother. And Jack's letters to Grace had been so open and so tender. When writing about the war, he had revealed much of himself. Yet, as Jack stood there, Katie became stiff with shyness. Once again he had become a stranger. She searched her mind for appropriate words. At times like this she desperately needed Alice. 'Tea?' she questioned weakly. 'Is it tea you've come for?'

William Howard Russell threw his head back and laughed. 'Tea is it?' he roared. 'At mess this morning, Jack O'Reilly hears tell of a tall, handsome American woman staying with Mary Seacole. "Saddle Embarr," he cries, and quick as a flash he's dashed from camp, with no leave or whatnot, me galloping at his heels. And do you really think he's come for the tea?'

Katie really did think she'd knock him down this time, but Mary Seacole did it for her, giving William Howard Russell a forceful push into a chair. 'You behave,' she admonished him. 'I don't think much of Americans as a whole, but this one is real genteel, a proper person. Now stop embarrassing the young ones.' She turned to Katie. 'I believe you are right, Miss. A hot pot of tea is just the thing. While I'm gone, you make friends with Mr William Howard Russell here. His bark is far worse than his bite.'

William Howard Russell was still laughing. Getting up from his chair, he took Katie by the hand. 'My apologies, Miss. It's just in times of war, I don't believe in tip-toeing about. And I'm not the friend you'll want to be making. I'll help Mary Seacole with the tea and leave the two of you to talk. And if the conversation must be of hot beverages, so be it.'

As he left the room, both Katie and Jack laughed. 'Well, that was like the most embarrassing thing ever,' Katie said, but at least she could look Jack in the eye now.

'He means well,' Jack told her. 'Russell is good at heart, and speaks out for the foot soldier. His articles in *The Times* will help to improve conditions for all of us. The only reason he came with me was to purchase supplies for our lads in the trenches. He's great company around the campfire, drinks anyone's brandy, and is often the only man in camp with a good cigar. He's also the source of all information. It was Russell who told me you were travelling to the battlefront with Miss Florence Nightingale.'

Katie tried to look dignified and seated herself. Was this what it was like to be courted? She'd never even been on a date. *Act normal*, she told herself sternly. She liked Jack too much to be silly. 'I suppose you've come to enquire about Grace,' she said. 'She really is much better.'

'You mean a lot to Grace. In fact, you mean a great deal to most of the members of my family.' Jack's blue eyes were still merry, but there was something deeper in them.

Katie felt the urge to run from the room and bang her head against the wall. Instead she changed the subject. 'Your brother, you know, James, is in Scutari,' she said. 'Miss Nightingale has put him in charge of sorting out the doctors.'

'Yes, I know he's my brother,' Jack teased, 'and he must be in seventh heaven, telling all those doctors what to do. James always thinks he knows best.'

'Well, most of the time he does,' Katie shot back loyally. Jack might be very attractive but her friendship with James was rock solid. 'He's extremely advanced in medicine, far above those doctors of your time, really almost up to practices in my time, I mean . . .' She stumbled slightly and fell silent. She'd forgotten for a moment that although Jack was James's brother, he still didn't know Katie's story. He didn't know the truth. She had to be more careful.

Jack looked at her curiously. 'What do you mean, *my time*? You seem so straightforward, but I'm puzzled by you,' he said. 'You might be an American, from a different place, but I assume we live in the same time.'

The conversation had turned serious. Katie fiddled with her cloak, trying to decide what to say. The silence grew long. Finally she looked up – she hated seeing that hurt expression on his face.

'I want to tell you,' she said. 'It used to be all about me, but it's not any more. There are so many other people involved. And even if I did tell you, I kind of doubt you'd believe me.'

Jack paced the room. She could tell he was frustrated. 'Is James involved?' he asked. 'And what about Grace?'

'James is in the middle of the whole thing,' she told him. 'He understands, and is helping in every way he can. We haven't told Grace, but . . .'

'And why would James understand, and I would not?' he interrupted.

Katie had forgotten that along with brotherly love, there was a lot of brotherly rivalry between James and Jack. She could have kicked herself. Taking a deep breath, she decided to trust him. 'It all has to do with time,' she began, 'something called the Tempus.'

At that moment the door burst open. Mary Seacole rushed in – had she been listening outside? 'Now, children,' she exclaimed, 'because tall as you be, you are still children. I've dished up something more substantial in the canteen for the two of you. Miss Katie has not eaten properly for some time, and Lieutenant O'Reilly I'm certain wouldn't say no to a nice hot supper.' She had Katie by the arm, and was literally dragging her from the room.

Jack just had time to whisper in her ear. 'I am grateful for your attempt to explain. I trust you. And you can trust me. I hope there will be another time, many more times.'

A great surge of affection flooded Katie, and she would have given much to sit with him and talk quietly. But that would have to wait.

They crossed the yard, where the boys were throwing grain to the animals. 'There chick-chick, there pig!' they yelled. The boys did everything at high volume, and now they had to shout across the sound of cannon fire. The canteen was in a separate building, made of rough timber. But the long plank tables were clean and the shelves filled with yet more boxes, bags and barrels.

William Howard Russell was already seated with a tankard of brandy and water, a circle of soldiers surrounding him. He waved them over cheerfully. 'You've heard of the gift of the Magi? Well, Mary Seacole has the gift of the magpie,' he joked. 'You can find anything and everything here – from a darning needle to a ship's anchor.'

As if to prove this point, Mary Seacole disappeared into her tiny kitchen – not unlike a ship's galley – and returned with half a dozen roasted fowls held high above her head. The men at the crowded tables banged their cups and cutlery in appreciation, and Katie suddenly realized she was very hungry.

Jack could almost read her mind. 'I remember you have quite a hearty appetite,' he said. 'I believe your first words to me were "I could eat a horse".' Russell hooked half a chicken with his fork and flung it onto Katie's plate. 'Horse flesh will be a delicacy here, particularly as the winter sets in. So I suggest you indulge your appetite with chicken while you can.'

The only sound at Katie's table was that of steady eating. Once Katie had demolished her half a chicken and a heap of fried potatoes, she looked around the room. It was a strange mixture of glamour and glitz, dirt and filth. The officers had a separate table, its prestige marked by a threadbare tablecloth. They drank warm champagne out of battered pewter cups. The other tables were a mix of men from different regiments – the 8th Hussars, the 93rd Highlanders, the 5th Dragoon Guards. Their tunics were draped in gold braid, but their boots were riddled with holes, some of them covered in the mud of the trenches. The close, snug room was heavy with competing smells: cooking oil and wood smoke, roasting meats, the slightest whiff of dung from the yard, mud and sweat. But the sweat definitely had the upper hand.

Mary Seacole had seated herself at their table, and was deep in conversation with William Howard Russell. Jack continued to eat, head down, fork continually on the move. Katie didn't want to disturb him. This war had swung into action, and who knew when he'd get a meal like this again? A man in the corner caught her eye. He was exceptionally slender and wore his uniform with great elegance. He sported a thin delicate moustache that turned up at the ends. His dark hair gleamed, his grooming was impeccable. Katie shifted in her seat to see who he was talking to. She almost fell off her bench. It was a very young man, really still a child. He pulled a richly embroidered cloak around his shoulders and hunched over the table, his white blond curls falling forward. It was Felix.

Katie turned to Mary Seacole. 'Why don't you rest a bit and let me help you,' she said and, picking up her own dishes, headed towards the kitchen. The men around the tables piled plates and cutlery into her arms as she passed. She barely made it out of the door without everything crashing to the ground.

Once she had deposited her load, she placed herself behind a pile of grain sacks, so that she could see and hear Felix without being seen herself. It was not difficult to eavesdrop on Felix. His voice was distinctive: high and whining, with a decided Prussian tinge. 'You are right, of course,' he was saying to his companion. 'It is all so mismanaged, this war. But the cavalry, the waste of the cavalry is criminal, particularly the Light Brigade. You are trained to attack, and yet you have seen no action. Your Commander, Lord Lucan – he left you sitting on your heels at Alma – he's more like Lord Look-on!'

The elegant man sitting opposite Felix nodded vigorously. 'You are so right. They need, they must, trust in the power of the cavalry. Even now the siege of Sebastopol is all infantry and cannons. This is not true military finesse. Lucan must use us, decisively, in action.'

Felix smiled – it made him look almost angelic, but it made Katie shiver.

'And you, Captain Nolan,' Felix continued, 'you who have written more than one excellent book on the tactics of the cavalry. They are fools not to turn to you for advice. You must make them listen. In the very next battle, the cavalry must take centre-stage. Go over Lord Lucan's head. Speak to Lord Cardigan – even Lord Raglan if you must. You can, you know, put yourself in a position to make this happen. Then everyone will see your fine abilities. You will become a national hero – I will make certain of that.'

Captain Nolan liked what he heard. 'With your influence we can overcome even the top echelons of the military,' he added. 'And with Lord Twisted's help . . .'

Felix laughed, a high-pitched and ugly sound. 'Lord Twisted? If you desire the help of Lord Twisted you'll need to ask for it in the Russian camp. Lord Twisted is more likely to hang than to be of help!'

Jack came up behind Katie. 'So,' he said, 'you eat like a man, and clean like a charwoman. What other hidden talents do you have?' He stopped smiling when he saw the look in her eyes.

'Who is that man?' she asked. 'Talking to the boy with the blond curls?'

'That is Captain Nolan,' he told her, 'one of the finest horsemen in the Crimea. If only his temperament matched his other abilities! I avoid him as much as possible.'

Katie's heart sank; Felix had found an excellent target. Should she tell someone about this? She looked over to their table, but both Mary Seacole and William Howard Russell were gone. 'Where is Russell?' she asked Jack. 'I'd like to speak to him.'

'You're too late,' Jack replied. 'He received a scribbled message from camp, and is already on his way back. He must report on Sebastopol for *The Times*. I too must leave, immediately.'

She looked at Jack – he was so like James – a less brilliant, more likeable version of James; and that bit more grown up. Yet his eyes were still those of a boy. She didn't know exactly how she felt about Jack, but she knew she didn't want him to get hurt.

'Your regiment,' she said, 'it's the . . .'

'17th Lancers,' he laughed. 'For an intelligent girl, you certainly have no military brain.'

'Are you in the cavalry?' she asked.

Jack shook his head. 'You really don't know anything, do you? Yes, the 17th Lancers is part of the Light Brigade, and yes, that's the cavalry – the best division the cavalry has.'

Her heart sank. 'Jack, if there's a battle, you mustn't rush forward,' she said. 'You must wait, be patient – don't mistake stupidity for bravery.'

For a moment he looked angry, but then his glance softened. 'Women and war,' he said, 'they're not made for each other. The 17th Lancers have waited and waited. We long to fight, and Katie, fight we will.'

She thought about telling him now – about Felix and who or what he really was; about Florence Nightingale and Mary Seacole. She wanted to tell him her own story too, but she could hear herself, inside her head, and every sentence she tried to form sounded crazy.

Jack took her hand. 'War is our job, Katie. Men must to work, and women must weep. But Katie, crying doesn't suit you. I like to think that we will have much time to laugh together.' He turned quite red, and giving her hand a final squeeze, bowed and was gone.

Mary Seacole returned; a stack of dirty dishes piled in her apron. 'Men must to work, and women must weep,' she echoed in her sing-song voice. 'He's right, that fine young man, but at least he goes to work with a full stomach and a full heart – thanks to the British Hotel. Now, child, dry your eyes and give me a hand with this washing. Lord but women have work too. Then we need to make up a batch of capsaicin salve and decant some bitter sherry. The bombardment of Sebastopol is bad enough; but I smell another battle coming and it don't smell good.'

They worked late into the night, in Mary Seacole's little kitchen, with the vats of bubbling syrups and the dried red peppers hanging in swags. These she used to make her capsaicin salve, and the fumes as they boiled made Katie's eyes sting with a different kind of tears. 'I should think

Miss Nightingale would have enjoyed seeing this,' she commented.

'Florence,' snorted Mary Seacole, 'Florence don't go in for making ointments. She hates fussing in the kitchen, and she don't much like bending over soldiers and soothing their brows either.'

Katie's eyebrows shot up. 'But she's a nurse, the greatest nurse in history. I mean, you're good too, but . . .'

Mary Seacole laughed. 'I am a far better nurse than Florence Nightingale. But she has that something else. She does think like a man. For her, it's all about the numbers and the shapes. She sees the big ideas and then makes them work in the day-to-day world. She pushes that brain of hers till it succeeds. Me? I see to the little things, the comforts, the womanly things. I'm like a mother to these men.'

Katie stirred the large pot and wiped the vapour from her face. 'But you're both trying to see something that's – I don't know – it's either the past, or the future, or some other world entirely. This I kind of know. And for some reason you need me, to see it better. I can't tell you how much this creeps me out.'

Mary Seacole looked at her for a very long time. Beads of perspiration stood on her brown forehead and seeped into the deep crow's feet around her eyes. But all she said was, 'We need to cool those peppers now, and push them through a muslin cloth – Lordie, but we'll sleep well tonight.'

Throughout the night the heavy artillery of the British army continued to fire on Sebastopol. Katie did not sleep well, and when she did sleep, the events of the past days flashed through her mind. She could see Alice in her nun's habit and hoped James was looking after her. Then Jack stared up at Katie; his eyes first merry, then angry, then blank. Pain and panic swept through her. 'Jack!' she cried, 'have I lost you?' and a sing-song voice replied, 'Lost for now, but found again, in another place and another time. *Tempus fugit, libertati viam facere*. Time flies, making a road to freedom.'

Then, in her dream, Katie was filled with light. But it was neither warm nor comforting. The light was like wires in her blood – sharp, cold, relentless and cruel. The persistent voice of Lucia pulsed through her body. 'The eve of battle,' Lucia cried with a high, clarion call. 'On the morrow, the British horses shall thunder below, and the skies shall flash above. The two wars shall rage, two wars from two worlds, the Verus and the Malum. *The Chosen and the Tempus will meet*.'

'It is coming,' Katie murmured, 'it is coming, but do – oh, do make it stop.' Then Jack's voice came to her, no longer laughing, but a dark and sorrowful dirge, repeating over and over. 'Men must to work, and women must weep.'

She tossed and turned, helpless in her sleep. 'I want to go home!' she cried. 'I want to go home!'

The dream changed, as dreams will. She was home, but no relief came to Katie. Women must weep. In Apartment 11C someone was crying out in protest and pain. It was a woman, weeping and weeping. The woman was Mimi.

Chapter Eighteen

The Two Battles

W as it possible to be awakened by silence? Sometime before dawn the guns had stopped. This was as unnerving as the muffled thuds of the previous day. Katie opened her eyes to find Mary Seacole seated in the dark. 'I was just about to wake you,' she said. 'We have to make a start, but I knew you needed the strength that sleep will give. It's going to be a taxing day.'

'How long have you been up?' Katie asked.

Mary Seacole laughed. 'At my age we need less sleep. Once you'd gone to bed, I set to cutting sandwiches and wrapping up the fowls, the tongues and the ham. There's wine and spirits too; they're already packed on the mules.'

Katie dressed quickly and Mary Seacole handed her a large canvas bag. 'It's for the wounded,' Mary Seacole told her. 'Lint, bandages, needles, thread and the medicines we've been making.' At the last moment, Katie grabbed the walking stick; its powers might be useful in whatever was to come. Outside stood two mules, weighed down with supplies. Two more were saddled for Katie and Mary Seacole. They left the British Hotel as dawn broke.

It was a crisp autumn day. The sunlight poured down straight and direct, turning the sky an odd, flat blue. The world seemed strangely bright, but somehow only two-dimensional.

'Just as I sensed, something's afoot,' Mary Seacole muttered. 'Even the weather is all wrong.'

Katie didn't ask where they were going. In the first place, she wouldn't have understood. The geography of the Crimea was beyond her. Besides, Mary Seacole had what Katie would call 'street smarts'. She was cunning, was known to tell a lie and definitely dabbled in some kind of voodoo. But Katie also knew she was a kind woman, with a big heart. If Katie had to face some kind of weird destiny, she wanted to do it with Mary Seacole at her side.

They followed the road between Balaclava and Sebastopol. The land rose sharply, and the mules groaned under their loads. At last they reached a plateau that lay between the valley of Balaclava and the trenches of the British forces. This was the site of the cannon fire; here lay the source of the siege. For now, the cannons were silent.

They dismounted their mules, and Katie made certain to hold onto the walking stick. She was amazed to find the plateau was already crowded with people. Soldiers just relieved from the trenches mixed with men in tweeds more suited to a shooting party. The ladies shaded themselves from the autumn sun with parasols.

'Who are all these people?' she asked Mary Seacole.

'War tourists,' Mary Seacole practically spat. 'They come to experience war, as if it were a theatre, a pantomime, or a cruise along the Thames. A useless waste of space, that's what I call them.'

William Howard Russell pushed his way through the crowds. 'I'm in agreement, Mary Seacole,' he added. 'Isn't there something in those capacious canvas bags of yours that you could give them? A fowl laced with arsenic, a cordial that produces dysentery?'

Katie laughed; she was getting the hang of Russell's Irish humour. 'Why are they all here?' she asked.

'Mary Seacole has a nose for conflict,' Russell said. 'And conflict is what we're about to get. The siege of Sebastopol has failed. Our military commanders thought it would take a day, several days at worst. But the Russians have dug in and built walls of mud around their city – and those walls have blocked our cannon fire. We can't surround Sebastopol completely, we don't have enough men. In setting up the siege, we've stretched our line of defence too far.'

Katie was used to a different kind of war: airplanes without pilots, that dropped bombs on whole villages; nuclear arms that could kill millions – wars that substituted weaponry for men. This was a war that depended on the men, and the sacrifice of their lives to attain victory. 'What happens next?' she asked.

Russell fished his field glasses out of his rucksack, and peered into the valley beneath them. 'The Russians are better strategists that we think,' he said. 'All our supplies for the siege are coming in by sea, from the harbour of Balaclava. The Russians are marching on Balaclava to try and cut us off from our supplies. They've already taken several of our defensive positions, and our guns. Directly below us is the only passable route to the harbour. I reckon that will be their next target. We can see it all from here – a bird's eye view.'

A woman's cry rang out, and Russell, despite his contempt for the war tourists, sprang to assist. Katie recognized the theatrical troupe that had travelled to Scutari with her on the *Vectis*. Her pulse raced as she spotted the Little Angel. The Countess Fidelia had stumbled on a stone and fallen hard. William Howard Russell helped her to her feet, and then, to Katie's surprise, embraced her. 'Well, if it isn't Mary Murphy, light of the Dublin stage, and admired throughout Europe as the Countess Fidelia.'

The Countess Fidelia did not take affront. 'My old friend Billy Russell,' she cried. 'God knows I'm pleased to see a friendly face, and such a well-fed one too!' But the joy of seeing a friend turned to agony as she tried to stand straight. 'Oh, but I've given my ankle a twist. I don't think I can stand.'

Russell turned to the others. 'I covered the famine in Ireland for *The Times*. The Countess here trod the boards night after night, touring the country to raise funds for the starving poor. It was an honour for us, to be entertained by such as she. She has won the hearts of many a royal sovereign, and emptied several of their pockets along the way.'

The Countess Fidelia leaned against him, half laughing at the chance meeting, half crying from the pain of her ankle. 'Ebb and flow,' she said. 'Life is always an ebb and flow. Truly, I've entertained kings and queens, but I've had my share of street life as well.'

Russell helped the Countess to a carriage filled with ladies. After many exclamations, and several protests from the silk-clad war tourists, he was able to procure her a seat with them.

Katie seized this opportunity, and slipped over to the Little Angel. This might be her only chance to really find out. Even getting near the Little Angel made Katie feel strange; she had a kind of glow – not hurtful, like Felix's, but warm and tingly. 'You know, I'm sorry, I just wanted to . . .' Katie began awkwardly, and then blurted out, 'Do you know me?'

The Little Angel's eyes became even larger. She stood very still. And then she took Katie's hand in hers. 'Everything but your name,' the Little Angel replied. 'I've known you for hundreds of years. And I certainly recognize your walking stick . . .'

A wave of relief washed over Katie. For the first time in her life, she could talk to one of her own kind. Princess Alice was as understanding as anyone could be, and Katie had won James over with time. But here before her was someone who had experienced what she had, knew how she felt and could share her burden. 'I'm Katie Berger-Jones-Burg,' she said. 'It's scary, isn't it? The seeing stuff, the knowing stuff.'

The Little Angel nodded. 'I've seen so much – war and revolution, plague and famine. I'm frightened and sickened by much of what I see. Perhaps it is a gift, to be part of the Tempus. But at times I am angry – it's as if I am being used, just a tool in *their* Great Experiment.'

Katie tightened her grasp of the Little Angel's hand. 'So you are the Chosen – the Tempus? I thought so. You know about Lucia and the Verus, Belzen and the Malum?'

The Little Angel smiled sadly. 'Not everything, but enough.'

They had begun their conversation in the middle, the way twins talk. Katie couldn't believe that she finally had an ally. 'Are they here? Lucia, Belzen?' Katie asked. It struck her that the Little Angel wasn't little any more. It was difficult to place her age. She seemed several years younger than Katie, but the look on her face was far from childlike. It was, indeed, hundreds of years old.

'Do you get it?' Katie quizzed her. 'That the Verus need our form of communication to live, that's why war has to be stopped? And the Malum – they feed off brute force, so they want this war? Belzen especially wants a war to end the world.'

'I *get it*, as you say,' the Little Angel replied. 'And I've had more time, so I know much more.'

Katie thought she'd never seen a person look so sad. Was it to be her own fate to become this sad? 'Can we get free of them?' she asked.

The Little Angel shook her head. 'I don't believe we can, and I'm not certain we should. What Lucia and the Verus want of me is not such a bad thing. I shouldn't have spoken of feeling sad, of being used. Lucia wants peace and I can help – it's my reason for being. This battle is important. I have a purpose and today it will unfold.'

They were interrupted by a burst of cannon fire. The battle had begun. Katie moved to the edge of the ridge and looked down. Beneath her was the valley, leading to the port of Balaclava. The sea sparkled in the distance. The Russian infantry advanced with solemn stateliness up the valley. They looked powerful, threatening. Was

Jack going to fight them? As she peered down, squinting, William Howard Russell seemed to read her mind. 'Yes, he's down there,' he said, with some sympathy in his voice. He rummaged in his pockets, and came up with a spare set of field glasses. 'Look through these,' he said. 'You'll find the cavalry forming up directly below. That bright line of red is the 93rd Highlanders. Sir Colin Campbell and his men will be our main defence of Balaclava.'

Sound echoed from the valley. Between the cannon bursts one could hear the champing of bits and the clink of sabres in the valley below. The Russians drew breath for a moment, and then in one grand line dashed at the Highlanders. There seemed to be so many Russians, and just a thin line of Highlanders to defend the British position. What, Katie thought, could this little wall of men do against such numbers and such speed?

Russell stood beside her, tense and watching. 'Steady now, Sir Colin,' he muttered. 'You have something those Russians don't – the Minié. No one else has such a powerful and precise rifle.' As the Russians swept up the valley, Sir Colin Campbell rode along the line, calling on his men to 'stand firm and die there'. Above them, Russell, Katie, Mary Seacole and the Little Angel stood stark still, as the mass of Russians galloped on. The small number of Highlanders looked like a thin red streak, tipped with a line of steel.

At around 1,000 yards the Highlanders fired their first volley, but the Russians continued on. The Highlanders fired a second time, but the Russians were undeterred. It was only with the third volley of rifle fire that the Russians wavered. They pulled up, surprised by the accuracy of the Minié rifle. Then they bent sharply to their left and rode back towards their own men.

'The Highlanders, they've done it,' Katie exulted. 'They've fought off the Russians.'

The Little Angel put a cautionary hand on her arm. 'This is just the beginning,' she said. 'This is not the time to celebrate.' Katie looked into her field glasses. The Russians were reforming, to attack again. But this time the Highlanders were not alone, as a flank of cavalry moved down the hills to join them. Frantically Katie scanned the ranks, dreading to see the face she knew.

'Lord Raglan has called in the Heavy Brigade,' Russell assured her. 'Your fine lad is encamped on the Highlanders' flank; his commander, Lord Lucan, is reluctant to fight. Young Jack, much against his will, just might be safe from harm.'

With a fierce battle cry, the Heavy Brigade charged. They smashed through the Russian cavalry, each side raising their swords in hand-to-hand combat. It was the Russians who lost their nerve and, turning, galloped back down the valley, pursued by the Heavy Brigade. From the hillsides, British infantry reinforcements were arriving. It was not likely that the Russian cavalry would attack again.

'Balaclava has been saved,' William Howard Russell cried. All around them, the spectators were cheering.

'It's over!' Katie exulted. Jack was safe.

William Howard Russell continued to scan the valley beneath them. He turned his gaze up the hills, to the defence positions the Russians had taken earlier. 'I believe it's far from over,' he said. 'I can see the Russians. When they first stormed the hills they captured British guns, and now they are removing them, rolling the cannons back into their own territory.'

Katie was busy helping Mary Seacole check the mule packs. There were certain to be wounded down in the valley. 'But we've won,' she said. 'Isn't it better to leave well alone? They just have a couple of our guns, two or three cannons.'

'Just a couple of guns,' Russell said. 'Lord Raglan won't see it that way. Legend has it the Duke of Wellington never lost a gun in battle. And you must know how Raglan, nay, the entire country, feels about the Duke of Wellington. Raglan will never permit his guns to be paraded by the Russians as trophies through Sebastopol.'

This all sounded very silly to Katie. 'So what's he going to do?' she asked.

William Howard Russell searched the hilltops for the British leader. 'He is certain to order the recapture of his guns.'

Katie's heart sank. She lifted her field glasses and turned her eyes to the heights where Lord Raglan was positioned, commanding the battle. He was far away, on the other side of the valley, and at first was simply a blur, a tiny dot of man and horse. She adjusted the field glasses. It was hard to see – dark clouds flitted across the flat blue sky; the light and shadow affected her view. Her eye was caught by a young man, really almost a child, riding up to Raglan and offering him something. Unusually for a soldier, the young man had long, fair hair that stood out against the dark that surrounded him – white curls waving down his shoulders. It was Felix, exactly where he ought *not* to be, at the heart of the British command.

'What the – !' Katie exclaimed. The Little Angel moved closer and peered over her shoulder, as if she could see without the aid of glasses. She put her arm around Katie, and then, as Katie watched, everything became much clearer. Felix was talking to Lord Raglan, and Lord Raglan was writing something down, almost as if he were taking dictation. As the letters sprang from his pen, Katie could read them. She might have been holding the paper inches from her face. It was the closeness of the Little Angel and the strange power that words had over her. The message leapt out:

To Lord Lucan: Lord Raglan wishes the cavalry to advance rapidly to the front – follow the enemy and try to prevent the

enemy carrying away the guns. Troop Horse Artillery may
accompany. French cavalry is on your left. Immediate.

In her excitement she said the words aloud. 'I too see clearly,' the Little Angel whispered, 'I can see the plan now.'

William Howard Russell looked at them both. 'You girls must have had a touch too much of the sun. Either that, or this is a hoax. You could not possibly see a message from this distance! It's hard enough to get a good view – the sky is so unsettled. Lord Raglan would have to be mad to give such an order.'

Mary Seacole put her arm out to Russell, trying to silence him. 'Hush now,' she said. 'Don't ask, just watch and listen. You will know more than any man alive about this battle if you do.'

Katie continued to stare at Lord Raglan's piece of paper. As she did, the words opened up a vista – she could see everything, close up and far away at the same time. She was like her own camera.

'Tell us Katie,' Mary Seacole said. 'Tell us everything.'

'Lord Raglan is passing the message to another man.' she said. It's that thin, elegant man I saw at the British Hotel. What's his name, Newland, Nolan?'

'Captain Nolan,' Russell answered. 'One of the fastest men on horse, but hardly a reliable messenger.'

'Nolan's down the hill now, with the other men on horseback, right below us,' Katie continued. 'Did you say that's the Light Brigade? He's talking to someone with a lot of gold braid on his uniform; they're directly under a large black cloud. It must be their leader.'

'That will be Lord Lucan,' Russell answered, 'and it won't be a pleasant conversation.'

Lucan was arguing vigorously. His arm swept to the right, towards the British guns in the hills.

William Howard Russell looked worried. 'If Raglan's message was as unclear as you say, then Lucan will have no idea what to do,' he said. *'Prevent the enemy carrying away the guns* – are you certain that was Raglan's message? Well, which guns? There are the ones the Russians captured; there are also guns at the top of the valley, and yet more on the lower slopes of the heights.'

Katie continued to stare at the two men, deep in dispute. Captain Nolan was not making the situation any easier. Katie could read insubordination in his every gesture. He was waving vaguely – not in the direction of the captured guns, but towards the far end of the valley, towards an area heavily fortified by Russian guns, cavalry and infantry. 'I think he's going for the other guns, the ones further away,' she said.

'Then God help us,' William Howard Russell replied. 'Captain Nolan is sending our men into the arms of death.'

A soldier must obey, even a soldier as adverse to danger as Lord Lucan. He reeled his horse around, and took the order further down the line.

'The argument is still going on,' Katie said. 'But now it's Lord Lucan and another guy in a very decorated uniform.'

'It will be Lucan and Cardigan,' Russell said. 'And here lies more folly. The two are brothers-in-law, but detest each other. They will never be able to resolve this.'

Lucan leaned forward over his horse, to get as close to Cardigan as he could. He nodded and gestured, at one point poking Cardigan with his finger. 'Lucan is furious; he insists Cardigan obeys the order,' Katie told them.

Lord Cardigan returned to his men. Katie could see the Light Cavalry taking up formation. She searched her mind for Jack's regiment. 'Are the 17th Lancers down there?' she asked.

Russell looked at her with pity. 'They are my dear. The 17th Lancers are the first in the line. They are being led by Cardigan himself.'

'But he'll be OK?' She wanted assurance, but none was forthcoming.

'If they actually do charge, I reckon it's a good mile to the Russian position,' William Howard Russell calculated. 'It would take the Light Brigade seven minutes to cover the distance – seven minutes surrounded by the enemy, with artillery and musket fire to the right of them, to the left of them and directly in front of them – all from an elevated height. If Jack can get through that, he'll be all right.'

It was ten minutes past eleven. The Light Brigade – all 661, man and horse – moved down the valley slope.

'I scarcely believe the evidence of my senses!' William Howard Russell exclaimed. 'The charge is on. The Light Brigade will have to ride all the way through the valley, between row after row of Russian cannon, and riflemen. Surely that handful of men is not going to charge an army in position?' The plateau was almost silent, the spectators frozen in horror.

The cavalry advanced in two lines, quickening their pace as they closed towards the enemy. Suddenly Katie could see Jack astride Embarr: his heels up in his stirrups, blue eyes ablaze, shouting. Next to him was Nolan, waving his sword and urging them on. The Light Brigade broke into a gallop as the first shells exploded. Faster and faster they went, as cannonballs tore the earth on every side and musket fire pierced from on high. The might of the Russians belched forth, a flood of smoke and flame. Then Katie could see only chaos and carnage – the men on the ground, dead or dying, horses flying, wounded or riderless across the plain.

Above them the skies flashed and swirled. At first Katie thought it was the firepower of the battle. But as she stared upwards, she could make out forms, shapes that mirrored the conflict below. What was happening in the heavens above? Then she knew. Her terrible dreams were coming true. This was not one battle, but two. Yes, the Russians were fighting the British. And yes, it had to do with Sultans and holy places, with trade and Empire. But it was also about Lucia and Belzen, the Verus and the Malum. High up towards the sun was a battle for the entire future of this world, being fought by those from another. It was a battle over nothing less than the possibility of eternal peace or the damnation of endless war. The time had come.

Lucia swept through the skies, her brightness piercing the black clouds. She sailed through the winds and opened her arms wide, using her light as a weapon. And then dark enfolded Lucia; she was wrapped, almost suffocated in the cloak of Lord Belzen. The elements around them took sides, scorching sun followed by brutal gales. Hail pelted the crowds below. The spectators, the war tourists, scrambled for cover. They had no idea what was happening. Next to Katie, the Little Angel trembled. Was this the war to end the world?

Even the raging heavens above could not halt the Light Brigade. With a sweep of flashing steel circling their heads, and with a cheer which was many a noble fellow's death cry, they rushed onwards. Soon they were amongst the guns, sabres flashing, cutting down the Russians gunners where they stood. Then turning, the Light Brigade reformed. They were going back over the same ground, littered with their dead and dying, and with the Russian weapons above still blazing. Katie wrenched her eyes from the storm above to the valley below. She was looking frantically for Jack. Mary Seacole seemed to be saying some kind of prayer or chant as she fingered the amulet hung around her neck.

'This is lunacy,' William Howard Russell repeated over and over. 'Lunacy. They can't sustain –'

He was cut off by an unearthly shriek. It was the Little Angel. She stood, pale as death, wringing her hands. 'They cannot face the cannon fire again. It will be a massacre. Oh the lives, the poor young lives! It was Nolan, I know it. He is but the messenger. I know who brings the message. I know who lies behind Nolan. I *will* end this!'

Before Katie could stop her, the Little Angel was over the ridge and down the hill, heading into the battle itself. How she travelled such a distance at such speed, Katie did not know, but the Little Angel was within reach of the back lines. This was dangerous enough. Coming towards the Little Angel Katie could see a very young soldier, mounted on a midnight black horse. He still wore the long fair curls of childhood. It was Felix.

Katie looked at Mary Seacole, and could see understanding dawning in her eyes. 'God preserve me,' Mary Seacole breathed, 'The Little Angel, *she* is the child who brings peace.' It was as if a curtain had been lifted. The Little Angel, Katie and Felix: the child who brings peace, the child who brings war and peace, and the child who brings the war to end the world. *The Chosen, the Tempus.* Was it as Lucia had predicted? Were they to fight each other now? From where Katie stood it looked as if Felix, sword in hand, was about to strike down the Little Angel, condemning the world to everlasting war.

Katie had long wondered what her purpose was. What should she do? For a long moment she panicked, toyed with the idea of doing nothing, staying put, seeing how things played out. She was not British or Russian. She wasn't part of the Verus, or the Malum. Neither of these wars was really hers. Didn't she have the right to protect herself? Someone else was sure to sort things out. But then she felt sickened by her own thoughts. It was up to her. The Little Angel must not die in this battle. Taking a deep breath, she lifted her skirts and, holding tight to the walking stick, she plunged down the hill.

William Howard Russell reached out to stop her, but Mary Seacole stayed his arm. 'She is the Chosen,' Mary Seacole said, clutching the amulet around her neck, rubbing her finger along its opening. 'Florence told me this might happen. She must go.'

As Katie raced towards the battle, the smoke was almost blinding. She struggled across the ground, knee-deep in the wounded and dying, looking up at the clashing armies. Horses and men were falling from every side. Dragging her way through the dirt and dust and blood, she caught up with the Little Angel. From every direction she was vulnerable, rifle fire, cannonballs, steel sabres and the thrashing hooves of terrified horses. But somehow none of this was as dangerous as Felix. Katie tried to drag the Little Angel out of the melee, 'You must save yourself,' she shouted into her ear.

'I will save them all,' the Little Angel cried back – and Katie realized she was heading purposefully towards the mouths of the Russian cannons.

Then Felix reared above them, a ghastly sight. His eyes were dead, trance-like. He was not a child or an adult – he was a being possessed by evil. As Katie stared up, Felix's curls became whiter and the light around him was unnaturally bright. But then it deepened to a dark purple-grey, like a diseased wound. There was terrible power, beyond Felix, in the skies above them. The longer she looked at Felix, the more he led her to a dark and strange place, a place she did not wish to be. Beyond him, above the horses, the men, the bullets and the cannonballs, the strange flashing white of the Verus grappled with the blackness of the Malum. 'Peace will be cut down,' she thought, 'the world will end. This world and many worlds.'

She tore her gaze from Felix and, grabbing the Little Angel's arm, began to drag her away. The death of the Little Angel would bring victory to the Malum. She had to stop Felix. Could she break his trance, or at least catch his attention? Was there any way to free him from this possession? If only he had human feelings. Was there anything she could say or do that would catch the attention of the real Felix, the child within? He was too far gone for human happiness or love. Was there anything left? Could she, perhaps, make him angry?

Katie remembered the day in the Palace gardens. He'd been furious when accused of playing with toy boats. His anger had been a very human emotion, so typical of a growing boy. He didn't want to be a child, playing with babyish things. It had hurt him. That is where he was vulnerable. Katie was still clutching the walking stick. She lifted it high and waved it at Felix.

'Baby!' she screamed. 'Felix, you are a baby – and a coward! Fighting a girl instead of the Russians. Wah! Wah! Felix is a baby!'

His dead gaze had fixed on the Little Angel, but now he turned so sharply that his horse reared into the hideous sky, bubbling with purple and black. 'You!' he raged. 'You are the weak one, to make your choice, to stand shoulder-to-shoulder with that girl! I am no baby. I am a man, a warrior! Just watch how I can strike you down!' He raised his sabre, and with a swoop, plunged towards Katie. For a split second Katie stared, the blade flashing down.

'He will cut me in two,' she thought. 'But he must not kill the Little Angel.' Was it worth living in a world without peace? She'd fought so hard, perhaps this was the time for surrender and oblivion. Had she done enough, in sacrificing herself to save the Little Angel?

The tip of Felix's sword sliced down, heading straight for Katie's heart. But then it froze, just at the top of her bodice. It wavered, struggling to reach Katie, to tear through her. Then it stopped, juddered, and shattered into a million pieces. Katie just had time to see Felix's face against the great flashing light of the sky, contorted and covered in messy tears. He was indeed crying, like a baby. What magic had shielded her in that final moment?

She could see almost nothing. The Light Brigade had turned and galloped back up the valley. They could not stop to avoid two girls, half-swooning, directly in their path. She saw the Little Angel go down, knocked unconscious by a vicious kick from a retreating horse. And then she was hit herself, and was sprawling backwards, into darkness. Again her mind changed, and her final conscious thoughts were of rebellion. 'I will NOT,' the words sang within her, 'I WILL NOT GIVE UP.'

When she finally came to, the world was a different place altogether. The great light of Lucia was gone from the sky, as was the poisonous black of Lord Belzen. Cannon smoke drifted across the floor of the valley, but there was not a cloud in the sky. The battle was over. But who had won? Katie turned her head to find Mary Seacole at her side, the great ornamental amulet pressed against Katie's heart.

'You were bowled over by a charging horse,' she explained in her low sing-song voice. 'My, but that animal knocked the wind out of you. You'll be fine, though, child, you'll be fine.'

'But the Little Angel!' Katie cried. 'Has she been killed? Will the world really . . . '

'It was touch and go,' Mary Seacole said. 'She's been hurt badly – trampled underfoot. Mr Russell has taken her – carried her all the way to the field hospital. If she mends, we'll take her on to the Scutari hospital. There's no one Florence can't patch up.'

Mary Seacole gave Katie a curious look. 'I notice you're not asking about yourself. Well, it's a miracle you are sitting up right now,' she said to Katie, whistling low. 'If anyone should have been killed, it's you, child. But that letter you're carrying in your bodice has some fine magic. Young Felix couldn't pierce it. Don't worry, I didn't take your mama's letter, just had a peek when I was checking you for breaks and bleeds.'

Katie looked about her, to a sad and sorry sight. Strewn across the valley were the dead and dying. Horses with their guts spewing out, men lying face-down, their hair matted in blood. Even more frightening were the living, crying out for help, for anything to stop the pain. 'I have my mules here,' Mary Seacole said, 'and I have my work cut out. You make your way up the hill, child, and rest. I could be here for hours.'

Katie got to her feet. Already the smell of gunpowder was overlaid with the stench of death. 'I think I'm fine,' she said. 'I'll stay and work with you.' She dreaded it, but she needed to know if Jack was lying there, in need of help. Mary Seacole looked at her with affection. 'You sure are one fine young woman,' she said, and handed Katie a canteen filled with water, a sponge and a tin basin. 'They're raving with thirst, some of them,' she said. 'Find the ones you think will live. Give them a drink, and wash their wounds before the gangrene sets in.'

All afternoon Katie moved among the broken men. Time and again she returned to Mary Seacole to fill her canteen and rinse her sponge. When they ran out of water, she washed her hands with sherry, and ladled it into the men's mouths. 'Probably better for them at this point,' Mary Seacole commented. 'They've been lying in the sun a long, long time and they're sinking fast. Best make their last moments more comfortable.'

They were not alone on the battlefield. Medics from the different regiments heaved the wounded onto stretchers and carried them to the field hospital. The wives of the cavalry came streaming down the hills, calling for their men, willing them to be alive. And then there were those less generous. The scavengers, picking through the bodies, looking for medals, coins – anything a dead man might not value. They took weapons, rifled through pockets, pulled rings from limp and lifeless fingers. Not far from Katie, a filthy urchin was cutting buttons from a dead man's uniform. As she looked closer, she noticed the child was opening the corpse's mouth, looking for gold fillings. She shuddered and turned away, not wanting to see what happened next.

'Katie, come quickly,' Mary Seacole called. She ran over, thinking Mary Seacole must need help, but slowed once she saw the look on her face. 'Come, my dear,' she said gently. 'There is no more I can do for this young man, not in this life. I can only do what I can at the very end. And I think he would rather spend his time with you.' Katie knew what she would see and, kneeling down, she took Jack's hand.

'Jack, it's Katie,' she said softly. 'I wish I could be James and Grace too.'

'And Riordan,' he said, barely audible, 'I would love to see that round little face. And beautiful Grace. And James, my dear brother. He will do great things, that brother of mine.'

Katie knew this was not the moment to cry. She must not break down. 'Where does it hurt?' she asked. 'How can I help?'

'It's such a strange pain,' he said. 'At first it was awful, but now it comes in waves, and after each one I feel a bit better, though so weak.' He stopped talking, as the pain moved through his body, and he twitched and gasped and closed his eyes. For a moment Katie feared he had died, but then he opened his eyes.

'It was terrible,' he told her. 'Not like I thought it would be. We were so excited, at the charge, but then it all went wrong.'

'Don't talk,' Katie said. 'It will just tire you.'

'But I must,' he answered. 'You must know, everyone must know. Nolan was wrong; he knew it. He led us the wrong way. I was next to Nolan when a shell hit him. He screamed like a child.'

Katie shuddered. 'Jack, I think Nolan had been led astray. I think he'd been used. I'll explain it all when you are better, when you are well.'

Jack's mind began to cloud, his voice to ramble. 'Where is Embarr? The smoke, the noise, it was dreadful. The men were dropping. Ahead of me, Captain Allread fell, I could see his brains on the ground. A cannonball hit my sergeant; his head went clean off. But oh, Katie, he carried on, like the headless horseman, for thirty yards, upright in the saddle, his lance at the charge, firmly gripped under the right arm. And then I felt this piercing, this burning, and I was down, and the horses thundered over me.'

Jack began to gasp, his breathing shallow and quick. Katie lifted his head into her lap, and smoothed back his hair. A grimace of pain passed over his face, and his eyes were frightened. But his head and face were untouched by his injuries; he was still the young handsome man she was just getting to know. She shifted him slightly, to try and make him comfortable, and realized he was lying in a pool of his own blood. 'I'll get Mary Seacole back,' she said. 'I'll get the medics, to put you on a stretcher. We'll take you back to Scutari. We have the best nurse in the history of the world there. Trust me, I know these things. She can make you well.'

With a faint smile, he tried to reach up, but was too weak. 'You are quite the girl,' he whispered. 'There isn't another like you, in any place or any time, as you say.'

Katie took his hand, and kissed it. She tried to smile back at him, but panic was rising up in her. Jack needed help, and not the kind that she could give. What did Mary Seacole mean – 'I can only do what I can at the very end'? Katie needed her now.

The day was still beautiful, not one cloud in the sky. 'I know what happened,' Jack said, 'we charged the wrong way, towards the wrong guns.' His body twitched again and he cried out. Katie bent down, resting her cheek against his, trying to soothe him in any way she could. And then Jack grew very still. The pain seemed to leave his body. For a moment Katie thought, 'he is recovering; he will survive.' Then, with a lurch, she realized it wasn't just the pain that was ebbing away, it was his life's blood.

'Oh Katie,' he whispered, 'someone has blundered.' The agony and terror drained from his face. He turned his gaze from her and looked straight up, his bright blue eyes meeting the flat blue of the sky. And as Katie watched, his eyes became as blank as the arch of colour above them.

Chapter Nineteen

The Plain Facts

The days that followed were a blur for Katie. Vaguely, she remembered Jack in her arms, and Mary Seacole swooping down, taking him from her. Mary Seacole had opened the amulet, the vessel around her neck, and held it to Jack's lips, then pressed it against his heart and head. She chanted softly, and Katie heard the same words she had heard in her dreams, on the eve of the battle.

Lost for now, but found again, in another place and another time. Tempus fugit, libertati viam facere. Time flies, making a road to freedom.

Sealing the flask shut, Mary Seacole kissed his forehead and closed his eyes. 'I can only do it at the end.

And I have done what I can,' she told Katie. 'You will thank me one day.'

But it seemed to Katie that, for all the chanting, Mary Seacole had not done much. Jack was still dead. Amidst all the carnage, chaos and confusion, decisions still had to be made. There was no question of Jack's body being shipped home. So many soldiers had been killed; and many, especially those of lower ranks, were buried together. William Howard Russell used his influence and charm to obtain a separate grave and headstone for Jack. He was buried on Cathcart's Hill, within striking distance of Sebastopol. The city was still under siege.

The Little Angel lay in the field hospital, and even before she could sit up, Mary Seacole whisked her, and the Countess Fidelia, to the British Hotel. 'I believe in Florence Nightingale with all my soul,' Mary Seacole said to Katie, 'and Florence has told me to bring this child back to her.' Once she had built up some strength, the Little Angel was stretchered onto a hospital ship to Scutari. The military baulked at this: only soldiers were allowed on these ships. But again William Howard Russell used his contacts. Not only the Little Angel, but Katie too, was able to board the ship.

The Countess Fidelia stayed behind. Her ankle was broken and travel at this point could lead to an infection, and much worse. She needed bedrest. It took all of Mary Seacole's powers of persuasion to get her to stay behind, leaving Katie to tend to the Little Angel. The Countess was distraught, but

Katie could see the beginning of an enduring friendship between the two colourful ladies. They had both led lives of great adventure. She would have liked to have heard the tales they would tell over Mary Seacole's cosy camp stove.

'Goodbye, dear Katie,' Mary Seacole said, giving her a hearty kiss as they boarded ship. 'As I've said before, I don't hold much store with Americans. They are harsh on people with a skin my colour. But it seems to me Americans might have changed over time. You are as good a girl as God could make. I am sorry for your troubles, dearie. I know you think the world has ended, losing that young man. Time's a strange thing though, as you know well. Jack's still with us. I'm keeping him close to my heart.'

She smiled down at Katie and fingered the amulet that always hung around her neck. Katie looked at her with curiosity. What was she really saying? But Mary Seacole felt she'd said enough. She only added, 'Believe in the future and trust your friends. Time might bring you what you least expect.'

Katie blinked hard. 'I don't know my future,' she said. 'Mother Seacole, I only know I want to go home.' She had borne everything until now, but Mary Seacole's sympathy made her tearful.

The Little Angel reached out from her stretcher and squeezed Katie's hand. Katie shook away the tears. There was still so much to do; there was no time for weeping. She looked towards Sebastopol, towards Cathcart's Hill. There

Jack lay, cold in his grave, no matter what Mary Seacole said. But she couldn't think of Jack. That would have to wait.

Mary Seacole noted the direction of her glance. 'I will go visit him, dear child,' she said. 'I won't leave him too lonely. I'm keeping him warm in my heart.'

The Little Angel and Katie sailed together. The journey back to Scutari was a sad affair. The Little Angel's mind would wander, and she spoke of many other times and many places: the great plague of Danzig, the famine of Bengal, the French Revolution. Then she sang herself to sleep with old French lullabies. And so she sang and rocked herself and talked until she lost her voice – and, Katie feared, her reason. Katie looked at the young beautiful face and felt infinite sadness. To see so much that is bad, and to live on and on. She did not leave her side.

Each knot they sailed took them further from Jack's grave and closer to Scutari, where Alice and James were waiting. News travelled slowly. Katie doubted they would know; she would be the messenger. Katie grieved for Jack, but she equally grieved for James. Something had been growing inside her – a tender green shoot of feeling. But that had been cut down, destroyed in a fierce and futile battle. For James, his brother was the attachment of a lifetime. He had fought with Jack, laughed with him and loved him. This, Katie knew, was a far greater loss. She dreaded what she must tell James.

They disembarked in the last hours of the night. Katie had hoped no one would meet them, it was so late. But Florence Nightingale stood at the quay, scanning the small boats. 'Thank God!' she cried, spying Katie and the Little Angel. Katie had never seen her look so emotional. With dismay she saw that Miss Nightingale was not alone. James and Princess Alice stood with her, looking tired and worried. They knew of the catastrophe of the Charge of the Light Brigade, but they did not know the details: who had lived and who had died.

As they touched the river bank, Florence Nightingale lifted the Little Angel into her own arms and carried her up the muddy slope. The medics protested, but Florence Nightingale replied brusquely, 'I will entrust her to no one but myself.'

Katie did not look at her friends. She simply took James by the arm and followed Miss Nightingale up the steep bank. 'Come with me,' she said. 'We need to talk in private . . .'

Katie didn't blurt out the news, but neither did she sidestep it. As clearly as she could, she explained the battle to James and Alice. She told them about finding Jack on the battlefield. She would never forget, in all her years, the look on James's face – it was almost more than she could bear. To stand with her two best friends in the world, and to bring them this terrible message.

She talked and talked, trying to soften the blow. 'There was nothing I could do,' she told James. 'Jack, he'd been hit.

His injuries were so bad. But I promise you, James, I was with him the whole time. I did everything I could.' James just continued to stand there, staring at her, defiant, as if she were making up some horrible lie. 'We talked,' she said, 'until he couldn't talk any more. We talked – mostly about you, and Grace and Riordan. He thought of you until the very end. It was the last thing to make him smile. Little Riordan, and beautiful Grace, and you, of course – he admired you so much. He wanted to be with you, James, he . . .' She couldn't stop talking; the silence would have been worse.

Finally James spoke. 'You say the Light Brigade tried to take the wrong guns? That they charged directly into the Russians?'

'Yes,' Katie replied. 'That's what William Howard Russell said. And Jack knew it too. The last words he said were "someone has blundered".' James's shoulders twitched at this, but his face remained stony, furious. Alice tried to comfort him. She rested her hand on his shoulder and squeezed it gently.

'We must honour the charge they made,' she said softly, 'we must honour the Light Brigade. Jack died a hero.'

James struck her hand from his shoulder as if it were on fire. 'A hero!' he cried, 'Jack died a fool! Following the orders of Cardigan – of Lucan! Vain, puffed-up, class-ridden parasites! They know the ballroom, and the gentle-man's clubs; they are not fit for the battlefield. And Raglan, doddering, elderly – if he had murdered the Light Brigade in their beds he could not have committed a more criminal act. "*Someone has blundered.*" Even Jack knew, though God knows Jack wanted to fight; he couldn't wait for action.' James shot Princess Alice a look of pure poison. 'Your mother will be happy,' he said bitterly. 'The Queen has another hero, a cold, dead, fool of a hero, lying . . . I don't even know where . . .'

Princess Alice flinched, but she accepted his rebuke. Katie tried to put her arm around him. 'Jack lies on Cathcart Hill's,' she said. 'We made sure he had his own grave. We did the best we could . . .'

James shook her off, staring at her as if she'd run his brother through with a sword herself. 'I've heard the facts now, and I must write to Grace,' he said. 'I hate to think how this will affect her health. Perhaps I should write to her about heroes, to try and spare her. Heroes – God help us all.' And turning heel, he left the room.

Only then did Katie break down, sitting on the floor, weeping. Princess Alice was at her side in seconds, arms around her friend, her wimple falling over Katie like a shelter. 'There, my dear, my good, brave Katie. James knows how hard you've tried.'

'I didn't know he'd take it like this,' Katie sobbed. 'I knew he'd be angry, but not with us. Alice, he's been just awful to you. When you, of all people, only want to help.'

Alice smoothed her friend's rough hair, and dried her face with the hem of her white nun's habit. Her hands were shaking, but her voice was steady. 'You know James,' she said, 'Anger is an easier emotion than hurt for someone like him. He doesn't hate you, or me. He hates losing his brother. He needs time . . .'

Katie sobbed and sobbed. All the journey back, she'd tried to hold it in. She had helped to get Jack buried, nursed the Little Angel and watched over her on the journey home. Now she was back, and James blamed her for everything. How would he ever get over this? She needed him now more than ever, but she feared they would never again be friends.

'No matter what James says; this is a noble cause,' Alice added. 'Jack died a hero's death, and we must celebrate his great achievements on the battlefield.'

Even as Katie sobbed into her hands, she knew she didn't agree with Alice. James had been right and so was Jack. Someone had blundered.

'Have your cry, dear Katie,' Alice soothed her. 'When you are calmer, there is much to do here. The wounded are pouring in faster than we can care for them. And while the doctors have relented, and let the Nightingale nurses help – there simply aren't that many of us. Between the lack of skilled nurses and our lack of medical supplies, we are fighting our own battle in the hospital.'

Katie tried hard to control her sobs. She looked up to study her friend. In the small time she had been gone, Princess Alice had changed. She was paler and thinner.

Her grave grey eyes were ringed with circles. More than that, she seemed to have changed inside. The suffering she'd seen had swept away her girlish sweetness. Her essential goodness was still there, as was her patience and loving heart – but she seemed years older.

'Of course you're right,' Katie sniffled slightly. 'I'm blubbering like a baby, while you do the work of a grown-up. You've become so strong.'

'We've both grown up,' Alice assured her, 'though I'm not as strong as I seem. I'm so pleased and so relieved that you are back. Your friendship makes it all bearable.'

Alice helped Katie up, and they made their way to Miss Nightingale's room. She had put the Little Angel into her own bed. 'Shhhh, she is finally sleeping,' Miss Nightingale admonished the girls as they entered. 'I have given her a draught – I hope she will sleep for many hours. You must know, Katie, that her return to health is vital. I have received a letter from William Howard Russell. He tells me that without you, Katie, the Little Angel would not be alive today. You are to be commended. I will relieve you of these duties and nurse her myself. That is the only way I can be assured of her safety.'

Katie stared at Florence Nightingale. For the hundredth time she wondered, *Who is this woman? What is the truth about Florence Nightingale?* Princess Alice looked at the Little Angel, lying in Miss Nightingale's bed; her dark lashes fluttering as she slept. 'She is so beautiful,' Alice said, 'but troubled, even in her sleep. What is her story? Why is she here?'

Florence Nightingale rested her hand on the Little Angel's forehead, and nodded in satisfaction. 'The outcome of her story will affect the entire world. I will tell you, and soon, but right now there are thousands of other patients, outside in the corridors, and they need our attention as well.'

They all slaved away, day after day. Miss Nightingale's influence spread throughout the hospital. She spent her days ordering supplies and making certain they were delivered – even travelling to Constantinople to purchase goods herself. She supervised the food the men ate, the medicines they were given, and tried to make certain the doctors weren't actively killing their patients. When she wasn't dashing about, she was at her small wooden table writing, writing, writing – orders, acknowledgements, receipts, reports to the government, missives of complaint, and tender letters of consolation to widows and mothers.

By night Florence Nightingale made her rounds through the long corridors of the Scutari hospital. 'I have no choice but to work through the night,' she explained to Alice and Katie. 'It is necessary to make my rounds before dawn breaks. The doctors must have my notes on the patients. They need to read them before they make their own rounds – whether they want them, or not.' Katie estimated that

Florence Nightingale walked more than four miles each night, holding her lantern before her.

The sick and wounded lay on the floor, row after row, only eighteen inches between them. Miss Nightingale glided through their ranks; smoothing a pillow, easing a bandage, bringing water, observing the men and writing notes for the doctors. She might prefer managing big institutions, but she was an excellent personal nurse whether she liked the occupation or not. Her normally brusque manner vanished – she was tender, kind and patient. It took her hours to walk the entire floor space of the Scutari Hospital. As she passed, the silence was profound. The men tried to stifle their moans and cries, and they kissed her shadow as she passed by.

Often Alice was Miss Nightingale's chosen companion, carrying her little basket of medicines and bandages. As long as Katie could stand up, she volunteered to come too. She was having disturbing dreams, surprisingly not about Jack or Lord Belzen, but about Mimi. It seemed from these dreams that she needed to get home, and she didn't know how to. Bernardo DuQuelle was thousands of miles away, and Florence Nightingale was too absorbed in the work at hand. Katie thought things over, through the night, as they paced the wards. Did Miss Nightingale know how to send her back to her own time? She needed to find the right moment to ask . . .

Stopping by one bed, Florence Nightingale placed her lantern beside a young man and, bending down, took his pulse. 'Too slow and too low,' she murmured to herself. 'He is barely conscious.' She turned to Alice and Katie. 'If you could take my notes to James O'Reilly please; I cannot leave this man. I will stay with him until the end.'

'But James . . .' Katie bleated weakly. For weeks now James had avoided them: doing the work of a dozen men, then falling into an exhausted stupor in the doctors' quarters. Miss Nightingale shot Katie a cutting glance. 'Any personal affront must be put aside,' she said crisply. 'James has a job to do, as do we all. Now, go!'

Princess Alice took the notes, and led Katie through the corridors. 'What do you make of Florence Nightingale?' Katie asked.

Alice's face was filled with admiration. 'She has followed her calling. She has found her work in life. But her health is not good. I am afraid that in doing her duty, she will push herself to the grave.'

'If she can die,' Katie replied. 'Haven't you ever noticed how creepy she can be? How her personality changes minute by minute. That she can read your mind? I often wonder exactly what is her relationship to Bernardo DuQuelle? And you know what *he* is.' But Alice was in another world of duty and service, sacrifice and holy reward. They walked on to the doctors' canteen in silence.

While Florence Nightingale brought calm and strength, the doctors' quarters were all irritation and confusion.

They soon found James, sorting through innumerable scribbled requests and arguing with a junior doctor. 'But if a man is ill, he needs a special diet,' James was saying. 'Not rancid mutton wrapped in old rags and boiled for hours.'

The doctor spoke slowly, as if placating a small child. 'We do provide special diets when needs must,' he explained.

'But not soon enough!' James cut across him. 'Look at these millions of scribbled requests. All applications must go from you to the senior doctor to the supplies' purveyor. If the supplies' purveyor doesn't have the right things, he writes back to the senior doctor, who then sends the message on to you. This can take days. No one in the kitchens is informed of anything. By the time it is resolved, the sick man will have starved to death!'

'I don't think James is ready to see us,' Katie muttered to Alice. 'I mean, it's all so awful for him. He needs more time. So maybe we should come back later.'

Once so uncertain, Alice now seemed able to face anything. She walked straight through the room full of doctors. They stepped back in respect for her nun's habit. To them, she was still Sister Agnes. Katie tagged behind.

'James O'Reilly,' Alice said in her soft firm voice. 'I have Miss Nightingale's notes from her rounds of the wards. Can you make certain the doctors read them before their own examinations? I draw your attention to Lieutenant Garnet Wolseley in the north corridor. He is scheduled for an amputation today, but Miss Nightingale feels he is recovering. His fever has dropped and the infection has subsided.'

Alice didn't say anything about Jack's death or James's outburst. She did not refer to his cruelty to Katie or his insult to the Queen. She didn't address him in a personal way at all. James ignored her, continuing to sort through the scraps of paper he held. She stood directly in front of him and looked at him steadily.

Eventually James lifted his eyes and met hers. They were completely still in the bustle around them. Without a word, they said a million things. James turned bright red, but Alice continued to regard him calmly. Finally he spoke. 'I am sorry,' he said. 'But of course, I am sorry. Please tell Miss Nightingale I will attend to this immediately.'

Turning to Katie, he tried to smile. 'You look terrible,' he said. 'You really need some rest. I do know – well, how hard you've tried, how much help you have been – and that this is hard for you too. I'm the one who's a fool, Katie . . .'

'We all need a good night's sleep,' Alice chimed in. 'Katie has always teased me about this. She says I think a nap will solve all the world's problems.' Again James and Alice exchanged glances. It all made Katie feel very lonely. She had suspected, and now she knew: Alice and James had been on one journey, and she had been on another. She desperately wanted to go home.

James passed the bits of paper to the junior doctor. 'Well, let's break off now,' he said. 'Nothing goes right in this hospital, and I'm not going to be able to fix it single-handed. I need some time to think clearly.'

'Miss Nightingale might be done with her rounds,' Alice added. 'Let's go and see her.'

The three of them entered the wards, now bustling with doctors, medics and nurses. Katie turned her head away as they passed the corner screened off for amputations. Despite what she'd seen on the battlefield, she still didn't have the stomach for the groans and screams of the men.

'You'll get used to it,' James said. 'Alice is often called in to help with the procedure.'

'I have found that if I am calm and cheerful and willing to stay with them, this strengthens their fortitude during the amputation,' Alice told her. Katie looked at her friend with admiration, but wondered – how could Alice ever go back to Palace life after this?

When they reached Florence Nightingale's storeroom-cum-office-cum-bedroom, she was not alone. She sat on one side of her little wooden desk, leaning forward and talking earnestly with a man on the other side. Though his back was to the door, Katie recognized him immediately. The broad shoulders, the large leather boots, the battered cap with the gold trim, which he'd removed in the presence of a lady. She felt a rush of relief. Billy Russell always made her feel better. He could fix anything.

'So she will live – that is a relief,' he was saying to Florence Nightingale. 'My heart was in my mouth when she rushed down that hill, straight into the battle – and then Miss Katie following in her wake! I've never been given such a jolt.'

As the three entered, Russell stood and, clicking his heels together, kissed Katie's hand. As he looked down into Katie's drawn tired face, his own cheery one became tender and gentle. 'Child,' he said, 'you've spent so much time tending the sick and minding the dying, that you're doing yourself some harm.'

Miss Nightingale was usually rather stern with Katie. But she too looked into her face with growing alarm. 'You are right, Mr Russell,' she said. 'I hadn't notice before. Miss Katherine Tappan, you are dismissed from your duties, indeed, you all are.'

'Please, Miss Nightingale, would you mind telling us, how does the Little Angel?' Alice asked. Miss Nightingale had forbidden her any companion other than herself. Katie found that she missed her, and wanted to talk more of their common secret.

'Much better,' she replied, 'as I was just telling Mr Russell. By the by, she is asking for Katie.'

There was a pause, and then James spoke up, politely, but firmly. 'I'd like to know why this girl called Angel is so important.' The pause grew longer, while everyone stared at Florence Nightingale.

William Howard Russell was practically exploding with curiosity. 'Yes,' he agreed, 'I could do with the plain facts.'

Finally, Miss Nightingale spoke. 'You've all played a part in her life,' she said, 'and several of you have saved her from death. And I did say I would explain.' She shot Russell a killer look. 'You must understand, though, this is not some lurid tale to sell newspapers. If I ever hear one word of this, or see one printed, I shall deny everything, and have you declared insane.'

Russell whistled low. 'She could do it too,' he said to the others. He pulled out the battered chair and offered it to Princess Alice. James stood behind her, while Katie simply dumped herself onto the floor.

Florence Nightingale paced the room and then turned abruptly to Katie. 'You know, of course.'

'Not really, not enough.'

'But you know.' And then she began to pace again.

James spoke up. 'We all know something. But we imagine, Miss Nightingale, that you know the most. If you'll excuse me, we're not quite certain that you are, well really, what you are, and . . .'

Russell cut across them all. 'Let's make this easy,' he said. 'I know nothing, except that something happened at Balaclava beyond the Charge of the Light Brigade. There was that storm for one thing; all blackness and white-hot heat. Then two young ladies behaving like lunatics – and still escaping certain death. Something strange and frightening, beyond comprehension or even imagination happened. So shall we start from the beginning? As I've said before, the plain facts, please.'

Miss Nightingale collected her thoughts. 'There are things in this world that are not of our world,' she began. 'I doubt you will believe me, but this is true. There is an entire civilization that uses us, takes from us. They use our ways of communicating; they harvest our words. In a strange way, they are an imperial power, just as we are. They wish to control our actions – a calm environment makes it much easier for them . . .'

It was a fairly staggering note to start on. Russell first looked shocked, and then his face became impassive. Katie could tell what he was thinking: that the strain of the work had unhinged Florence Nightingale – that she was the one who was insane. But he was too good a newspaper man to stop her. He would fight his doubts, and try to keep quiet until he had the story.

Miss Nightingale could read his thoughts too. She smiled slightly to herself, knowing how ridiculous it all sounded, but continued on gamely. 'This civilization works within our own to a certain extent. They look like us, hold offices and positions, but they are not *of* us.' The three friends glanced at Florence Nightingale, with questioning looks. Her face gave away nothing. 'There is a war,' she went on. 'Not this war, not the Crimean War, but one within this other civilization that takes from us.'

'Two factions, the Verus and the Malum, want to control the way they use our world. They exploit the children to try and achieve their ends. The children are the tools. It is known as the Great Experiment. They send children through time to try and change history. These children are called the Tempus, the Chosen. Some – the Tempus Fugit – fly through time. And the others, the Tempus Occidit, I am afraid they fall through time. There are three we know of: the child who brings peace, the child who brings war and peace, and the child who brings the war to end the world.'

At this point William Howard Russell couldn't contain himself. 'Miss Nightingale, an entire nation is grateful to you for your unceasing work. But you are telling me a yarn best kept for a peat fire and a whisky in a Kilkenny pub. No drunkard could speak more foolishness.'

Katie stood up, and faced Russell. 'It is all true,' she told him. 'I know, because I am one of them. I am the Tempus.'

Russell began to get angry. 'This is all an elaborate hoax,' he said. 'Now, just confess it – the joke is over.'

'You yourself said there was more to Balaclava than the Charge of the Light Brigade,' Miss Nightingale continued. 'You saw the skies above you. You saw the battle of light and dark. That was not just a British military fiasco.'

Russell leaned against the wall, as if his sturdy boots couldn't support him any longer. 'Go on,' he said. 'What was that battle then?'

Anxiety and anger crossed Florence Nightingale's face. 'Both the Verus and the Malum believe these three children, the Tempus, are to take up arms against each other on the field of battle – that they will fight to the death. Their victory or defeat will change the course of our history. I find it cruel in the extreme.'

Katie breathed a sigh of relief. Now she knew what she had always hoped. Florence Nightingale might not be quite human, but she was not bad. She was with them, of them, for them. That was a great comfort.

'I still think that . . .' Russell interrupted. He looked decidedly shaken.

'You still think this is rubbish,' James cut in. 'So did I, for the longest time, though Princess Al— I mean Sister Agnes, always understood.'

Alice smiled, and Miss Nightingale nodded. 'Perhaps you would like some proof?' she suggested. 'Let us go to the Little Angel. She is not yet well enough for visitors, so we will have to be brief.' She led them into the next room, where the Little Angel was still lying back in bed. She sat up weakly and reached out to Katie. She wanted to say something, but her voice came out in a hoarse croak.

'Now, now, you mustn't speak,' Florence Nightingale admonished. 'It is too tiring, as is this string of guests. But they were with me, and I wished to deliver this letter as soon as possible.' She took a folded paper from her pocket, and as the Little Angel opened it, Miss Nightingale whispered to the others, 'It is from her guardian, her adopted mother, the Countess Fidelia.' As the Little Angel read, emotion overcame her. She tried to speak, but no words came. As her lips opened, an arc of light and colour rose from them, into the air – a bouquet of roses, of lustrous blue and white, waved and trembled above her.

Florence Nightingale stroked her forehead. 'But of course,' Miss Nightingale murmured, 'the colours of pure love and faithfulness. I will write back to the Countess and tell her what you feel; though I am certain she already knows, and has always known.'

The Little Angel nodded, and a single tear streaked down her white cheek. She closed her eyes; the effort had exhausted her. Soon she was asleep.

The others said nothing as they followed Miss Nightingale back to her cramped little office. Russell broke the silence. 'It could have been a conjuror's trick,' he said defensively. 'After all, they are street performers. They are masters of illusion.'

'At a time like this, in the midst of a war, bedridden, ill, weak and alone – I wouldn't think she was in a fit state for a vaudeville performance!' Princess Alice exclaimed.

'I've learned that you must put aside sense,' James added. 'Some things are beyond the rational mind.'

'Then what freak of nature is she?' Russell asked.

Katie looked at them all. She could tell that James and Alice were curious too. With every question, the distance between them grew. 'The Little Angel is as I am,' Katie said. 'She is one of the chosen. She is part of the Tempus. I am certain she is the child who brings peace.' For some strange reason, Katie thought she might cry, and she was so tired of crying.

Princess Alice took her friend's hand. 'Are you certain?' she asked. 'I have always thought that you, Katie, were the child who brings peace.'

'Look at my own time,' Katie replied with some bitterness. 'There's war everywhere. People fight each other – over money, over politics, over religion. My world, in my time, is a total mess. But we haven't given up hope. I might think I'm a jerk sometimes, but I'm not the one who ends the world.'

James began to laugh, and they all looked at him with some amazement.

'I know it's not a laughing matter,' he said, 'but it still makes me laugh to think of our Katie as either a Goddess of Goodness or a Dark Master of Evil.'

Katie didn't mind that James was laughing at her – at least he was laughing. 'No, I'm not the good one,' she said. 'That's definitely the Little Angel. And we pretty much know who the evil one is.'

'But of course, it is Felix!' breathed Alice. 'He is the Tempus Occidit – the child who falls through time to bring the war to end the world. Yes, I see now; that means you are all here, as in the prediction.'

Katie shuddered. She'd been wondering about this. 'The three are here, and we've met in the field of battle,' she said slowly. 'But we're still all alive. Does that mean we still have to fight to the death?'

They all looked to Florence Nightingale for answers, even William Howard Russell. 'I think not,' she said. 'I've never thought so, and now I am certain. Katie, you have seen Lucia?' Katie nodded. Florence Nightingale smiled drily. 'There is much to admire in Lucia, but she has a purity of purpose that at times clouds her reason.'

'A woman too purposeful for Miss Florence Nightingale,' Russell muttered. 'Now that's a woman I'd like to meet.'

Miss Nightingale ignored him. 'The Tempus – all three of you have gathered on the field of battle. In this Lucia was correct. But Katie, Lucia could not control you in the end. You chose for yourself. You chose not to kill, but to save.'

Katie was sitting on the floor and felt the tears pouring down her face. She had suffered greatly, seen things girls of her age should not have to witness, and she grieved for Jack, for all the fallen men. Sometimes she thought she was made out of tears. But this was different. It was as if an enormous stone had been lifted from her chest. She was weeping with relief.

Princess Alice clapped her hands. 'I knew it!' she cried. 'I knew that Katie could only do good.' She caught James's eye and they smiled at each other.

'In this case, you are correct,' Florence Nightingale

continued. 'Katie, have you noticed there is a difference between you and the other two Tempus?'

Katie brushed the tears from her face. 'Well, they're both a lot better looking,' she said rather lamely. James groaned and Katie pulled herself together. 'When I sailed with the Little Angel, she was suffering from delirium,' she added. 'She talked of living through so many times. Yet I only remember my own time – New York City, in the twenty-first century.'

James's scientific mind kicked in. 'And Felix isn't really a child at all. It is Felix's body, but it's been taken over by Belzen.'

'But there is some part of Felix that's still a child,' Katie told him. 'That's the only way I was able to defeat him.'

'If it is the Great Experiment, then it's a flawed experiment,' James said. 'If the children are not the same, then any conclusions will not be valid . . .'

'Really,' Katie said indignantly. 'I'm not a guinea pig.'

Billy Russell's eyebrows shot up. Florence Nightingale looked as if she might break into a laugh. 'Well, you are actually,' she said. 'But James is right. To a certain extent, you have freed yourself. The Great Experiment is a failure. Katie, if you had not saved the Little Angel, we would be heading towards destruction. You have acted as an individual, with your own voice. You made an independent decision. You chose peace.'

William Russell still wasn't certain he believed this story;

to him it sounded too fantastical. He knew he would never commit it to paper, and *The Times* would never print it. The readers of *The Times* would swallow many untruths, but this was going too far. He looked down at Katie; they all looked at Katie.

She could feel Alice's gentle love and total belief, James's loyalty and friendship – and finally, the approval, the commendation of Florence Nightingale. 'I chose,' Katie said to herself. 'I have a voice. I count. I matter.'

A brisk knock at the door interrupted her thoughts, and the Reverend Mother entered. 'I am sorry to disturb you,' she said, 'but the entire world seems to be looking for William Howard Russell. I have several messages marked "urgent" and a telegram from London.'

Russell raced through the messages, and then ripped opened the telegram. He read it through three times, stopping each time to look at Florence Nightingale and Princess Alice. Shaking his head, he let out a hearty laugh. 'Well, here are several stories I could write up,' he said. 'The first has to do with treachery. A traitor has been caught. Lord Twisted, young Felix's guardian in the Crimea, has been picked up leaving the Russian camp. It seems he has been selling military secrets. A spy – now that is a story our readers will attend to! Strange, my source says Twisted looked almost relieved when they arrested him.'

'And Felix?' Katie asked.

'He's in the field hospital,' Russell replied. 'He claims to be suffering from "Crimea fever" – and has agreed to disclose all the information he has on Lord Twisted in exchange for his own removal from the case.'

'The hospital is a good place for Felix,' Florence Nightingale commented. 'If there's one thing we know about, it's hospital conditions in the Crimea. Let us hope for an infection. I'd recommend a bout of cholera for that young man!' Miss Nightingale had a way with black humour. 'Mr Russell, you said there were several stories. What more do you find in your correspondence?'

Russell read through the telegram one last time. 'It is with pleasure that I learn of the birth of another royal child.' He bowed his head, more of an impudent bob, and handed the telegram to Princess Alice. 'Sister Agnes, I congratulate you. You have a little sister. Her name is Beatrice.' Alice turned bright red, and James moved protectively to shield her.

Florence Nightingale sized up the situation. 'What do they know in London?' she asked. 'This could be a major scandal.'

Russell smiled with satisfaction. 'They know little, as did I, until this moment. But my hunch has proved correct.' He bowed his head again to Princess Alice. 'I did wonder that such a young novice could project such great dignity. And then Master O'Reilly here *would* keep getting your name wrong.'

James was furious. 'You can't destroy her life like this,' he shouted. 'Exposure would mean the end of her prospects. There would be no future as a member of the Royal Family. You might as well lock her up in a real convent!'

'It was a deception, but the motives were pure,' Florence Nightingale added. 'Princess Alice wished to learn about nursing; I was on my way to the Crimea. Why can a woman not pursue worthy goals?'

Katie took William Howard Russell's arm. 'You can't do this to Alice,' she begged him. 'Not only is she my best friend, but she's really got talent as a nurse. She can help the world, but only if you let her get away with this.'

Princess Alice looked up into William Howard Russell's eyes. His face softened – she had that effect on people.

'I repeat, little is known in London yet,' he said gruffly. 'The Queen gave birth in the Highlands. She is convalescing at Balmoral. My editor telegraphs that she is asking that her entire family join her, and they are having trouble locating certain members.'

'But where am I supposed to be?' Alice asked.

William Howard Russell read through the telegram again. 'Well, let's see . . . ah, that great panjandrum of the Palace, Bernardo DuQuelle, has played a part in this. It says here . . . DuQuelle insists you are taking the air in the Alps with your governess, the Baroness Lehzen. Yet there are rumours that the Baroness Lehzen is actually in Baden-Baden, the worse for wear from fortified wines and gambling.'

Alice too clutched Russell's arm. Both she and Katie had him in a stronghold of pleading. 'Will you tell?' she asked. 'Please . . .' They all held their breath.

He looked, for a very long time, into each face. A good journalist could read character, and he read the same thing in all four faces. With a sigh, Russell folded the telegram and put it in his pocket. 'The treason story is more immediate,' he replied. 'I'm right here, at the scene of the crime. I should return to Sebastopol and try and finagle an interview with Lord Twisted. The man has always been a scoundrel. Indeed, I have some choice bits of information about his past . . . I just might choose to share these with Lord Raglan. This is a story that will run and run. And by the time I'm done with it, I assume Princess Alice will have joined her family in the Highlands . . .'

He examined the sole of his thick leather boot, and shook his head. 'Perhaps I am in the wrong profession after all. What kind of newspaper man am I? To let my best leads slip through my fingers. The Verus and the Malum, the war to end the world – you've given me a story so fantastical that no one would believe me. Then there's Princes Alice, smuggled out to the Crimea as Sister Agnes, nursing her mother's soldiers back to health. Inspiring, yes, but a story so scandalous, it would destroy not just the princess but the entire Royal Family. I don't want that burden on my back. So I am left with Lord Twisted. The facts are plain enough there: debt, greed and arrogance led him to treachery. I'll write such a story; he'll rue the day he betrayed his country. As for his young ward, Felix, God help him. Miss Nightingale is rarely wrong. He might just come down with cholera.'

Chapter Twenty

The Journey Home

The sea was smooth as silk. It had been agony on the outward voyage; now it was over in a flash. The Little Angel was too weak to leave her bed and stayed behind with Florence Nightingale, while Katie travelled with James and Alice. Katie longed to speak to the Little Angel – to talk over the recent events and delve into their shared secrets – but time was against her. 'I've only just found you,' Katie said, 'and now I am leaving you. Am I ever going to learn anything?'

The Little Angel smiled, and did manage to say a few words. 'Don't worry, we will meet again. You'll be surprised who you might be meeting again. But there's someone who needs you more right now. Katie, find a way to return to your mother.'

Florence Nightingale booked them on the fastest steamship possible. She knew that a scandal about Princess Alice would not only ruin her life and damage the Royal Family – it would also destroy the nursing profession for decades to come. Bringing Alice to the Crimea had seemed a gamble worth taking, but she was close to losing the bet. Everything was done to ensure the three reached England safely – and in secrecy. Bernardo DuQuelle's servants met them in Marseilles, and whisked them through France and across the Channel. They had a private train compartment to cross England, and a heavily curtained carriage met them at London Bridge.

At last the three rattled across the cobblestones to Half Moon Street, and were bustled, unceremoniously, through the servants' basement entrance, then up to DuQuelle's dark study. There had been no time to rest or wash or change. Princess Alice was still in her nun's habit, now a dull grey. James's clothes were stained with the gore of the operating table, and Katie's grey tweed gown was encrusted with the dirt of the battlefield.

DuQuelle shuddered at the sight of them and held a handkerchief to his nose. His sense of smell was painfully acute. 'Greetings,' he said. 'Grubby,' he added. 'It is one of the adverse side effects of your civilization. Personally I bathe three times a day, but still the residue clings.'

'That's great,' Katie retorted. 'It's like we've gone through all this, only to get a report on your personal hygiene.'

James's mouth twitched and Katie noticed that Alice did not seem too shocked. Scutari had rubbed that out of her.

DuQuelle looked at the tattered trio before him. 'Do excuse me. You are correct, Katie,' he said. 'You have gone through a great deal.' His eyes rested on James O'Reilly. 'And you have suffered terrible losses. If I am sharp-tongued or mocking it is only as a release. Katie, you always say I have no emotions. Well, I do. I am relieved that you have arrived safely. And now, we must return Princess Alice to the Palace, as if nothing had ever happened.'

'As if nothing had happened!' Katie cried. 'That's impossible. Alice can't go back. She's learned a lifetime in these weeks. She's a brilliant nurse. You've got to let her use her abilities. And James, he can't just return to his old life, helping his father in the Palace. The government, the officials, the army – they're making a mess of this war in the Crimea. James can expose the blunders. I mean, he knows what happened at the Charge of the Light Brigade. I've told him everything. He needs to do something about it. He owes this to Jack. And Jack, I mean, I feel . . . there was the battle, no, *two* battles, the Verus and the Malum . . . have the Malum been defeated? I've found the Little Angel. She's safe for now, but will she stay safe? . . . and Jack is gone . . . and none of us will ever, *ever* forget that . . .'

Alice had tears in her eyes, and even James looked as if he might cry.

DuQuelle realized he had pushed them too far. 'I know, I know. Sit down, sit down . . .' he soothed them. 'I am sorry for your loss. Jack was a fine young man, and will be again. I believe Mary Seacole was on the battlefield? *Tempus fugit, libertati viam facere* . . . Jack has taken the road to freedom. Will he live again?' DuQuelle's comments were baffling and the three still looked miserable. 'What was I thinking,' he continued. 'There is only one thing to comfort the English . . .' He rang for his footman. 'Tea,' he ordered. 'Strong and hot; and I believe cook has baked some little cakes.'

It was always a mystery to Katie, this thing about tea. But when the tea arrived, it was a comfort. She even ate three little cakes.

'And now,' DuQuelle continued after a long silence, 'we need to marshal our thoughts and act. Princess Alice, the Baroness Lehzen has returned from Baden-Baden, where she was gambling under an assumed name.'

'Gambling?' Alice looked puzzled. 'I cannot believe this. The Baroness Lehzen is not a particularly nice person, but she is not a gambler.'

DuQuelle's eyebrow went up. 'Well, someone has lured her into gambling.'

Katie shot him a sideways glance. She could guess who that *someone* was.

'She has lost a great deal of money,' DuQuelle continued. 'I have agreed to cover her debts and shield her identity. In exchange she will write to the Queen saying you have been in the Alps for your health, and are now on your way to Balmoral. She will accompany you, and swear to that story. As you know, the Queen has great faith in the Baroness Lehzen. She is a great Queen, but at times . . .'

James snorted, but looked at Alice with fond concern. 'The Princess does not look as if she's been walking in the Swiss mountains,' he said. 'She looks very pale and tired.'

DuQuelle glanced from Alice to James, and then caught Katie's eye. He seemed to understand. 'Nevertheless, that is the story,' he said, a crisp note returning to his voice. 'The Princess can stick her head out of the train window on the way to Scotland, and then I'll order an open carriage for the rest of the journey. The Queen's beloved fresh air – that should put some roses in Princess Alice's cheeks.'

Alice didn't respond for a long time. 'So we will be separated,' she said finally. 'It is a hard bond to break.'

Katie noticed a flicker of alarm in DuQuelle's eyes. 'But break it you must,' he said, 'and the sooner, the better. It will need to be quite a lengthy separation. The Queen will convalesce at Balmoral for many months.' Alice sipped her tea and sighed.

'I'm certain my father will be at Balmoral,' James said encouragingly. 'I will be able to join him, as soon as I sort things out about this war. First I'll contact the War Office, and if that doesn't work, I'll turn to the newspapers.' He shot Alice a half-fearful, half-defiant look. They did not agree on the war, but they had agreed to disagree.

'You will not need to contact anyone,' DuQuelle told him. 'It is all in hand. William Howard Russell's account of the Charge of the Light Brigade appeared in *The Times* three days ago.' He took a newspaper from a pile and passed it to them. James seized the paper, and read aloud:

'They swept proudly past, glittering in the morning sun in all the pride and splendour of war . . . with courage too great almost for credence, they were breaking their way through the columns which enveloped them . . . to our delight we saw them returning, after breaking through a column of Russian infantry, and scattering them like chaff . . .'

James was stormy-faced, furious. 'This simply cannot be,' he spluttered. 'Russell's written complete rubbish. He's made it read like a victory, as if we should applaud the Light Brigade for throwing themselves in front of the Russian guns.'

Princess Alice tried to placate him. 'These words are not the truth as you see it,' she said; 'but there is truth in them. Jack did die a hero, and he is honoured in these words by Russell.'

Bernardo DuQuelle turned to Katie. 'What do you think?' he asked her.

Katie thought of her own time. Mimi was, after all, a celebrity. Sometimes the newspapers were kind – writing about her charity projects or her New Age enthusiasms. At other times they were cruel – telling all about her string of failed marriages, ridiculing her attempts to stay a pop star despite her age. Katie remembered one particularly harsh photo of Mimi staggering out of a nightclub at 3 a.m.; the headlines shrieked '*MIMI AT DEATH'S DOOR: AGE SERUM FAILS*'. Mimi had cried for weeks, and then had a facelift. Katie felt a pang of anxiety at the thought of her mother. 'Well, I mean, newspapers are a business,' she said. 'They have to sell copies, so they need to make it entertaining.'

'Entertaining,' James spoke through gritted teeth. 'How can you, of all people, call the death of my brother entertaining.'

Katie looked miserable. 'James, I saw the whole thing. I know it didn't happen like this. But Billy Russell isn't doing a really awful thing. He's putting a spin on it. And yes, he's making it exciting for the readers. But, like Alice said, he's creating a bunch of new heroes. And Jack was a hero – he was terrific. He . . .' Katie felt as if she might cry again, but this did stem James's fury.

DuQuelle watched them. His face was unreadable, but his silence spelled sympathy. Finally he broke the silence. 'Katie is right. Her flights through time sometimes give her the edge of experience. There is no point fighting the press. Even when they are wrong – and they are often wrong – they will still win.'

James hunched over his cup of tea, while Alice discreetly took the copy of *The Times* from him and hid it under the other papers.

'Now I have some good news for you, James O'Reilly,' DuQuelle continued. 'I have taken the liberty of enrolling you for a series of lectures to be given in Paris – by Auguste Comte. I know you are interested in the interdependence of the sciences; indeed, I lent you the *Course of Positive Philosophy* myself.'

James sat up, interested, but he was too angry to accept gifts from DuQuelle. 'I have duties in London. Little Riordan is here, and Grace will need me,' he said gruffly. 'In fact, I cannot wait any longer to see them. They will require my help.'

'I notice you do not mention your father,' DuQuelle's face took on its arch, mocking mask. 'You are right there; your father needs no help. He has played the loss of his son to perfection. The Queen is showering him with attentions. I even believe there is talk of a knighthood. He has taken advantage of his high favour at court and sent for young Riordan to come to Balmoral. He will now be tutored along with little Prince Arthur . . .'

Dr O'Reilly would always put himself first, James knew that, but it didn't make him feel any better. 'And my sister?' he persisted.

DuQuelle's face looked more human at the mention of Grace – less happy, but more human. 'Grace did not take the news of Jack's death well,' he murmured. 'She is convalescing in a sanatorium outside Paris. It is one of the best in this world. That is another reason why I chose these lectures. You will be near each other. You can visit her daily.'

'It does make sense,' Alice agreed. 'And I envy you the lectures. Even I have heard of Comte's new science. He calls it "sociology", and it sounds fascinating. You must write and tell me all.'

As Alice approved the plan, James thought it might be best to go. 'I will send you the lectures word for word,' he told her. 'I will write to you every day.'

Both Katie and DuQuelle looked uncomfortable. 'My personal view is that Comte is a rather silly philosopher,' DuQuelle said. 'It's all very fine to link things together – but to create a new religion, new holidays, and new saints – St Shakespeare! St Adam Smith! But then, James, you might become one of the new elite industrialists – St James O'Reilly, I can see it now . . .' They all laughed at this. But Alice sighed again.

'Princess, I can see you are afraid of what is to come: a life divided between social visits and embroidery,' DuQuelle continued. 'How can you have learned so much, travelled so far, and simply return to your old life?'

Katie couldn't help but notice how Alice had aged. The hands, always slender, were now so thin, and the bones of her face jutted from the stark outline of her wimple.

DuQuelle, too, looked at her with something that smacked slightly of concern . . . and affection. 'What you need, my dear Princess is rest,' he said gently. 'But it is your nature to comfort others, without comforting yourself. So I have taken the step of corresponding with Lord Aberdeen. He is setting up a dispensary for the poor in Deeside, not far from Balmoral. I have told him of your interest and training in medicine – not, of course, about Scutari, but of the instruction you have received in the Palace. I believe he will recommend to Prince Albert that you help this new institution in some important way.'

Alice was pleased. 'Do you think my father will agree?'

DuQuelle smiled, ever so faintly. 'I think it is in all our best interests for him to agree. I will persevere.'

Katie glanced around – at the firelight flickering through the book-filled room; at DuQuelle's face, not unlike the wooden figures carved in the ancient furniture; at Alice, pale but resigned; at James, so sad still, but excited by his life of the mind. 'What about me?' she thought. 'Is there nothing for me?' She must have said it out loud, because everyone turned to her, and the only other sound was the leaping fire.

'You will go to Paris with me,' James said gruffly, 'and continue to care for Grace.'

'If Grace needs her, of course,' Alice said. 'Though I'd like Katie to come to Balmoral. I am less than happy when we are apart and there's so much we could achieve together.'

Bernardo DuQuelle turned to Katie. 'What do you want?' he asked.

Katie looked at her friends, and then stared down at DuQuelle's beautifully polished shoes. She didn't answer, but raised another question. 'How ill is Grace?'

DuQuelle nodded to himself, as if Katie had passed some sort of test. 'She is ill,' he said 'but she is in capable hands. The Sisters of Mercy are quite progressive in their treatments. I've sent them detailed notes of your care of Grace. They are quite impressed. They will follow your lead.'

'Now you can answer, Katie,' Alice said gently, taking her friend's hand, 'though I fear I already know what you will say.'

'I want to go home,' Katie burst out. 'There's something going on there, something really wrong. I keep dreaming about Mimi. And I had some kind of vision in the Crimea, some hocus-pocus with Florence Nightingale and Mary Seacole . . . it's all kind of fuzzy. I'm not really needed here now – not by Grace, not by Riordan. DuQuelle doesn't need anyone, and you and James have each other – well, kind of, I mean, not really but . . .'

Everyone looked a bit embarrassed. DuQuelle stepped in. 'Yes, you're all very keen on being needed. Though I thank you for placing me above hoi polloi,' he said as he sniffed the air. 'I think Katie is right to take leave of us. I too fear something is amiss in Apartment 11C.'

Anxiety pulsed through Katie.

'Then we're agreed,' she said. 'James will go to Paris, Alice to Balmoral, and I'm off to New York City circa the twenty-first century.' She turned to Alice, preparing herself for a hard goodbye.

But Bernardo DuQuelle stopped her. 'I'm not quite certain,' he said.

Katie gave him a sharp look. 'Not quite certain of what?'

'I'm at a loss, unsure how to return you . . .' He seemed unmoved by this disclosure. His heavy lids drooped over eyes that showed no remorse.

'But you knew how to get her here,' James exclaimed. 'You must know how to get her back.'

DuQuelle almost smiled. Katie thought about hitting him. 'I knew how to plant the seeds of Katie's visit,' he said. 'It was always up to Katie to harvest them.' He could be infuriatingly cryptic.

'Well, start planting seeds again,' Katie said.

'Is it that urgent, that you leave?' Alice asked.

'Alice, I just know something is wrong at home. My mother, she's not like your mother.'

James made a sound between a bark and a snort. 'Sometimes, Katie, I do think you're dim,' he said. 'Of course your mothers are not the same. Alice's mother is the Queen.'

Katie turned her back on him. 'Mimi doesn't have a house filled with servants. She doesn't have millions of children and she really, really doesn't have a loving and devoted husband,' Katie explained. 'She just has me and she needs me. That's it – the bottom line.'

'Yes, we understand now. If you think she's in danger, then you must return, immediately,' Alice said. She looked up at Bernardo DuQuelle. 'I know you can do this.'

DuQuelle's face was still impassive. 'It might be that bit easier,' he said, 'now that I've heard Katie say those words. *Need* has a great magnetic force.'

James got down on his hands and knees and began to rummage through Katie's belongings. He didn't look too happy about touching some of her stuff, but he had been amputating limbs not a week ago and had handled worse. 'The last time Katie travelled through some letter Princess Alice wrote, and returned by her own diary,' James muttered. 'There must be something in here that she's written. And she's got the walking stick. Isn't that important somehow? Is there anything you have, DuQuelle?'

'There was a book,' Katie said, '*Tempus Fugit, Libertati Viam Facere* – and the card: the aide-memoire.'

'Katie arrived with quite a bit of cargo,' Bernardo DuQuelle said, and opening a drawer, he took out the original book and the embossed card that had flown Katie through time.

'What about the mirror?' Katie asked. 'I arrived *deep in the looking glass*.'

'It's in the Palace,' DuQuelle replied, 'but it was a conduit only; it didn't actually give you the power . . .'

'There were those loose fitting garments she arrived in,' Alice added.

'Pyjamas,' Katie interjected. 'My pyjamas, they're in the carpet bag, James.

They piled all of the belongings into the centre of the room. DuQuelle circled the small mound of odd and ends and sniffed about; then shook his head. 'This won't work,' he said. 'Katie's gift comes from the words. She has great power, when the right words come. I don't believe the right words lie before us.'

Katie couldn't believe DuQuelle. If ever she needed an optimist, this was the time. She looked beseechingly at Alice and James.

'Why don't you put on those ghastly pyjamas of yours,' James said, 'to get you in the mood.'

'At least I'll be comfortable,' Katie replied gloomily.

She scooped up the pile of her things, and disappeared behind the carved wooden screen in DuQuelle's study. Her clothes were so filthy, she almost had to peel them off. Letting out a sigh, she loosened the corset and rolled down her stockings. Her skin was grey with the dust and travel. She smelled sour and sweaty. All Katie really wanted to do was have a bath and go to bed. But an underlying anxiety drove her forward. It was as if an entirely different life was going on beneath the surface. If only she could reach it.

'There is something I want to ask you,' she said from

behind the screen. 'Florence Nightingale, what's going on with her?'

'And what do you mean, *what's going on with her?*' DuQuelle replied. 'That is a question with no meaning.'

Katie peeked around the edge of the screen. 'You know perfectly well what I mean,' she said. 'Is she as you are, Bernardo DuQuelle – or is she as we are?'

DuQuelle examined his nails as if they contained an epic tale. 'It is a woman's prerogative to keep her own secrets,' he said finally. 'If Miss Nightingale hasn't spoken, then I certainly won't.'

'Katie,' Alice said. 'I can see your shoulder from here, and Jamie is looking very embarrassed.'

'I am not,' James protested. 'After what we've seen, do you really think I would react to Katie's scrawny shoulder?' They began to bicker, lightly but, Katie thought, happily; the way great friends or couples do.

Katie shrugged into her pyjamas and, separating out the walking stick, the book and the card from her things, began to pack the rest into her carpet bag. As she folded up the grime-encrusted bodice, a piece of paper fell to the floor. Picking it up, she found Mimi's letter:

Katie-Kid: I'm off to the Hamptons!!!

The words, they always had such power over her, and Katie's recent experiences had increased this. Her brush with Felix, her association with the Little Angel, her interaction with the Tempus: it gave her more ability, but also made her more vulnerable. The magic was within her, but she could not control it.

Even as she read, the room began to change. Alice's and James's voices grew faint. The dark carved wood of DuQuelle's study disappeared. Instead she was on 89th Street, in Apartment 11C. She was in Mimi's bedroom, standing before the mirrors, but there was no reflection of herself. Instead she saw Mimi. She was sitting up in bed now, her eyeshade pushed back over her mussed hair. One tasselled earplug dangled over her shoulder. She clutched her cashmere throw to her chest. Something was swirling through the house. Katie could hear the splintering of glass and wood snapping. Mimi fumbled for the telephone, but then dropped it and dashed for the door, towards the noise and destruction, as a single thought overtook her mind. 'Katie! My baby!'

'Mimi!' Katie shouted, running after her. The noise and destruction – it was Diuman. His fury had welled up, sweeping all before him. In the distance James's and Alice's bickering died away. DuQuelle's face appeared before her, but only as a ghostly reflection. She just had time to clutch the walking stick, the very thing Professor Diuman was searching for. Then she was swirling through light and noise, Alice was calling for her, Mimi screaming. Words swirled around her: *Tempus fugit, libertati viam facere . . .*

And then Diuman was before her, glasses glittering, his braided beard writhing like three tiny snakes. He was standing in her own pink bedroom. Mimi faced him, on fire with defiance. She lashed out, kicking towards him, blocking his way, hissing between her teeth 'not my child'. But Diuman was strong. Before Katie could stop him, he struck hard, and Mimi fell to the ground.

In a frenzy, Diuman rampaged through the room, slashing at the bed with his metal pipe. But what he wanted wasn't in that bed. It was right behind him – and it had powers beyond that of a normal New York girl. She could choose, and she could act. 'Not my mother!' Katie shouted, and brought the walking stick down on his head with all her might. The world around her exploded.

Here and Now:
Yet Again

She ached – everywhere: the top of her head, under her knees; her back felt as if it had been welded into one solid throbbing piece. Katie had never known her earlobes could hurt, but they did, like the blazes – and the tip of her nose. She could smell some kind of burning, electric smell. She turned her head, and winced. There was a sound – voices, low and excited, and running footsteps. Bracing herself for what might come, she opened her eyes.

She was in the bathroom on 89th Street, in Apartment 11C. How had she got there? Groaning slightly, she raised herself to look in the mirror. It wasn't broken any more.

When she looked into it, she could see herself but nothing more. The door handle rattled, and then there was urgent banging. 'Is anyone there,' a man shouted. 'Open up. It's the police.' Katie was frightened now, and didn't answer. So much had happened, in so many different times and places. What was reality? Katie had no idea. She felt paralysed. And then there was another voice.

'Katie, honey, open up the door now. Everything will be fine, sweetheart.' It was Dolores, and she sounded even more frightened than Katie felt.

Getting to her knees, Katie unlocked the bathroom door with shaking hands. Why was the door locked anyway? She'd left it open when she'd crept towards the mirror; but that seemed so long ago.

On the other side, flanked by two policemen, was Dolores. She swept Katie into her arms in an enormous bear-hug. 'All safe now,' she crooned, 'all safe and sound now.'

Katie rubbed her eyes, confused. 'Why am I here,' she said. 'I don't know . . . what's up?' And then the anxiety washed over her again, drowning out the pain. 'Where's Mimi?' she asked sharply.

The two policemen looked at each other. 'Thank God, the kid slept through the whole thing,' one said. 'He didn't even know she was here.'

'Thank the Lord,' Dolores echoed, holding on even tighter to Katie.

'Where's Mimi?' Katie asked again, a rising note of hysteria in her voice. 'I want to see Mimi.'

'Don't you worry,' Dolores soothed her. 'She's gonna be fine, but they needed to take her to the hospital.'

'We'd like to take a statement, as soon as the mother comes to,' the policeman added. 'You bring the kid with you as soon as you can. We'd better get on.'

Katie was now almost speechless with fear. 'Dolores,' she whispered, 'what happened? Where is Mimi?'

'Sit down, child,' Dolores said.

'I don't want to sit down,' Katie said, though she could barely stand. 'Where is Mimi?'

Dolores stroked her back. 'They loaded her in the ambulance as quick as they could,' she said. 'She's bad hurt. You see, I was worried about you, honey, so I slipped back to check on you. And I found this man, that Professor we always thought so nice. That man, he broke into the house. He tried to kill your mama.'

Katie groaned as she remembered her visions. She'd known, all the time she was in Buckingham Palace, in the Crimea. She'd known that Diuman was in the apartment. She should have tried harder, come home earlier. An even more horrible thought crossed her mind. 'Mimi's not going to die?' she whispered.

Dolores held her even closer. 'No, my honey, Mimi's not going to die. She got hold of that walking stick of yours. The one I'm always complaining about. Well, I'll never complain again. She must have attacked him with it. Somehow she brought him down. They were both unconscious when I got here. If she hadn't found that thing, she really might be dead. My, but it's lucky she found that stick.'

Katie detached herself from Dolores, and sat down on her bed. 'It's not luck,' she said. 'I don't know what it is, but it's not luck. Dolores, the world . . . it's just not what we think it is . . .'

Dolores shook her head. 'No, it's a bad world, dearie, a world of sin. To be woken in the dead of night, given such a shock – that can't be good for you. You look like you've been in a fight yourself. But we need to get to the hospital. Now, let's get you dressed and I'll find a taxi.' Dolores sniffed Katie and wrinkled her nose. 'What have you been up to? I swear you had a bath before I left last night . . . I'll just wet down a washcloth and find you some fresh clothes.'

As Dolores bustled out of the room, Katie got down on her hands and knees under her bed and surreptitiously searched for her diary. She had to get to Mimi, but there was something else she had to do. This time she wasn't going to forget. She would write it all down. The power of words – DuQuelle was always going on about the power of words. She would start at the beginning. Stick to the plain facts as William Howard Russell was fond of saying.

'Visions,' she wrote, 'mirror – walking stick – DuQuelle, Alice, James. Tempus – Occidit – Fugit – Verus – Malum –

Lucia – Belzen – Grace – corset – Angel – fleas – Felix – Florence – Seacole – Russell – salve – charge – Jack – Jack – Jack. Was DuQuelle right? Would Jack live again? She wanted to write his name a hundred times, so she wouldn't forget. The door buzzer rang but she continued to scribble.

'Well!' came a loud brisk voice, and Katie jumped. Dolores was standing in the doorway, hands on her hips. 'You are a strange one, Katie,' she exclaimed. 'I know you are worried sick about your mama. We have to go to the hospital. The taxi is downstairs, and you are a-sitting there scribbling in your diary!'

Katie looked up, and the tears finally fell. 'I'm sorry, Dolores,' she whispered. 'It's just that . . .'

Dolores' face softened. 'That's all right, honey,' she said soothingly. 'It's just the hospital called. Mimi's regained consciousness. And the first thing she asked for was you.'

Katie took the wet washcloth and quickly rubbed her face and behind her neck. It turned dark grey. Snatching her winter coat, she threw it over the pyjamas. 'I'll be fine like this,' Katie said as Dolores started to protest. 'Honestly, I've worn worse things than this.' She smiled slightly as she thought of the horrid nurse's uniform and the grey worsted jacket.

'Katie,' Dolores said, as they headed for the elevator, 'sometimes I think you're on a different planet.'

'No, Dolores,' Katie said, 'not a different planet. A different place, a different time – but not a different planet.'

Dear Reader,

I received a really wonderful email from one of you recently. He said, 'I consider myself a great authority on time travel and you are the first person I have encountered who actually knows how time travel works.' Flattering, yes – but I think every single one of us is an authority on time travel. Who hasn't imagined what it would be like to live in another time? Or wondered about the real lives of those we learn about in history?

It's fun to mix fact with fiction. Some of my characters, like Princess Alice, are real. James, though entirely made up, is based on someone I know and love well. Both Florence Nightingale and Mary Seacole are important figures in history. I've drawn their personalities from their own letters and memoirs; though I can provide no proof for the more magical elements of their personalities.

I did want to get things right, so I spent a lot of time researching *The Queen at War*. Much of what I needed was right on my doorstep in London. If you are interested in the Victorians and the 1800s, the Victoria & Albert Museum is a good place to start. The Florence Nightingale Museum is a hidden gem, chock full of Florence memorabilia. The National Army Museum has information and artefacts on the Crimean War.

Next year, the third book in the Chronicles of the Tempus trilogy will come out. *The Queen Alone* brings Katie, James and Princess Alice together again. War, intrigue, madness and murder are all on the menu. Be prepared.

Respectfully yours,
K. A. S. Quinn

Follow K.A.S. Quinn on Facebook, Twitter or contact her by email (kasquinn@hotmail.com)